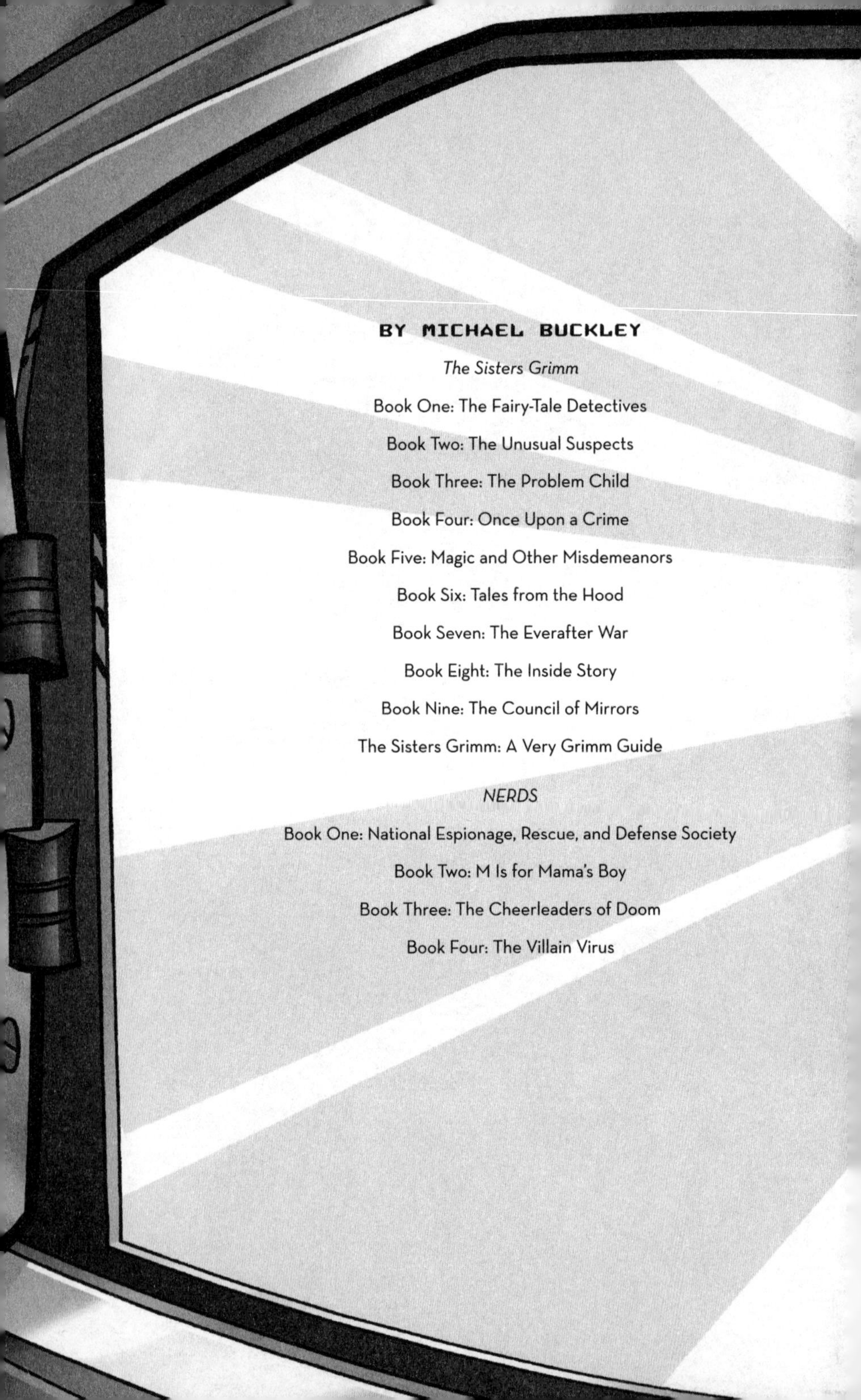

BY MICHAEL BUCKLEY

The Sisters Grimm

Book One: The Fairy-Tale Detectives

Book Two: The Unusual Suspects

Book Three: The Problem Child

Book Four: Once Upon a Crime

Book Five: Magic and Other Misdemeanors

Book Six: Tales from the Hood

Book Seven: The Everafter War

Book Eight: The Inside Story

Book Nine: The Council of Mirrors

The Sisters Grimm: A Very Grimm Guide

NERDS

Book One: National Espionage, Rescue, and Defense Society

Book Two: M Is for Mama's Boy

Book Three: The Cheerleaders of Doom

Book Four: The Villain Virus

NERDS

THE VILLAIN VIRUS

• BOOK FOUR •

MICHAEL BUCKLEY

Illustrations by
ETHEN BEAVERS

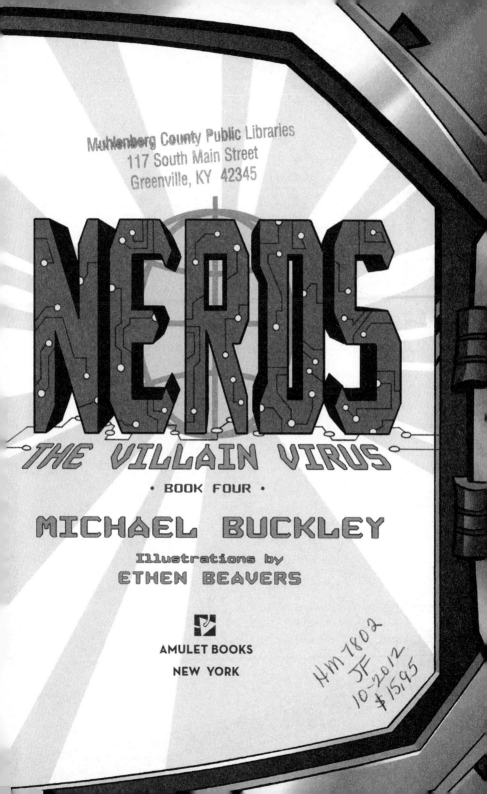

AMULET BOOKS
NEW YORK

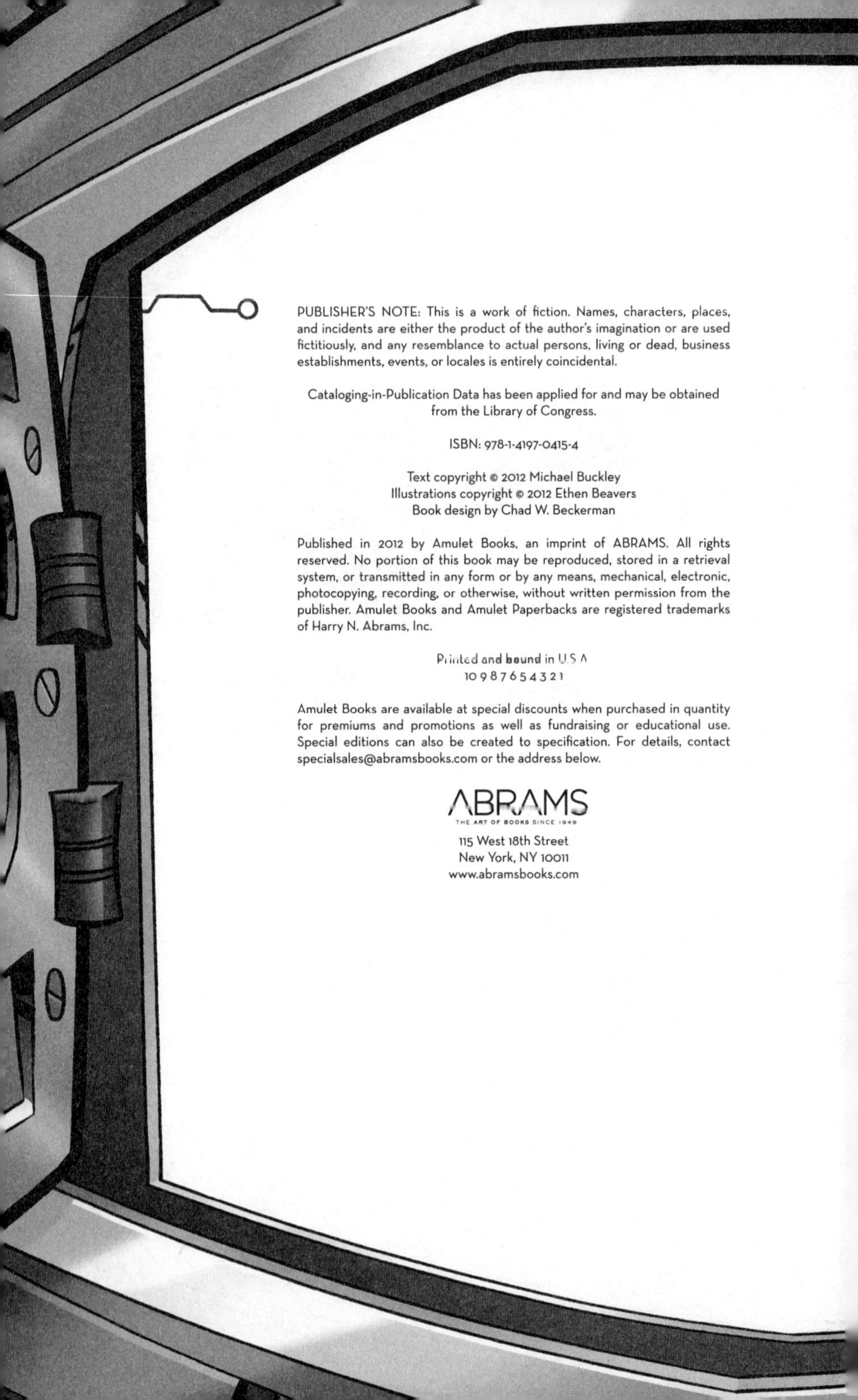

PUBLISHER'S NOTE: This is a work of fiction. Names, characters, places, and incidents are either the product of the author's imagination or are used fictitiously, and any resemblance to actual persons, living or dead, business establishments, events, or locales is entirely coincidental.

Cataloging-in-Publication Data has been applied for and may be obtained from the Library of Congress.

ISBN: 978-1-4197-0415-4

Book design by Chad W. Beckerman

Printed and bound in U.S.A.
10 9 8 7 6 5 4 3 2 1

Amulet Books are available at special discounts when purchased in quantity for premiums and promotions as well as fundraising or educational use. Special editions can also be created to specification. For details, contact specialsales@abramsbooks.com or the address below.

ABRAMS
THE ART OF BOOKS SINCE 1949

115 West 18th Street
New York, NY 10011
www.abramsbooks.com

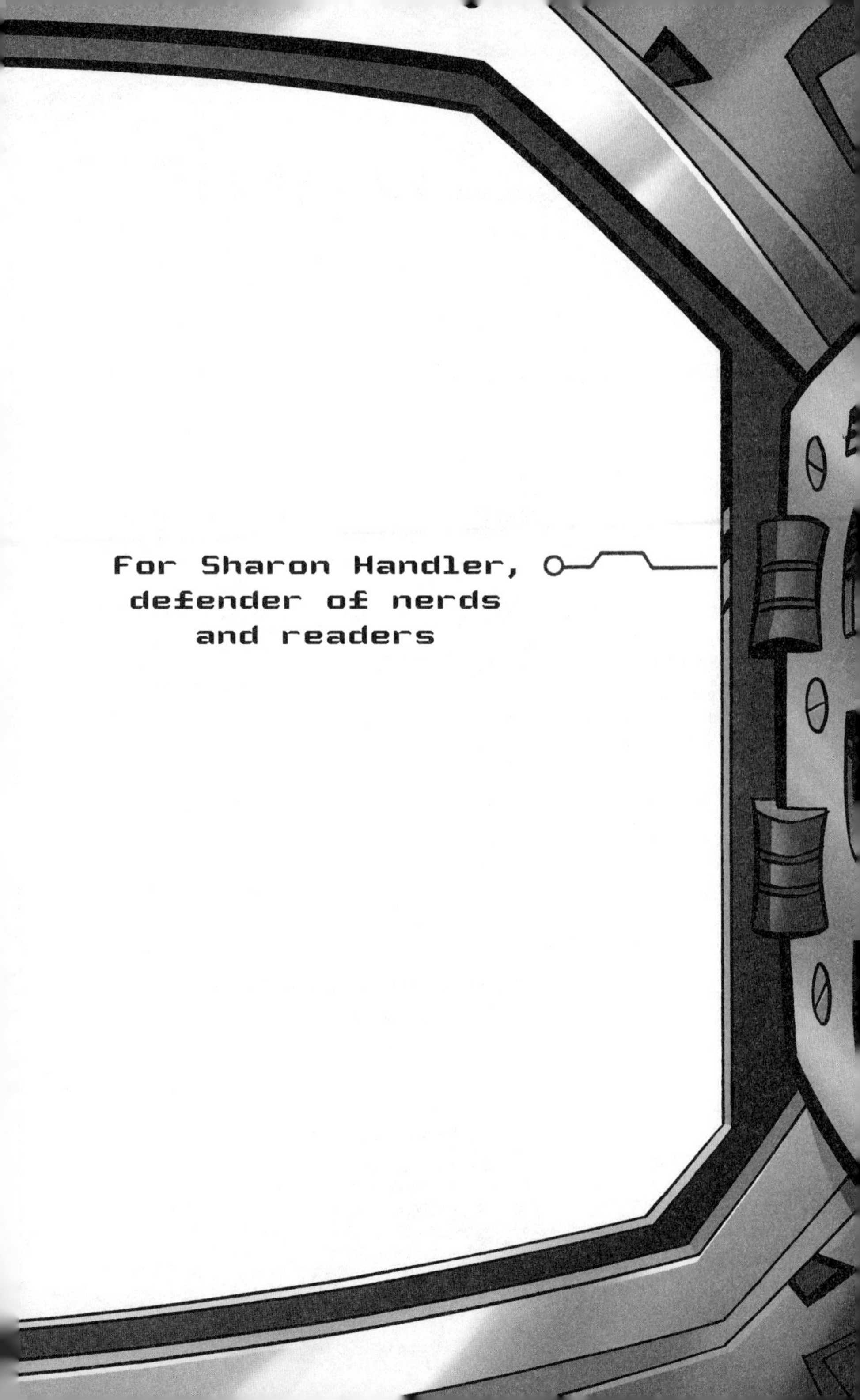

For Sharon Handler,
defender of nerds
and readers

Prologue

38°87' N, 77°10' W

In this great big world, there are plenty of lousy jobs, and if you aren't careful, you might grow up to have one. Without the right encouragement and education you could get stuck being:

1. An alligator massage therapist
2. A cat food taste-tester
3. A toilet bowl shiner
4. A roadkill collector
5. A screenwriter
6. The guy who scrapes boogers off the bottoms of movie theater seats

Which one of these jobs is the worst is open to debate, but all of them are soul-crushing nightmares. Still, none of them are as bad as Sherman Stoop's job. Sherman guarded a humongous head.

To be clear, it wasn't just a humongous head. It had arms and legs, but they were teeny-tiny and useless. The head had feet and hands, too, but they were even smaller and less useful. But if you were pressed to describe the bizarre creature to a friend, it would be safe to call it a head—a gigantic, RV-size, tiny-limbed head.

Sherman's bosses told him that this head was evil and could destroy the world, so it was put into a drug-induced sleep. Sherman was also told that if the head were to ever wake up . . . well, it would be very, very bad—so Sherman had to watch it very, very carefully. It snored, mumbled in its sleep, drooled, and frequently passed gas.

Worst. Job. Ever.

Or was it? It seemed to Sherman that there had been a time when he loved his job. In fact, it seemed like just yesterday. Maybe it *was* yesterday. He couldn't be sure. Things were foggy lately, but somewhere in the hazy reaches of his memory there were hints of a time when he thought his job was cool. Didn't he use to think it was epic to be working around spies in a secret headquarters built beneath a school? Hadn't it been thrilling to help a secret organization save the world on a daily basis? Wasn't it awe-inspiring to wear a uniform that was covered in fancy body armor that made him look extremely tough? And what about his oversize laser gun that could burn through metal? None of his friends from high school had a laser gun! And the dental insurance! The dental insurance ruled!

Or did it? He couldn't be sure. He was so angry now and much of his frustration had to do with his job. What was once exciting and new about working for the NERDS was now tedious and stupid. What used to make him feel important now made him feel disrespected. And the spies and scientists he once admired now seemed like a pack of mouth-breathing apes.

He couldn't be sure when his change in attitude had occurred, but it all seemed to begin with the flu. It hit him all at once—dizziness, sore throat, and a fever so hot he felt like a marshmallow roasting over a campfire. He tossed and turned in bed, too sick to even call a doctor, and then suddenly the fever, nausea, and aches were gone, replaced by a newfound clarity about the world and his place in it. His job guarding an evil, gigantic, RV-size head was not a matter of national security but a task for a monkey, and his employers knew it! They were jealous and fearful of his brilliance. They wanted to squash his potential and steal the glory that was rightfully his, so they stuck him with a thankless chore. Well, he wouldn't stand for it. Sherman Stoop was destined for greatness, and it was about time the whole world knew it!

"Sherman, you don't look well," Andrea said. She was a coworker on the security staff, and lately the two of them had been eating lunch together. They had a lot of interests in common—kung fu movies, Hungarian goulash festivals, and kitten calendars. Sherman had been building up the courage to ask her out on a date for months, and finally he had the perfect romantic evening—the annual goulash cook-off was a week away. What could be more romantic than taste-testing a hundred different goulashes? He was sure to sweep her off her feet! But now . . . well, what had happened to all those good feelings? Instead of being smitten by a beautiful woman who shared his love of heavy Eastern European cuisine, he saw a manipulative, cruel jerk who laughed at him behind his back.

"I'm fine," he seethed. "Not that you care."

"Sherman, what does that mean?"

"Be gone, woman! Can't you see I'm thinking?" he replied, enraged.

Andrea's face fell. As if he had hurt her feelings! What an actress. She should have been in Hollywood, making movies. She probably didn't even like goulash! He turned and walked toward the door.

"Sherman! You can't leave your station—"

"Watch me!" Sherman took off his helmet and tossed it to the floor. It bounced around. CLANG! CLANG! CLANG!

The noise caused everyone in the lab to gasp, and all eyes turned to the slumbering head. Its horrible, stretched face grimaced, and it snorted. Was it waking up? What were they supposed to do if it woke up?

But then it licked its lips and went back to its incessant snoring, and the staff breathed again.

Sherman wasn't going to wait around for the scientists to scold him like a child. He stormed through the exit doors and nearly ran straight into his boss, Dave Hobin. Dave was a short, dumpy man with a full mustache.

Several nights a month, he and Sherman got together to play a card game called euchre.

"Sherman, why are you leaving the holding cell? Are you not feeling well?" Sherman's answer came in the form of a punch to Dave's nose.

"You wouldn't listen to my ideas, and you laughed at me! All of you laughed at me!"

"What ideas?" Dave cried as he held his sore snout. "Is this about wanting Cheese Curls in the employee snack machine? I told you I'd look into it."

For a moment the anger faded and Sherman realized what he had done to his friend. He was horrified and wanted to apologize. But before he could, Andrea rushed into the hall and helped Dave to his feet. Sherman could see the hurt and confusion in their eyes.

"Sherman, explain yourself!" Andrea cried.

Sherman's tongue felt as if it were in the grip of a boa constrictor. He couldn't form an explanation, and even if he could, his actions were just as baffling to him as they were to Andrea and Dave. Why was he so angry at his friends? Why was he so angry at his life?

And then the fever returned and his regret turned to scorn. These two simpletons should have been apologizing to him for masquerading as his friends. They were no different than the others—just trying to keep him down.

"You are all going to pay!" he shouted as he stomped away. "I've already begun work on a plan that will show the world my brilliance, and everyone will beg for mercy when I take my rightful place as their ruler."

"Did you eat at the Goulash Hut again?" Dave shouted after him. "I told you that place has about a thousand health code violations. You probably have food poisoning. Come on, I'll take you to the infirmary."

Sherman turned one last time. "My name is not Sherman! From this day forth, those who are lucky enough to live will call me Captain Kapow!"

"Captain who?" Andrea asked.

But Sherman did not reply. He stormed away, his brain hard at work on complex math equations and chemical formulas. His ideas had never been so clear, so crisp, so brilliantly dangerous! All he needed were the materials to construct his inventions and the money to buy the parts. But that wouldn't be a problem. He knew exactly where to turn for the cash. All he had to do was find the man in the skull mask. Sherman's dreams the night before had been filled with the mysterious stranger. Whoever he was, Sherman was certain the masked man would help him take over the world.

But first he was going to stop by the Goulash Hut. He was starving.

NO WAY! YOU'RE BACK! GEEZ! I CAN'T GET RID OF YOU. EITHER YOU REALLY WANT TO BE A SECRET AGENT OR YOU'RE JUST A GLUTTON FOR PUNISHMENT. YOU ARE AWARE THAT THIS LINE OF WORK HAS A HIGH DEATH RATE, CORRECT? YOU COULD BE KILLED IN A NUMBER OF TERRIBLE WAYS! PLUS, YOU HAVE TO BUY YOUR OWN TUXEDO!

FINE! THERE'S NO TALKING YOU OUT OF IT. I GUESS THAT'S HOW IT SHOULD BE. MEMBERS OF NERDS ARE MENTALLY TOUGH AND AREN'T SWAYED BY A LITTLE THING LIKE EXCRUCIATING DEATH. STILL, DON'T COME CRYING TO ME IF YOU GET YOURSELF KILLED, 'CAUSE ALL YOU'LL GET FROM ME IS AN "I TOLD YOU SO."

OK, PAL! LET'S GET STARTED. WRITE YOUR CODE NAME BELOW.

____

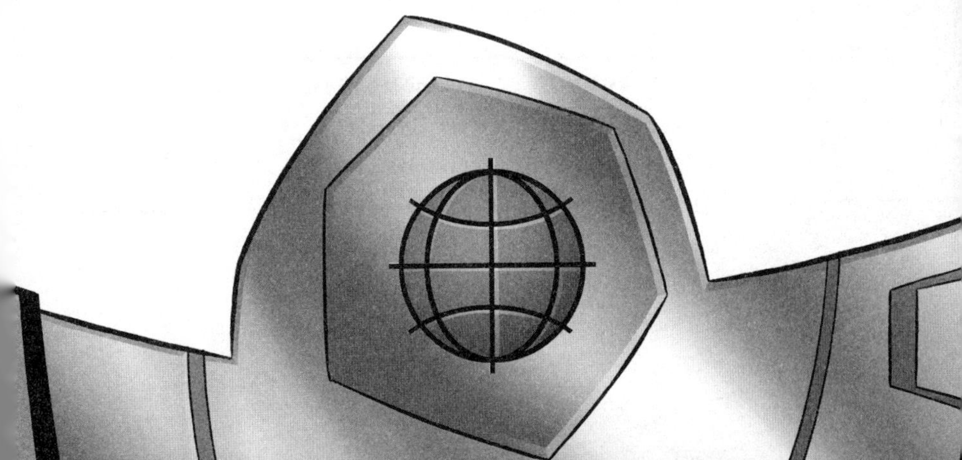

HA! THAT CODE NAME IS DOWNRIGHT GOOFY. YOU SHOULD HAVE A SUPERCOOL CODE NAME LIKE MINE: BEANPOLE. THAT'S THE KIND OF NAME THAT STRIKES FEAR IN A VILLAIN'S HEART. YEAH, BEANPOLE! WHAT'S SO FUNNY?

GRRR. ENOUGH WITH THE GIGGLING! I HEARD YOU WERE BELLYACHING BECAUSE YOU HAVEN'T BEEN SENT ON ANY MISSIONS YET. WELL, THERE'S A PERFECTLY GOOD REASON FOR THAT. YOU HAVEN'T SIGNED THE WAIVER. WHAT'S A WAIVER? IT'S A LEGAL DOCUMENT THAT FREES OUR ORGANIZATION OF ANY RESPONSIBILITY IF YOU HAPPEN TO SUFFER A LOSS OF LIMB OR DIE. YOU NEED TO SIGN IT BEFORE WE CAN GET STARTED.

THE "I KNOW I COULD DIE" WAIVER

I, ______________________________,
AM PERFECTLY AWARE THAT THE LIFE OF A SPY IS ONE WHERE I COULD BE KILLED IN A NUMBER OF VIOLENT AND TOTALLY GROSS WAYS, INCLUDING, BUT NOT LIMITED TO:

A BEAR ATTACK; A KILLER BEE ATTACK; FALLING OUT OF A PLANE; BEING PUSHED OUT OF A PLANE; FALLING THROUGH THE GLASS ROOF OF A SWORD FACTORY; A RACE CAR ACCIDENT; A MOTORCYCLE ACCIDENT; A GOLF CART ACCIDENT; AN ATTACK BY MUTATED OR HYBRID CREATURES; BEING BEATEN TO DEATH BY GOONS, THUGS, TOADIES, MINIONS, OR OTHER LARGE-MUSCLED CHARACTERS; A SPEED BOAT CRASH; DROWNING; BEING FED TO: SHARKS, PIRANHAS, ELECTRIC EELS, ANY OF THE GREAT CATS, OR ANY OF THE LESSER CATS; BEING LOCKED IN A SAFE AND TOSSED INTO THE OCEAN; A LASER BLAST TO THE FACE; BEING TIED TO A ROCKET AND LAUNCHED INTO SPACE; BEING VAPORIZED; BEING DISINTEGRATED; BEING RUN OVER BY A TANK; BEING RUN OVER BY A BUS; BEING RUN OVER BY ANYTHING; HAVING MY HEAD CHOPPED OFF; BEING BLOWN UP; AND PRETTY MUCH ANYTHING ELSE I CAN IMAGINE AND QUITE A NUMBER OF THINGS I CAN'T.

I AM ALSO AWARE THAT I COULD BE TERRIBLY INJURED IN A HOST OF

TROUBLING SCENARIOS THAT WOULD CAUSE MY OWN FAMILY TO AVERT THEIR EYES FROM MY HORRIBLY DISFIGURED FACE AND BODY, INCLUDING, BUT NOT LIMITED TO, BEING: BURNED, PUSHED INTO A TUB OF ACID, DRAGGED BY A SPEEDBOAT ACROSS A CORAL REEF, USED AS A GUINEA PIG BY AN EVIL SCIENTIST, USED AS A GUINEA PIG BY A GOOD SCIENTIST WHO IS FORCED BY SOMEONE ELSE TO PERFORM EVIL SCIENCE, MELTED, PUSHED INTO A WOOD CHIPPER, STRAPPED TO AN OUTRAGEOUSLY LARGE PENDULUM FEATURING AN ALMOST RIDICULOUSLY GIGANTIC RAZOR AND THEN SLICED IN HALF, ATTACKED BY VARMINTS, DUNKED IN HONEY AND BURIED NEAR A FIRE-ANT COLONY, PLUS SUBJECTED TO A WHOLE HOST OF REALLY GROSS THINGS I WOULDN'T EVEN FIND IN A HORROR MOVIE.

I AM ALSO AWARE THAT IN THE LINE OF DUTY I COULD BE SO BADLY

MAIMED THAT I WOULD STRIKE FEAR INTO BABIES AND PETS OR I COULD SUFFER MALADIES, INCLUDING, BUT NOT LIMITED TO: FACE-THIEVERY, HAVING MY ARM EATEN BY AN INSANE BEAVER-CHAINSAW HYBRID, PRETTY MUCH ANYTHING EATING A PART OF MY BODY, AND HAVING MY NOSE CUT OFF IN A SWORD FIGHT. (I THINK YOU GET THE IDEA—AND I DIDN'T EVEN INCLUDE ALL THE NORMAL WAYS A PERSON CAN DIE.)

BEING FULLY INFORMED OF ANY POSSIBLE DAMAGES TO LIFE AND LIMB, BOTH REALISTIC OR SOMETHING THAT I COULD NEVER IMAGINE WOULD BE POSSIBLE BUT THEN ONE DAY I GO TO WORK AND—BAM!—IT'S VERY MUCH POSSIBLE, I RELIEVE THE NATIONAL ESPIONAGE, RESCUE, AND DEFENSE SOCIETY OF ANY RESPONSIBILITY AND CLAIMS TO DAMAGES. 'CAUSE, LIKE . . . THIS IS A DANGEROUS JOB NOT MEANT FOR CRYBABIES.

SIGNED,

____

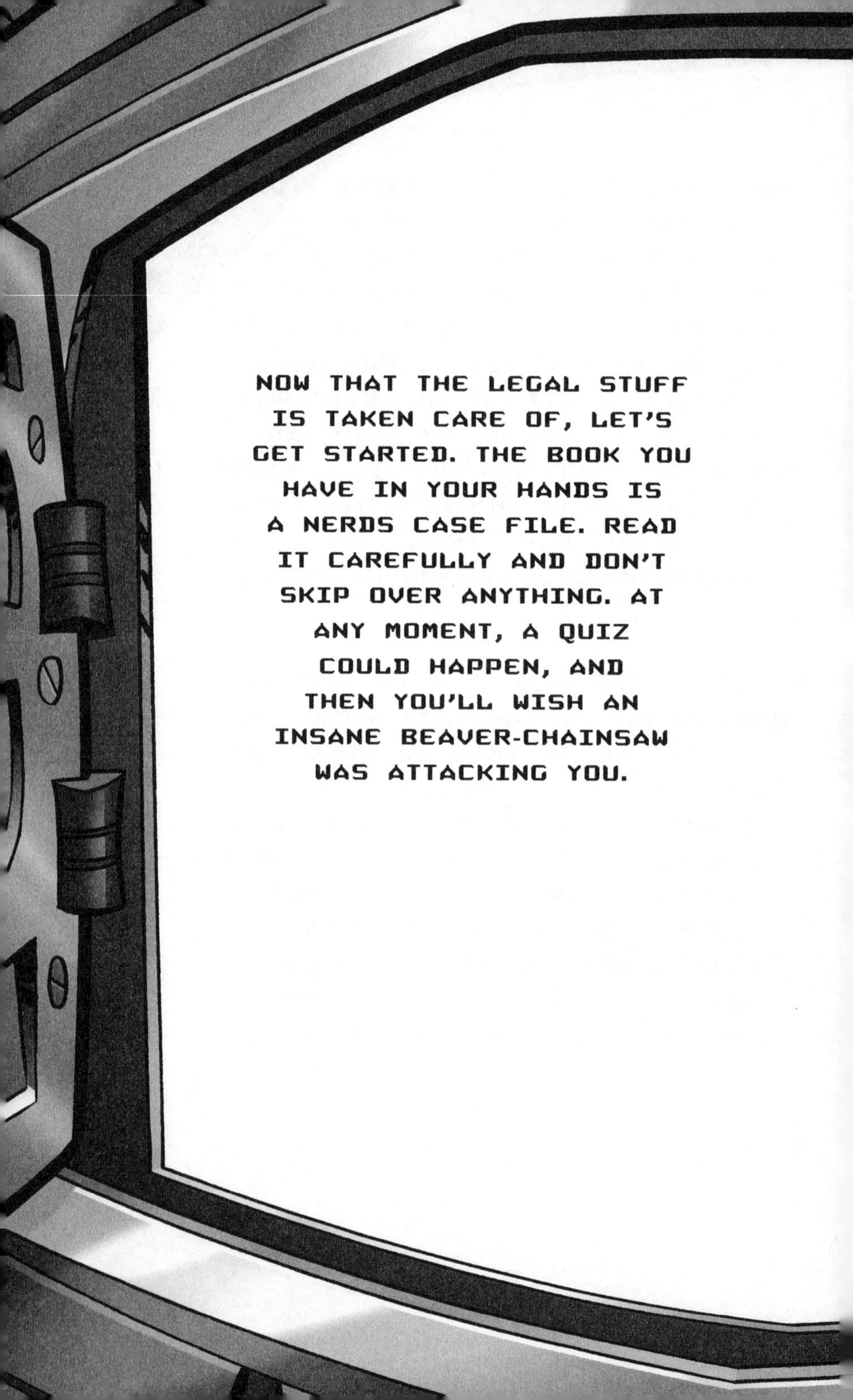
NOW THAT THE LEGAL STUFF IS TAKEN CARE OF, LET'S GET STARTED. THE BOOK YOU HAVE IN YOUR HANDS IS A NERDS CASE FILE. READ IT CAREFULLY AND DON'T SKIP OVER ANYTHING. AT ANY MOMENT, A QUIZ COULD HAPPEN, AND THEN YOU'LL WISH AN INSANE BEAVER-CHAINSAW WAS ATTACKING YOU.

LEVEL 1
ACCESS GRANTED
BEGIN TRANSMISSION:

Duncan Dewey
Code name: Gluestick
This paste-eater sticks to any surface
Jackson Jones
Code name: Braceface
High-tech braces form any gadget
Ruby Peet
Code name: Pufferfish
Allergies detect danger and dishonesty
Matilda Choi
Code name: Wheezer
Flies and blasts enemies with inhalers

Julio Escala
Code name: Flinch
Hyperfast, hyperstrong, and just plain hyper

1

38°87' N, 77°10' W

Secret Agent Alexander Brand was a man of danger, action, and intrigue. He once subdued a raging elephant with nothing but a dress shoe and an apple pie. He incapacitated a dozen trained jujitsu fighters while simultaneously deactivating a bomb. He hang-glided into a raging forest fire to recover the plans for a deadly laser cannon. All this and more had earned him the title of America's Greatest Secret Agent.

But now, as he looked up at the imposing building before him, with its chained doors and barred windows, he felt nervous about his latest mission.

Ms. Holiday, his partner and fellow spy, stood next to him. The two had worked together for nearly a year. They'd been at the center of saving the world more than once, and they had become close. Lately, she had been urging him to express his feelings. But it didn't feel natural to talk about such things. Luckily, she seemed to be able to read his mind even when his lips were closed tight.

"It's going to be OK, Alexander," she said, patting him on his arm and smiling. "We've had tougher assignments than this one. Remember Syria? Remember when we infiltrated that street gang in Mexico? Or the time we were tied to a rocket and shot into space?"

Brand nodded. Perhaps she was right. The current mission

was no more dangerous than any of the others. Mustering his courage, he hobbled up the steps, using his cane for support. Once at the top, he cupped his ear to the building's massive door. Inside there was a tremendous racket. It sounded like a battle zone or a full-scale riot—obviously, a bigger job than two secret agents could handle.

"We're going to need backup. Call SWAT, the FBI, CIA, Special Forces, the Green Berets—whoever can get here the fastest. Tell them to bring tear gas and riot gear. We're probably going to need some air support, too."

Ms. Holiday joined him at the top of the steps and pushed the double doors open. "Alexander, calm down. It's just middle school."

The duo stepped inside and were immediately surrounded by chaos. Spit wads flew through the air, children ran in all directions, trash spilled across the floor, and slamming locker doors assaulted the ears. Near the front door was a portrait of Thomas Knowlton, one of the United States of America's first secret agents. Knowlton was a striking man with a thick head of hair and a courageous face. Unfortunately, someone had drawn a curly mustache on him and blacked out a few of his teeth. Brand wondered what kind of juvenile delinquent would be so disrespectful to a national hero, and then he realized any one of the kids in the hall could be a suspect. They darted about like maniacal jackrabbits, while the teachers staggered down the halls, shell-shocked and disillusioned.

"Alex, I know you don't like change, but we couldn't keep the kids at Nathan Hale Elementary any longer. It was time to move on. It's part of what happens with the NERDS," Ms. Holiday said.

"But I had just gotten my office the way I like it," Brand said. "Now we've got a new school, new teachers, a new Playground—"

"Everything is online and fully operational," Ms. Holiday said. "The new Playground is even better than the one before. Don't worry, you're going to think of this place as home in no time.

A soccer ball whizzed through the air and, instinctively, Brand tapped his cane on the floor, releasing the dagger-sharp tip. Right before the ball smashed him in the face, he impaled it on the end of the cane. A tubby kid with an upturned nose rushed toward him. "Hey, that's my ball!"

Brand pulled the now-flat ball off his cane and stuffed it into the kid's hand. "Try to be more careful with this in the future."

The kid looked down at his ball and frowned. Then he walked away, just as deflated.

"Oh, our new friends are here!" a voice cried from down the hall.

Brand squinted into the sea of children and spotted a little woman barreling toward them. She was short and stumpy, like a smushed Twinkie, with long hair the color of straw and the wide-eyed expression of a porcelain doll. She gave Brand a hug he did not expect and could not escape from.

"Welcome to our nest, new friends!" the woman cried.

"Our nest?" Brand asked Ms. Holiday, still trying to squirm out of the woman's iron embrace.

The woman turned to Holiday. "You must be our new librarian. No one told me we were getting a peacock. What a beauty. I have no idea how our boys are going to concentrate with you checking out their books! Well, we've got a lot of reluctant readers flying around these halls, so you have your work cut out for you! We'll have to do lunch and you can tell me all about your favorite reads! How is Wednesday?"

"Well, I just—"

"Wednesday it is!" the woman cried, clapping her hands like a happy baby. She turned back to Brand. "And you must be our plover."

"Plover?"

"It's a bird that cleans the teeth of alligators," Ms. Holiday told him.

"Our Ms. Holiday is beautiful *and* bright!" the woman cried. "You are correct. A plover cleans up messes, swooping in to snatch the debris and take it off to who-knows-where.

Just like you! I like this place to be spic-and-span, Mr. Plover."

"It's actually Mr. Brand."

The woman waved a hand in the air as if his contradiction was a swarm of pesky gnats. "You'll have to get started right away. One of the bad birdies has played a little prank and clogged all the toilets on the first floor. A couple were so backed up, they exploded, and now there's water everywhere. Naughty, naughty birdies! You're going to have to have lunch with me and we can talk about ideas to keep things clean. I'll pencil you in for Thursday."

"Um, and you are?" Brand asked.

The lady clapped her hands and giggled. "Oh, I'm a silly bird. I didn't introduce myself. I'm Principal Dove. Get it? Dove! Like the bird!"

The spies stared at the woman for a long time until they realized she expected an answer. "Yes, we get it," Ms. Holiday said.

If Ms. Dove's smile could have gotten bigger it would have required surgery. She gestured to the students. "And all these children are my little birdies."

Brand glanced around the hallway. A girl was shoving a smaller boy's face into the drinking fountain, soaking his hair and shirt, while other kids cheered and laughed. Two boys were tossing balloons filled with shaving cream at each other. A young girl was wiping dog poo off her shoes and onto the wall.

"I think some of these birdies need to be in a cage."

"Oh, you scamp!" Principal Dove said. "They only act like this because they are so eager to fly, and it's our jobs to get them up into the sky and let them soar! So, can I count on you to help me teach them to fly? Peacock? Plover? Are you ready to join our flock? You know, we should all have lunch together, too—the three of us! I'll pencil it in for Friday. No, let's commit. It's going down in ink."

Just then a bell rang.

"Well, I'd better get my chicks to their coops," Ms. Dove said. "We can't stand around chirping all day. The two of you need to get to work. We're so excited to have you here!"

Dove walked down the hallway, flapping her arms like an excited hen. "Let's fly off to class, now, birdies," she called out to the students. "Your teachers are going to lay some eggs of learning and you want to be there when they hatch!"

When the hallway was clear, the two spies stood, stunned.

"Can't we just flunk the team and send them back to the fifth grade?" Brand asked.

"Let's take a look at the Playground," Ms. Holiday said. She removed a small, metallic orb covered in blinking blue lights from her handbag. It floated into the air, spinning and clicking with the sounds of internal electronics. Then it spoke in a dignified, old-fashioned accent. Its creators had programmed it with the personality of one of America's most famous spies, Founding Father Benjamin Franklin.

"Good afternoon, team," it chirped as it hovered in front of them. "Welcome to Thomas Knowlton Middle School, named after the father of military intelligence. I suppose the two of you are excited to get started. If you'll step into Locker 41, I can take you to the new HQ."

"You've got to be kidding me," Agent Brand said. "We have to take the same entrance as the kids?"

"I'm afraid so. I've taken the liberty of filing a requisition form for a new entrance, but until it is approved, there is only one way in and out," Benjamin said. "Locker 41."

Ms. Holiday opened the locker door and peered inside. "This won't be so bad." She squeezed into the tiny compartment and closed the door. When Brand opened it a moment later, she was gone.

Now it was his turn. But he was larger than Holiday and had an injured leg. He cursed quietly during the entire humiliating experience, praying some child would not walk out of a classroom and see the new janitor struggling to fit into a box half his size. When he was completely inside, Benjamin darted in with him, filling the tiny amount of space left over. Brand closed the door, plunging them into darkness.

"Cozy," Benjamin chirped.

Brand grumbled. "File another request, Benjamin. Pronto."

"Will do, boss."

The locker was suddenly illuminated in green light, and a computerized voice said, "Identity scan. One moment, please. Identity confirmed. Director Alexander Brand. Prepare for delivery to the Playground."

The floor beneath Brand vanished, and he tumbled down a narrow tube like some kind of secret agent Alice in Wonderland. He was right side up, then sideways, then diagonal, then upside down. There were blasts of bright light and frosty air, but they were brief and he was in the dark more often than not. He braced himself for an ugly crash, but then gusts of air as powerful as those of jet engines roared from below. Now he was no longer falling to his death but floating gently down, as delicately as a flower petal. He fluttered through a hole at the top of a huge glass dome and marveled at what he saw.

The dome's walls acted as one enormous television screen, airing thousands of images from all over the world. Desks and tables, each covered with strange inventions and space-age weaponry, filled the floor of the dome. An army of lab coat–wearing scientists hovered over their projects like worker bees. Ms. Holiday watched as Brand floated down to join her. She was no longer wearing the pretty pink cardigan and gray skirt of a librarian but rather a formfitting black bodysuit with boots and a belt. It was then that Brand realized his own janitor's uniform was gone, replaced with a sleek black tuxedo complete with a bow tie and cuff links.

When his feet touched ground, the wind stopped. "Well, that was different."

"Welcome to the new Playground, agents," Benjamin said, appearing from above. "Maintenance crews have kept the place quite tidy as we waited for our team to arrive in middle school, and our scientists have outfitted it with all the latest technology. My recent diagnostics have shown every system is fully operational and online, ready to be put to use saving the world."

"And the head?" Brand didn't care about gizmos and gadgets. He had one worry and it was a gigantic head—Heathcliff Hodges.

Benjamin twittered. "Heathcliff's transfer to this facility went as planned two weeks ago. He is heavily sedated and safely secured in holding cell 4A. He is under constant medical and security surveillance to keep him from waking up and will remain that way until his condition can be reversed."

Benjamin's assurances did little to ease Brand's mind. Heathcliff was dangerous and had been since the day Brand met the boy, who back then was known as Agent Choppers because of his enormous front teeth. He had the unique ability to draw attention to his teeth, and with the help of some hallucinogenic toothpaste, could bring any person or animal under his complete control.

But being a hero in secret was hard for the boy. Like most nerds, he was picked on and humiliated, and one day he decided he wanted revenge. He spiraled into a power-hungry maniac, with an endless stream of plans to take over the world, and soon he turned his back on the team and started a new life as a supervillain. Choppers became Simon, then Screwball, then Brainstorm—his identity changed with each new plan to conquer the world, which were all foiled by his former teammates. During a violent confrontation with the NERDS, his teeth were knocked out of his mouth, and he became obsessed with getting them back. What he got instead was a million times more dangerous—a brain with unlimited potential and a skull to match. His new mental strength had proved to be nearly impossible to stop, and it was only by luck that he had been captured and sedated. Heaven help the world if he woke up again.

"Keep me posted on his status at all times, Benjamin. He's too dangerous and too clever to underestimate—even if he is asleep."

"Will do, sir," Benjamin clicked.

"Now, where is my team?" Brand asked. "I thought the kids would be down here first thing, exploring the place."

"The children are on a mission," Benjamin twittered.

"A mission?" Brand cried. "By whose authorization?"

"I have General Savage with an incoming message," Benjamin said. "May I transfer it to the dome screen?"

Brand nodded, and in a flash the giant, meaty head of General Savage looked down on the spies. There were stories about the General's toughness that would have made a professional wrestler wet his pants. Savage was even more intimidating as a hologram with a noggin over thirty feet tall.

"Hello, sir," Brand said.

"Brand, Holiday. I trust you are settling in at your new headquarters."

Just then, there was a huge explosion, and a team of security guards raced across the massive room with fire extinguishers. Smoke was drifting from flames that engulfed a workstation. One of the scientists was dancing around in a panic.

"It's just like home, sir," Brand said.

Savage had one eyebrow that spanned his forehead, and his eyes were sunk deep into his face. It often made him look as if he had no eyes at all, especially when he was concerned about something, as he was now. "I'm afraid you're going to have to work out the kinks later, agents. We have a situation under way in Paris."

Savage's head was replaced by the image of a man dressed in a black trench coat. Attached to his coat were probably fifty ticking alarm clocks, and he had a smile that you didn't need a psychiatric degree to call crazy.

"This joker is calling himself Captain Kapow."

Brand rolled his eyes. It always seemed as if the bad guys they encountered had goofy names: the Savage Scooter, Monkey in the Middle, the Ant Queen, Mrs. Jeopardy, Oilslick, Commander Canine, Heat Miser. And who could forget Dr. Wind and his toxic fart-making machine? (Detroit would never be the same.) These fools spent so much time on their costumes and weird names that they neglected their master plans—which made stopping them a lot easier.

"But his plan is not so funny. He's about to blow up half of Paris," Savage growled. "I went there on my honeymoon. That would really ruin the photo album. So I scrambled your team, and the lunch lady has already delivered them to the scene. There was no time to wait."

"The children are in Paris? Right now?" Ms. Holiday said.

Agent Brand was stunned. "General Savage, with all due respect, I direct this team. I know their strengths and weaknesses. The children need to be prepped and equipped with—"

"I didn't intend to step on your toes, Brand, but this was an emergency. Our intel says that if the bombs aren't deactivated in the next half hour, half of Paris will be in ruins."

"Understood, sir. Who's leading this mission?" Brand asked.

"The hyper one. What's his name? The one who can lift a car over his head."

"Flinch is on point?" Brand cried. He had never put Flinch in charge of anything. The boy was so high-strung and jumpy. Most of the time Brand couldn't understand a word the kid said. Young Julio Escala had as much leadership experience as a roomful of excited puppies.

"Yes—Flinch. He and the team have located the bombs and are working on dismantling them as we speak," the General said. "I'm turning the mission over to you now. I have the fullest confidence in your team."

The dome went black, leaving Brand and Holiday alone, and stunned again.

"He put the hyper one in charge," Brand said. "Heaven help Paris."

2

43°67' N, 4°113' W

Julio "Flinch" Escala was freaking out. Ten bombs were planted beneath the streets of Paris, set to go off at any minute. The destruction they would cause would be cataclysmic—hundreds of thousands of people would die, and one of the world's most beautiful cities would be rubble. It was his job to prevent it, but at that moment he was too busy with his freak-out mentioned above. He screamed and kicked and struggled and screamed some more. And then he did it again.

It wasn't supposed to happen like this. The NERDS had easily located Captain Kapow's bombs stashed in the Paris catacombs, a series of intertwining mazes that made the French city's underground resemble Swiss cheese. All the team had

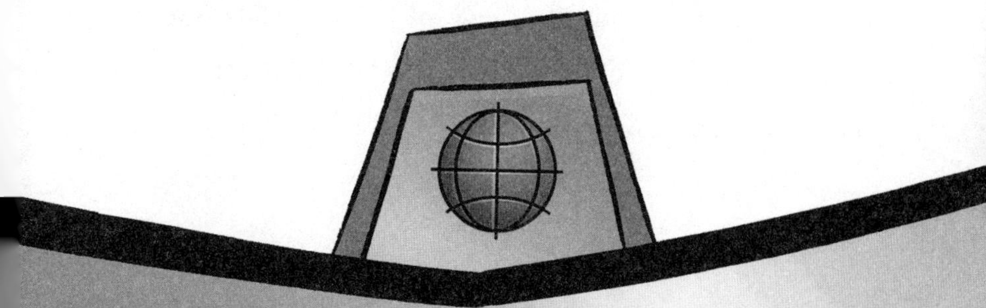

to do was go into the tunnels, find the bombs, and deactivate them. Easy, right? Well, it probably would have been if General Savage hadn't put Flinch in charge.

The General must have thought having the fastest and strongest member of the NERDS in charge made sense, but Flinch was hyperactive and he had a hard time concentrating, especially when he was full of sugar, which was most of the time. Put on the spot, Flinch had flashed through hundreds of plans, all competing for center stage in his mind. It gave him a headache trying to untangle them. So he did what came naturally—he plunged into the tunnels headfirst, all by himself, and was promptly surrounded by a gang of thugs. He fought most of them with ease but one clocked him in the back of the noggin, and then it was lights-out, Flinch!

And when he came to and discovered he was tied up, the freak-out began.

He wasn't sure how long he had been out, but figured it wasn't long. After all, the bombs hadn't exploded and he was still alive—though he had no idea how much time was left before they sent Paris, and himself, sky-high.

Suddenly, Flinch felt a powerful tickle in his nose and he let out one of the loudest sneezes of his life. Aside from the outrageous noise, the sneeze had one other peculiar feature. It activated a tiny communication device buried deep inside his nose. There was a crackle in his ear as a com-link came to life, and soon he could hear a familiar voice inside his head.

"Agent Pufferfish to Agent Flinch, can you hear me? Please respond."

"I'm here," Flinch said.

"What are you doing?"

"Having a nervous breakdown!" he cried. "I'm tied up in a tunnel surrounded by bombs!"

"Flinch!" Pufferfish said. "Stay calm. You can't freak out. Take some deep breaths. Are you breathing?"

"I think so," Flinch said.

"Good, now use your superstrength to snap the ropes," Pufferfish told him.

Flinch tried and failed. The more he pulled, the more the ropes dug into his wrists, which meant he had an even bigger problem. His hyperactivity was channeled through a harness he wore at all times. It gave him superhuman strength and speed. If he couldn't break the ropes, there was only one conclusion—the harness was malfunctioning, which meant he was just an ordinary boy, albeit a very hyperactive ordinary boy.

"No can do, Pufferfish," he said. "My upgrades are offline."

He heard the sounds of scratching and itching through his com-link.

"What's that noise?" he asked.

"It's me. I'm freaking out," Pufferfish said. "And I'm allergic to freaking out. You've only got fifteen minutes before Paris goes bye-bye."

The two of them screamed and shrieked—freaking out together—until another voice came on the line. This one belonged to Agent Wheezer. From the sound of the wind breaking up her voice, Flinch guessed she was soaring over the City of Lights, using her inhalers to propel her through the sky. "This is Agent Wheezer, your eye in the sky. Captain Kapow is making his way toward the river Seine, where he has a getaway boat waiting for him. I'll do what I can to slow him down, but I could really use a hyperactive strongman with superspeed to help out."

“I’m a little tied up at the moment,” Flinch said as he pulled at the ropes once more. He wished he could see what was bound around his hands. If only it wasn’t so dark. Wait! Hadn’t the scientists given him something special for just this situation? Yes, the contact lenses! But how did they work? If only he had paid attention during the briefing, but there were bear claws in the briefing room and they weren’t going to eat themselves.

“Uh, Gluestick, how do the contacts work again?” he said.

Duncan came on the com-link with a sigh. “I knew you weren’t listening!”

“Bear claws!” Flinch cried.

“The T-477 Contact Bulbs have a nuclear core that—”

“Just tell me how they work!”

“Geez! OK, blink your eyes three times fast and say ‘spotlight,’” Gluestick said.

Flinch did what he was told and suddenly his eyes lit up like the high beams on a Gran Torino. He immediately wished he could go back to not knowing where he was. He was in a narrow tunnel with walls lined from floor to ceiling with bones—hundreds and thousands of bones. Hips, legs, feet, fingers, ribs: all different sizes of bones stacked on top of one another in neat rows. Suddenly it seemed as if the tunnel was getting smaller and the bones were getting closer. The skulls were turning their lifeless gaze on him, and their cackling jaws unhinged to eat his soul.

"*MUERTO!*" he cried.

"Here comes the freak-out again," another voice said. This one belonged to Agent Braceface. "I don't know why Savage didn't just send me. My braces could have gotten this done fifteen minutes ago and we'd have time to see the Eiffel Tower."

"Flinch, you must calm down," Pufferfish said. "There's nothing to be afraid of. This was all explained in the briefing. You're in the Parisian catacombs, also known as the City of the Dead."

"City of the Dead!!" Flinch cried.

"Shut up and listen! It's a big underground cemetery. Nearly six million people were moved there in the late eighteenth century from a place called the Cemetery of the Innocents. The original tunnels were carved out by limestone miners and are centuries old."

"Less history lesson and more rescuing me from the skeleton people!" Flinch shouted, pulling fruitlessly at his bindings.

"The tunnels are why we have to stop the bombs from exploding. If they go off, every house, business, car, and person above them will collapse into the earth."

"I didn't know that!" he said.

"IT WAS IN THE BRIEFING!" his teammates shouted through the com-link.

Duncan's voice returned. "All right, buddy, take a deep

breath and calm down. Try to relax and stay positive. What is it that your grandma always says?"

"*De que tocan a llover, no hay más que abrir el paraguas,*" Flinch said.

"What does that mean?" Wheezer asked.

"If it's raining, all you have to do is open your umbrella."

"So what are we going to do?" Pufferfish said.

"We're going to find his umbrella," Gluestick responded. "Now, feel around for something to loosen the ropes."

Flinch reached out until something sharp jabbed his wrists. Was it a knife? What did a skeleton need a knife for? Were the skeletons not satisfied with scaring him to death, and now they wanted to stab him? He pushed the thought out of his mind and focused on his situation. He had learned in his secret agent training that anything could be a tool—even a pointy thing in a stack of dead people. So he fought the urge to pee his pants and rubbed the ropes against its sharp edge.

"Maybe I need to go in after him," Braceface said. "I'll just morph my braces into a motorcycle and zip down there. If we don't act fast this place is going to be French toast."

"They don't eat French toast in France," Pufferfish grumbled.

Flinch continued tearing at his bindings. Soon he heard a snap and his hands were free. Against his better judgment he turned to see what the sharp object was. It was a skull with a jaw full of broken teeth. He had put his hands into its mouth!!! Ugh!!! He danced around, trying to shake the creepy feeling.

"Now, for the harness," he said when he got himself under control. He eyed it closely, searching for damage. As one of the most hyperactive kids in the world, Flinch was doomed to a life full of the jitters until he received his upgrades. Tiny robots called nanobytes turned the sugar that he consumed into raw power, then channeled it into the harness, which focused it and allowed him to dial it up or down at will. Without it, he was just a kid who ate too many cupcakes and rambled when he spoke. But how had the thugs known to disable it?

One of the harness's power cords had been yanked out. Flinch reinserted it, and the chest plate glowed to life with a familiar blue light. Immediately, he felt the energy coursing through him.

"*Problemo numero dos* has been solved. How much time do I have?"

"Nine minutes," Pufferfish said.

"I need someone to guide me through these tunnels. Can we scan them for the bombs?"

"Already done," Pufferfish said. "Each bomb is producing a low-grade electronic signal, which I can detect because there is very little power down there. But they're spread out, and worse, these tunnels are hundreds of years old and some have collapsed, so be careful. The first one is only a few yards ahead of you."

Flinch blasted forward, fueled by the harness. He left a trail of dust and bone behind him.

"Make a left at the fork ahead," Pufferfish said. "Radiation signatures tell me the explosive device is just beyond."

Flinch did as he was told, tearing through the tunnels. He rounded a bend in the path, noticing stones inscribed with strange dates and numbers. One read OSSEMENTS DU CIMETIÈRE DES INNOCENTS DÉPOSÉS EN AVRIL 1786.

"What's with the markers down here?" he asked.

Pufferfish cleared her throat. "They're sort of on-site lists of when people were taken from the original cemetery and brought to the catacombs. They're not important to the mission."

"I'm trying to keep my mind off all the dead people," Flinch said.

"The bombs aren't enough distraction?" Wheezer asked.

"There!" Pufferfish cried.

Flinch came to a screeching stop. The first explosive was crammed into a dark corner of the tunnel. It was about the size of a small paperback book, with a timer on the front and several glowing lights. "Got the first one!"

"Describe what you see," Pufferfish said.

"It's small and metal and there's a clasp on the side. Hold

on, I'll open it. OK, there are two long tubes filled with liquids. One looks like cream filling and the other like fruit punch. At the ends of the tubes are needles, like in a doctor's office, and they are inserted into two small bricks of white clay that look like saltwater taffy. And it's all hooked up to a black box—the timer."

"Plastic explosives," Wheezer said.

"Only worse," Gluestick said.

"Huh? Why is it worse?" Flinch asked.

"Don't panic," Gluestick said.

"Don't tell me not to panic! Now I'm panicking!"

"It's a hybrid bomb. The plastic explosive is probably enough to knock the ceiling down, but the explosion isn't enough for the whole tunnel, so Kapow added a chemical element. I can't know for sure what is in the tubes without doing tests, but I suspect it's a form of acid. The bomb knocks out the tunnel and the chemicals eat the limestone from below. It spreads and disintegrates everything it touches until there's a gigantic hole that can't be filled in or built upon. Not only is this lunatic trying to cave Paris in on itself, he's making sure no one can fix the damage."

"And how do I stop it?"

"Just a second. I'm accessing the information now," Pufferfish said. "OK . . . remove the cover of the black box, and inside there should be some wires."

Flinch reached down and delicately removed the cover, but he didn't see just a few wires, as he had expected. Instead, he saw dozens . . . scores . . . hundreds. The guts of the timer looked like multicolored spaghetti spilling out all over the place.

"Find the green wire," Pufferfish said.

The green wire? There were a hundred green wires! The more he dug, the more he found. There was no way he was going to be able to do such delicate work.

"OK, Plan B!" Flinch said, shoving the bomb into his pocket. "Where's the next one?"

"Flinch—"

"*Andale!*" Flinch cried. "We don't have time!"

"Fine! Keep moving down the tunnel, then make a left at the curve ahead and go up to the next level. Wow! Some of these tunnels run parallel to one another. It's like an ant farm down there. Anyway, the next explosive is in an alcove," Pufferfish said.

"This is going to take forever! What if I just knock down the wall?"

"Well, I—" Flinch slugged the wall and the limestone collapsed, opening a passage to another tunnel. There he found the second bomb. Finally, one of his decisions had worked. "We're on a roll now. Where's the next one?"

Pufferfish led the boy through the catacombs. One by one he smashed through the ancient limestone walls and found Kapow's bombs. He tucked each new device into his pants and hoped that he wouldn't accidentally set off the chemicals inside.

"How many left?" Flinch asked.

"One," Pufferfish said. "It's in a section of the tunnels called the Port Mahon Quarry."

Following her instructions, Flinch smashed his way to the last of the explosives. What was it the teachers said in math class? "The shortest distance from point A to point B is a straight line"? They were right. It was even shorter when you had a superpunch.

Finally, he found himself standing before an iron gate with a concrete wall on the other side.

"OK, I'm here," Flinch said. "Looks like they don't want anyone to go past this point."

"Records show the city closed up this tunnel because the ceiling was collapsing. A few workers died here about a decade ago."

"How did he get a bomb back there?" Flinch asked.

"There are other ways into the quarry," Pufferfish explained. "This is the most direct. How are you doing?"

Flinch looked down at the light on his harness. Knocking down walls and running at over seventy miles an hour had used up a lot of fuel. He turned the knob on his harness to the highest level and then pulled with all his strength at the iron gate. It came away in his hands. Now he just had to punch through the concrete.

He gave it two wallops. There was a huge orchestra of rumbling, a thick cloud of dust, and a blast of cold air. When the dust settled, he could see the last bomb waiting on the other side. He scooped it up and shoved it into his pocket with the others, then turned to make a dash for the exit. But he wasn't feeling all that fast. The powerful punches had sapped almost all of his strength.

"I hope there's an exit nearby because I'm on empty," Flinch said.

"It's just off to the left," Pufferfish told him.

Suddenly, everything went black.

"What happened to my contacts?!" Flinch cried. He blinked furiously but nothing happened. He still couldn't see anything.

"The battery must have died," Gluestick explained. "They last only a few minutes. Don't you remember the—"

"Yes, I KNOW! The briefing!" Flinch growled. "I'm in the dark. I'm out of power. I've got ten bombs shoved in my pants, and I'm surrounded by skeletons. This is the worst mission ever!"

Desperate, he reached out for the wall and felt the cold, ancient bones on his fingertips. Fighting the urge to gag, he started walking as quickly as possible, stumbling occasionally on something—what, he dared not imagine. But after a while he saw a shaft of light shining down on a spiral staircase. With what was left of his power, he raced up the steps and darted out onto the streets of Paris. Gluestick and Braceface were waiting for him at the exit.

"I have to get rid of these bombs!" Flinch said, gasping for breath. "Do you have any sweets?"

The boys fumbled in their pockets, searching for a stick of gum or a forgotten piece of taffy, but there wasn't any. Even the emergency lollipop Flinch kept in his shoe was gone. He cursed himself for his late-night snacking.

"I have to use the emergency stash," Flinch said.

He pushed a button on his chest plate, which activated a panel that slid away, revealing a glass plate and a tiny red hammer. On the plate was written the warning BREAK IN CASE OF EMERGENCY. EAT ONLY IN DESPERATE SITUATIONS. He shattered the glass, reached into the tiny compartment, and pulled out a candy bar. It was called the Heart Attack Bar—a nine-thousand-calorie concoction of nougat, coconut, chocolate, caramel, and almonds, with a filling of high-fructose syrup. It was a candy bar on steroids shot out of a cannon at a mountain of firecrackers.

"There must be another way!" Duncan cried. "They tested that thing on a dozen hamsters, and eleven of them exploded. Literally blew up!"

"What happened to the twelfth one?" Jackson asked.

"He stole a semitruck and drove it through a shopping mall," Gluestick said.

"I saw that on the Internet!" Braceface said. "That was real?"

"I have no other choice," Flinch told them as he unwrapped the candy. The chocolate glistened. It was a creamy, dreamy work of art. He had no idea what it would do to him, but the situation was desperate. "Well . . . here goes nothing."

He took a bite of the candy bar and his taste buds exploded. The nuts and nougat swirled around his mouth, sticking to every surface, causing him to drool. Each bite assaulted his teeth like a jackhammer. It was the most delicious and painful thing he had ever tasted, and he let out a little scream that was part joy, part horror. His heart began to pound, and blood raced through his body like a tidal wave. He was pretty sure he saw angels telling him to "not go into the light."

"Grrrgggaggggabbb! I AM MIGHTY!" he shouted as he beat on his chest.

"Flinch! Flinch!" Gluestick shouted over the boy's excited yelps. "Are you OK?"

Flinch wanted to respond, but he couldn't work his mouth right.

"Is there any chance that he died and his body is just so wound up, it doesn't know yet?" Braceface asked.

“Flinch! If you can hear me, we need to get the bombs away from the city,” Gluestick said.

Flinch shook the clouds from his head and started to speed down the road. He underestimated the power at his command, and slammed face-first into a bus, nearly tipping it over. “Sorry!” he cried.

“What are you doing with the bombs?” Pufferfish asked through the com-link.

“NO . . . TIME . . . GRRAAGGH!!!” Flinch said as he ran. “NEED . . . GAAARGGGH . . . TOSS . . . RIVER . . . AIYYYYYYY!”

“You can’t toss them in the river!” Gluestick said. “The chemicals will destroy the fish life and then flow out into the English Channel. It will be devastating.”

“YAAAAAGHHH?” Flinch cried, though what he was wondering was where he could dump the bombs if the river was out of the question. Scanning the horizon, he found his answer. In the distance he saw a tower soaring high above the Paris skyline. It was made of wrought iron girders and its tip touched the clouds.

“TOWER?”

“Tower? You mean the Eiffel Tower,” Gluestick said.

“YESSSSSSSSS! WHEEZER! TOWER! MEET!” Flinch screamed, slipping into a string of nonsense words because the sugar had overwhelmed him. He took off like a streak, leaving his teammates behind, and bounded down crowded cobblestone alleys.

"BOOM! KAPOW! EXPLOSIONS! AAARGGGH!" he shouted to the people in his way, but it didn't seem to have any effect. They just looked at him like he was crazy. So he had to dart back and forth like a spastic bumblebee, zigging and zagging down one street and then another, all the time checking the horizon for the Eiffel Tower.

He sped across the Charles de Gaulle Bridge, scattering terrified pigeons. The bridge spanned the Seine, the waterway that cut Paris in two, and led him closer to the tower. After dashing through a park, he reached the tower's base. The place was full of tourists, and the French police were trying to evacuate them. He spotted a couple of familiar faces—Pufferfish and Wheezer—and a strange man wearing a mask with a clock painted on it and an overcoat covered in real alarm clocks. He was in handcuffs and yammering about his master plan.

"You foolish children. Don't you know with whom you are dealing? I am Captain Kapow, the mad bomber! Do you think you can stop me? My intellect is beyond anything you can even imagine."

"Agent Brand is going to love this," Braceface said as he and

Gluestick arrived on a motor scooter formed out of Jackson's superbraces. "Aren't we supposed to keep a low profile?"

"You're the one riding a moped that is coming out of your mouth," Wheezer said.

"We'll worry about the fallout later," Pufferfish said. "Flinch, what's your plan?"

Flinch pointed a shaky finger toward the top of the tower. "UP!! SKY!!!" he said, still struggling to speak through the sugar overload.

"That's crazy!" Pufferfish cried.

"That's Flinch," Gluestick said.

"You'll never make it!" Kapow roared, his words broken by a series of obnoxious high-pitched giggles. "Your time is almost up. I may not have gotten to cave in the city, but by bringing the bombs here, you have unwittingly helped me destroy one of the most recognizable tourist attractions in the world!"

"Yawn," Matilda said, as she intertwined her arms around Flinch's waist. "You clearly have no idea who we are. We're the kids they send when James Bond can't get it done."

With a squeeze of her inhalers, she and Flinch blasted into the sky. The tower's graceful girders flew by in a blur. Wheezer landed on the highest platform, where she and Flinch now stood completely alone.

“Hand over the bombs,” Wheezer said. “I can fly up into the stratosphere and let them go off where no one will be hurt.”

“NO! GRAAAGGGH!” Flinch dug into his pants and removed the explosives. Then, using every ounce of power he could muster, he hurled the bombs, one by one, into the sky. They flew higher and higher until he could no longer see them. When they exploded, there was a massive fireball, and the shock wave sent Wheezer and Flinch tumbling off the observation deck and into the air.

Flinch saw the ground approaching fast, but then Wheezer’s inhaler rockets were blasting in his ears and he was no longer falling.

“You’ve got quite an arm there, buddy,” Wheezer said. “You know, if this whole ‘saving the world’ business doesn’t work out, I hear the Nationals are looking for a new pitcher.”

Flinch could hardly speak. The shock of the Heart Attack Bar, and then the subsequent draining of all its power, had exhausted him. “I am mighty,” he said with a whimper.

“Good job, shaky,” Pufferfish said through the com-link. “Your first mission in charge and you save Paris. Pretty sweet.”

Suddenly, there was a rumbling sound from below. Flinch and Wheezer hovered to get a good look. Several avenues and streets began to crumble and give way. A few apartment buildings sunk into the ground and were swallowed whole.

Cars vanished, trees disappeared, and even a small park was pulled into the destruction. The damage snaked through five neighborhoods before it stopped.

"I thought we got all the bombs!" Wheezer said.

"That's not from the bombs," Pufferfish groaned as her voice came on the com-link. "Flinch must have knocked down too many tunnel walls. There wasn't enough to hold up the streets, and they collapsed under their own weight."

Flinch gaped at the destruction and then did what he did best. He freaked out.

3

38°86' N, 77°11' W

The Antagonist was irritated. When he got irritated bad things happened. Nasty, irrational ideas sprouted in his mind and spread like little angry weeds. The weeds grew and grew, choking anything sensible, until his mind was a garden of death, destruction, chaos, and fires. He knew he should try to calm down. But he just hated to shop. He hated it!

And Staplertown—the tristate area's largest office supply store—was not helping. He was lost inside its labyrinth of aisles, all stacked nearly to the ceiling with copy paper, shredders, computers, packing tape, and toner cartridges. All he wanted was a three-ring binder, but he had been up and down every aisle, searched every bin and shelf from top to bottom, and there

wasn't one to be found. He would have loved to ask for help. Actually, he would have loved to have asked for help a couple hours ago, but the store didn't seem to have any employees. He was all alone, among the Post-its and label makers, struggling with the urge to burn the building to the ground.

Suddenly, he spotted something moving. Down at the farthest end of the aisle, seemingly miles away . . . It was an employee! He wore a Staplertown vest and a matching hat. The Antagonist raced after him, desperate not to lose him in the maze they called a store, and finally reached him—a pimple-faced mouth breather playing a game on his phone as he walked through the store.

"Excuse me, but I require a three-ring binder," the Antagonist said. The sound of his voice startled him. In the last few weeks his vocabulary had grown dramatically, and he'd lost the Brooklyn accent he acquired as a kid hanging around the waterfront. Now when he spoke, he sounded intelligent—almost sophisticated—and he wasn't sure how the change had happened. But then again, he'd been going through a lot of changes lately.

The glassy-eyed teenager looked up from his game. "You're wearing a mask."

The Antagonist sighed. The mask was another of the big changes. It was causing problems. The white skull painted on it shouted "LOOK AT ME!" Whether he was at a drive-thru or a greeting card store, taking a walk in the park, or watching the puppies in the dog run, someone always wanted to know about the mask. Sometimes he hated wearing the stupid thing, but a little voice in his head wouldn't let him stop. It demanded that he wear it, even in the shower.

"Yes, I'm wearing a—"

"And you have a hook for a hand."

"Can we get back to the three-ring binder?"

"What is it?" the teenager asked.

The Antagonist wanted to crush the boy's spine. "You mean to tell me that you do not know what a three-ring binder is? It is used to hold documents so that they can be stored indefinitely in an organized manner. This type of binder is quite popular with businesspeople, students, teachers, and evil geniuses."

"We don't have those," the teenager said, and turned back to his game.

The blood boiled inside the Antagonist and a fever swept over him. With a fierce, violent slash, he impaled the teenager's phone with the sharp tip of his hook.

"Dude, that is so not cool. I'm calling my manager," the boy said. "Belle! Belle!"

Another employee came around the corner. She had thick glasses and pasty skin. Beneath her Staplertown smock was a black sweater and she wore dark purple eye shadow that made her look like a vampire in a very cheap horror movie. She was playing a game on her phone as well, and seemed irritated that she had to look up from it.

"What's going on, Darryl?" she asked.

"This psychopath attacked me!"

"Young lady, I'd like to see your manager," the Antagonist said.

"I'm the manager," the girl replied.

The Antagonist was dumbfounded. "You? You manage this entire store? You can't be older than nineteen."

"I'm eighteen. Now, what's going on?"

"My name is the Antagonist. I am a supervillain. I'm building an organization that deals in chaos and world war. Right now, I have twenty different operatives in ten international cities. Each is planning a terrible crime. I even have a lab where I combine animals with people to create horrible mutant hybrids. As world conquerors go, I am the real deal. To keep all these moving parts running smoothly, I need to be organized. I need to keep meticulous records, including maps, plans, blueprints, and tax forms. So . . . I need a three-ring binder."

"They're in the next aisle over by the color-copy paper," the manager said.

"Thank you," he said. Then he turned to Darryl and lifted him off the ground by his neck with his good hand. Darryl's face turned red and puffy. He tried to say something, but it came out as chokes and spittle. While the clerk struggled, the Antagonist turned his attention back to Belle.

"Young lady, I'm going to take your friend with me to the next aisle. If the three-ring binders aren't there, something terrible will happen to him. So, are you sure they are in the next aisle?"

Belle thought for a moment. "Actually, I'm not sure I know what a three-ring binder is."

What happened next is far too terrible to record, but suffice it to say that Darryl and Belle learned a valuable lesson about

work ethic and taking pride in their jobs. Of course, they spent the rest of their lives in hospital beds convalescing, but they did realize that they had been rude. And the happy ending for the Antagonist was that he found the three-ring binders by the cash registers on his way out of the store.

In the parking lot, he was loading his purchases into the Antagocar, which was really a Subaru Outback with a skull painted on the hood, when a woman came racing toward him. She was lean and tall, but he could not see her face because she was wearing a black mask with a white skull painted on it.

"I saw what you did to those oafs," she said.

The Antagonist was surprised. He hated surprises. He snatched the woman by the collar, but she caught his wrist and gave it a quick turn to free herself. He was about to attack again but realized by her stance that she knew a great deal about the martial arts. Fighting her would be useless. And painful. "And?"

"I thought it was awesome."

"Yes," the Antagonist agreed. How strange it was for him to receive compliments. Even stranger was how desperately he seemed to need them. "It was most certainly awesome."

The woman nodded. "I hate this store. I come here all the time to buy stuff and they never know what I'm talking about. I'm glad someone finally did something about it."

The Antagonist smiled under his mask.

"My name is Miss Information. I heard you talking about your evil organization. You wouldn't happen to have any openings for an assistant?" she asked. "I'm very good with calendars and I know my way around a fax machine. Plus, I'm really pretty evil."

He eyed the woman up and down. It seemed that lately everywhere he went people were eager to join his cause. It had become a little overwhelming. Still, he could use an assistant to help around the office. The files were getting out of control, and his henchmen kept complaining that the watercooler was always empty. This was a woman who could handle the details.

"You're hired. You start immediately. The first thing you're going to do is burn this office supply store to the ground."

Miss Information held up a box of matches. "Already on it, boss."

THE POWERS THAT BE THINK YOU'VE SHOWN SOME REAL SPUNK GETTING THIS FAR IN YOUR TRAINING, BUT I'M NOT SO SURE. I MEAN, ADMITTEDLY, YOU'RE A LOT CLEVERER THAN YOU LOOK (YOU LOOK LIKE A GROUNDHOG WITH A HEAD COLD). BUT WHAT ABOUT YOUR PHYSICAL ABILITIES? BEING A SPY ISN'T ALL ABOUT YOUR BRAINS. SOMETIMES, IN DANGEROUS SITUATIONS, YOU NEED TO BE STRONG, FAST, AND AGILE.

SO IT'S TIME TO START YOUR NERDS SECRET AGENT ATHLETIC EXAMINATION. NOW, I REALIZE THAT YOU MAY NOT BE STRONG, FAST, AND AGILE. IN FACT, ONE LOOK AT YOU TELLS ME YOU ARE WEAK, SLOW, AND . . . WELL, LET'S JUST SAY I HAVE MY DOUBTS YOU COULD LEAP A FENCE. THIS IS YOUR CHANCE TO PROVE ME WRONG.

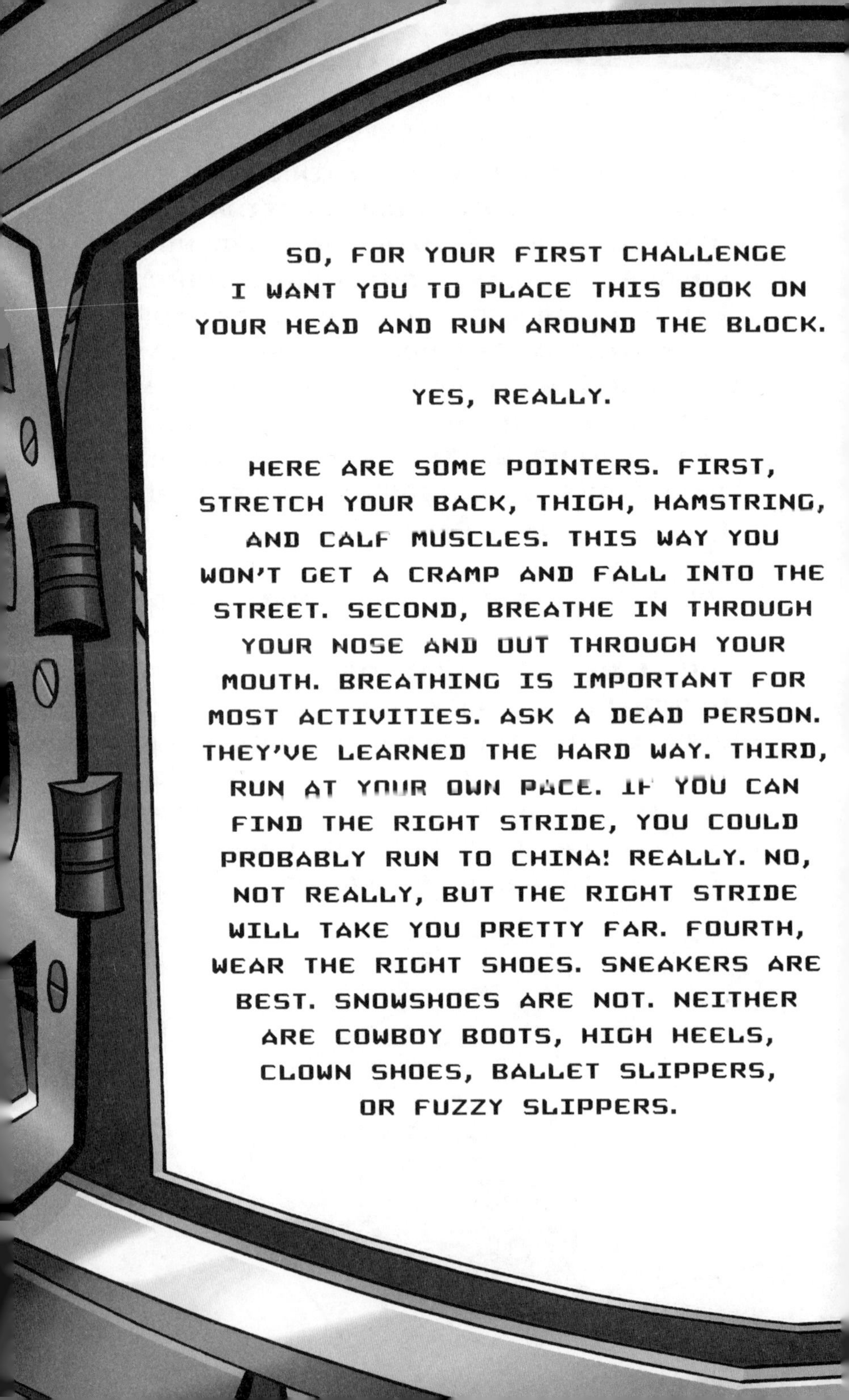
SO, FOR YOUR FIRST CHALLENGE I WANT YOU TO PLACE THIS BOOK ON YOUR HEAD AND RUN AROUND THE BLOCK.
YES, REALLY.
HERE ARE SOME POINTERS. FIRST, STRETCH YOUR BACK, THIGH, HAMSTRING, AND CALF MUSCLES. THIS WAY YOU WON'T GET A CRAMP AND FALL INTO THE STREET. SECOND, BREATHE IN THROUGH YOUR NOSE AND OUT THROUGH YOUR MOUTH. BREATHING IS IMPORTANT FOR MOST ACTIVITIES. ASK A DEAD PERSON. THEY'VE LEARNED THE HARD WAY. THIRD, RUN AT YOUR OWN PACE. IF YOU CAN FIND THE RIGHT STRIDE, YOU COULD PROBABLY RUN TO CHINA! REALLY. NO, NOT REALLY, BUT THE RIGHT STRIDE WILL TAKE YOU PRETTY FAR. FOURTH, WEAR THE RIGHT SHOES. SNEAKERS ARE BEST. SNOWSHOES ARE NOT. NEITHER ARE COWBOY BOOTS, HIGH HEELS, CLOWN SHOES, BALLET SLIPPERS, OR FUZZY SLIPPERS.

OK, THAT'S ALL YOU NEED TO KNOW. THE SENSORS WILL RECORD YOUR TIME, AND WHEN YOU GET BACK WE'LL SEE HOW YOU DID.

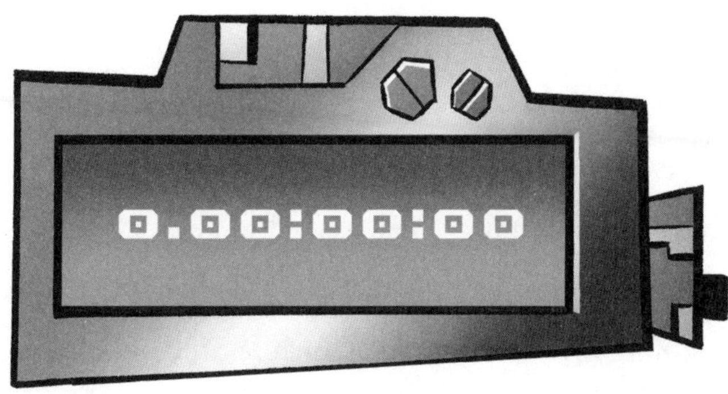

MAYBE YOU NEED A FEW MORE PRACTICE ROUNDS. IN THE MEANTIME, HOW ABOUT A SHOWER? YOU STINK.

LEVEL 2
ACCESS GRANTED

BEGIN TRANSMISSION:

4

38°87' N, 77°10' W

Flinch had never met anyone like Principal Dove. Her eyes were as big as dinner plates, and she had a dainty nose and a mouth that seemed to always be open in a perfect circle. When she moved, her whole body shook as if she were ruffling invisible feathers. Flinch felt the impulse to toss her some bread crumbs.

"Tsk, tsk, tsk," she said, shaking her head in disapproval. She leaned over her desk and eyeballed each of the NERDS, finally landing on Flinch as if he were some peculiar animal at the zoo. He was already jumpy from the morning's semi-successful mission in Paris, and the massive sugar shock from the Heart Attack Bar was still taking a toll on his nerves. Her scolding smile didn't help.

"Late on the first day?" she asked.

Flinch looked to Pufferfish. Her real name was Ruby Peet, and as the team's official leader, she usually called the shots and did the talking. That's how Flinch liked it. The others were quick with their thoughts. He was quick with his feet.

"We missed the bus," Ruby lied.

"All five of you?" Ms. Dove said, her smile widening. "Well, that must be quite a story. What happened?"

"Oh, um—it's just one of those mornings," Jackson said, flashing his biggest grin. Even with his braces he had a charming smile, and he wasn't afraid to use it.

"Now, you wouldn't be trying to pull my leg, would you?" Dove said with a giggle.

The children looked at one another. It was clear to Flinch that none of them knew what to say, and despite the principal's smile, the tension in the room was building by the minute. What were they supposed to tell her—that they were spies? That they had little robots inside their bodies that gave them superpowers? That they had flown to Paris that morning and stopped a lunatic from destroying the city, yet managed to create nearly a billion dollars in damage in the process?

Back at Nathan Hale Elementary the team occasionally encountered a teacher who asked questions about the sudden and frequent disappearances of the children, but somehow

Agent Brand and Ms. Holiday made it all go away. Then again, back at the elementary school they were taught by Mr. Pheiffer, who spent most of his time talking about his tan. A tornado could have swept through his class and he wouldn't have batted an eyelid. Their old principal, Dehaven, could be difficult, but he enjoyed bullying his staff a lot more than he did the children. So for the most part, the members of NERDS came and went as they pleased.

It appeared as if all that was going to change.

"It seems a rather odd coincidence that all five of you missed the bus this morning," the new principal said. "It boggles the mind."

"Actually, the odds of such a thing happening are really not that far out of the realm of possibility," Duncan said. "If you consider the distance of the bus stop to our neighborhood as well as the average speed in morning traffic—"

Ms. Dove put her finger to her mouth. "Shhhhhhhhh!"

She stared at the children for a long moment with a smile on her face, as if what she read in their eyes was amusing. Flinch knew that she couldn't read their minds, but he covered his ears just in case that was how the woman accessed his thoughts.

His blood sugar was still out of whack. Something sweet would calm him down, so he reached into his pocket and took out a Chocolate Coconut Bomb Bar he'd grabbed when he got back to the Playground. He tore it open and chomped down with delight. Yum! It was like heaven inside his mouth, and he was starting to feel better when, suddenly, with a hand faster than lightning, Ms. Dove snatched the treat from his hand and tossed it into the wastebasket next to her desk. Flinch shrank back in horror. His treat was covered in paper clips, dust balls, and a few thumbtacks. It took every ounce of self-control not to shriek.

"Mr. Escala, our school has a 'no junk food' policy," she said. "There is no junk food of any kind anywhere on my campus. No candy bar or soda machines. No sugary treats at lunch. Not a single drop of chocolate milk in the cafeteria. Little birds need healthy food to fly."

"Uh-oh," Matilda said.

And that's when Flinch's shriek escaped. No candy machines? No soda pop? What kind of a madhouse was this woman running? Someone had to be alerted. When he finally stopped screaming, he reached for his phone. He had the president's number on speed dial—he would help! But before Flinch could hit the number, Matilda reached over and gave the knob on his harness a twist. The harness captured some of his energy and he managed to calm down a little.

"Children, I know the first day in a new nest can be confusing," Principal Dove said.

“Nest?” Ruby asked.

“There are so many new and strange birds in the air, and I like to keep a careful eye on the hatchlings.”

“Hatchlings?” Duncan asked. “Are you talking about us?”

“Some birdies need a lot more attention than others. Some birdies need to be placed under the strong, watchful wing of a mama bird. I’m thinking that you five might need that wing hovering over you, keeping you safe and watching every move you make.”

“Does she think we’re really birds?” Flinch whispered.

“I think so,” Jackson replied.

“It all depends on you and what kind of birdies you are. Are you the kind that can fly free, or the kind that need to be in a cage?” Ms. Dove asked the group.

“Um . . . we’re free birds?” Pufferfish said.

Ms. Dove clapped her hands. “I’m as happy as a hummingbird. I’d hate for you to leave the nest not knowing how to fly.”

She handed each of the children a piece of paper.

Flinch looked down at his. “What’s this?”

“They are your new class schedules. I took a quick look at your files and noticed that all five of you have the same classes at the same time. That’s not good for little birdies, especially ones that need to stretch out and meet other members of our flock. So I made some changes.”

Flinch looked at Pufferfish again. This time the team leader wasn't so calm. Her hand swelled to the size of a small pumpkin. She was allergic to logistical nightmares. Keeping the NERDS together in one class made it easy to reach them quickly. What would they do now?

"OK, little birdies, fly back to your classes," the principal said, and waved them out of her office. Flinch got up slowly, still wondering if maybe he should snatch the trash can from under her desk and liberate the poor, innocent candy bar. Matilda seemed to read his mind and pulled him out of the office.

Once in the hall, the NERDS stared at their new schedules.

"That woman is going to be trouble," Pufferfish said.

"What if she starts watching us?" Matilda said. She took a shot of her asthma inhaler. "Look, she's got me hyperventilating."

Flinch shuddered. "Did you see what she did to my candy? What kind of a heartless person throws away a perfectly good Chocolate Coconut Bomb Bar?"

Jackson waved them off. "Everyone relax. She's no different than any other teacher. She just wants you to know who's boss around here. All we have to do is dazzle her with a few smiles or ask for extra help we don't really need—you know, pretend that we look up to her. We'll have her eating out of the palms of our hands in no time. Trust me. It'll work like a charm."

"That would work well if she was sane," Duncan said. "But

you heard her in there. She thinks we're birds. I bet the woman is sitting on an egg right now. It's best if we just stay off her radar. We can't be late or act suspicious."

"I hate to say this, but I miss the old days when Heathcliff could just hypnotize our teachers so they wouldn't remember us dashing off to save the world." Ruby sighed.

"Well, I liked him a lot better back then than I do now," Jackson said. "The 'I'm a creepy giant head that can take over the world' thing is really obnoxious."

"So now what? We just go off to our separate classes?" Flinch asked.

The children shrugged. For some, it was the first time they had been separated in years, but what could they do?

Flinch watched his friends drift away down the hall and realized there was a comfort in being part of a group. When they were gone, he looked down at his schedule. His first class of the day was math—his worst subject.

"There's another thing we should consider," Flinch shouted to the others. "Ms. Dove might be evil."

Math was hard, even on the first day, and science class was no better. With his brain drowning in algebraic equations and plate tectonics, Flinch headed off to history class, where he was bombarded with dates and names from hundreds of years ago. To top it all off, he had Latin, which he was surprised to learn, was a language that no one spoke anymore. What kind of a madhouse was Ms. Dove running? Worst of all, without sweets Flinch actually had the ability to pay attention. It was an unusual feeling for him to hear facts and remember them. Somehow it felt wrong.

He drifted from one class to the next, catching only brief glimpses of his teammates as they hurried down the halls. He didn't like being alone. Before he became a spy, being alone meant being a target for bullies. Like jackals, they hunted those who were separated from the pack. Once the weak were identified, the bullies would descend, dishing out brutal wedgies and painful flicks to the neck, sticking wet fingers in the ears and spitting paper wads in the eyes. Nothing was quite as terror-inducing as the bullies' high-pitched giggles as they cornered their prey. Flinch scanned the halls. If bullies came at him, he would have to take their abuse. He was too strong and fast to fight back. He could hurt someone, or worse, blow the team's cover.

But being lonely, concentrating in class, and fearing bullies were nothing compared to the heart-racing experience called lunch. Normally, lunch would have been a feast of chocolate-covered morsels, caramel layers, and cream filling, all soaking in the finest high-fructose corn syrup money could buy. But Ms. Dove's school had no such pleasures. For the first time in as long as he could remember, Flinch had to eat what most scientists would call "real food." Some of it was green and leafy, some of it was broiled and baked, and there was a slice of something labeled "whole grain bread" and a few little orange logs he was told were called carrots. There wasn't a peanut butter cup or red rope in sight. He appealed to the lunch lady, who knew what Flinch usually ate, but the big, burly figure said his hands were tied. Ms. Dove had already set up a lunch date with him to discuss what to serve in the cafeteria.

"It's just going to get worse, kid," the lunch lady warned. "Tomorrow we're serving hummus on pita bread with baba ghanoush."

“Baba ghanoush doesn’t happen to have little colored marshmallows in it, does it?”

The lunch lady shook his head.

The rest of the day didn’t get much better. When Flinch’s last class was over, he just wanted to go home and drown his sorrows in a couple of cases of juice boxes. But before he could even close his locker, he found himself surrounded by four very large boys. Every school has a few bullies whose growth spurts defy all logic. They are impossibly tall. They have mustaches. The four kids who confronted Flinch looked like gorillas wearing human costumes.

“Hey, kid, you didn’t pay the new student fee,” one of the

boys said. He was skinny with a mop of red hair that hung in his eyes.

"New student fee?"

"Yeah, we're here to collect. It's five bucks, which is a great deal. Last year it was ten," the second boy said, and the others chuckled. This one was a bit too chubby for his T-shirt.

Flinch sighed. He would have happily handed over five dollars just to avoid the hassle, but he was broke. He said as much, and suspecting the boys would not accept an IOU, he prepared for the inevitable: pushing, manhandling, maybe a purple nurple, maybe a pink belly—typical bully stuff—and there wasn't a thing he could do about it without blowing his cover. Sometimes, being a superpowered spy was a real bummer.

The third boy stepped forward. He was the shortest of the bunch, but to call him the shortest was like saying he was the smallest giant. He had a wide, thin smile and big buggy eyes like an amphibian. He opened Flinch's locker and went through everything, tossing books and papers aside in search of some money. "I think he's telling the truth. He's broke. Must have spent all his money on candy. There's a trash bag's worth of wrappers in here."

The fourth boy was average-looking, but every time he breathed, a high-pitched whistle filled the air. "Well, you know what happens when you can't pay the fee." He laughed, then grabbed Flinch by the shirt and shoved him inside the locker.

The door slammed in Flinch's face and he was plunged into darkness. His first thought was to wait until the boys were gone and then free himself, but suddenly he didn't feel well. Nausea came on like a hurricane. A fever raced through him, making him feel like someone had lit a bonfire in his head. But the most peculiar sensation was his anger. He was angrier than he had ever been—even angrier than when they stopped making tropical fruit–flavored Now and Laters. He wanted to punish these kids for making him an easy target. Who were these . . . these fleas to treat him so disrespectfully? Couldn't they see his intelligence and power? They needed to be taught a lesson!

With a swift kick, his locker door flew off its hinges and crashed against the far wall. He stepped out, fists clenched. The first bully shook off his surprise and charged at Flinch, who caught him in the chest with a punch that sent him skidding down the hallway several yards. The other three boys stared at their fallen friend in bewilderment, and the universal truth about bullies was revealed once again: They are usually cowards.

The boys tried to run, but Flinch wouldn't let them. He raced down the hall like a jaguar and blocked their way. They turned to run back the other way, but he blocked them again, in the blink of an eye. He grabbed two of the boys by their shirts and launched them down the hall like twin bowling balls. They slid into their fallen friend and crumpled into a pile with him at the bottom. Then Flinch grabbed the fourth boy, the one with the whistling nose, and lifted him off the ground over his head. He wanted to toss him out a high window. He wanted to slam his body onto the floor. He wanted to crush the fool so that no one would dare challenge his mighty power. It would be a message to the world that he was someone to fear.

And then the fever was gone and his head cleared. What was he doing? He couldn't treat normal kids like this. Where had all this anger come from, and why could he hardly control himself? He gently set the boy back down on the floor.

"Are you OK?" he asked the confused bully.

The boy couldn't seem to speak, but Flinch didn't think he was injured.

"Tsk, tsk, tsk," a voice said from behind him.

Flinch turned and saw Ms. Dove standing there. She still wore her fixed-on smile, but her eyes were those of someone who finds her new puppy has chewed on her shoes.

"And what just happened here?" she asked.

"Just a little horsing around," Flinch said.

"Jessie, get your friends and meet us in room eleven," she said, then she led Flinch down the hall by the arm.

"I truly hate to do this, Mr. Escala. If it were up to me, I wouldn't even have this room, but it does seem to help with those little birds who need time to think about how to straighten up and fly right."

She stopped at room eleven and opened the door. A collection of juvenile delinquents and criminals to rival the inmates of Alcatraz looked up at Flinch.

"What's this?" Flinch asked.

"Detention," Ms. Dove said, with an exaggerated frown. "We can't have a bully in our nest, Mr. Escala."

A bully! Flinch could hardly believe his ears. He wasn't a bully. He was the opposite of a bully. He was an anti-bully.

"Have a seat," she continued.

He found one and collapsed into it, feeling foolish and humiliated. He gazed around at the other children looking for some sympathy and found none. When he looked back to the door, he saw Ms. Dove watching him from the hallway, her big owl eyes round and full of suspicion. She would be watching him now. Flinch was under her wing.

5

38°87' N, 77°10' W

Heathcliff's head was kept in a large two-story holding cell that was encircled by a catwalk on the second floor that was used by the doctors and scientists for observation. It was a bustling room filled with busy people who checked Heathcliff's heart rate, breathing, and sedative levels around the clock. Armed guards were on alert twenty-four hours a day.

But it was not enough. Not for Agent Brand. If Heathcliff woke up, a bunch of guards were not going to be able to stop him—not much of anything would stop him. So, Alexander often found himself wandering away from his desk to check in on Heathcliff and make sure that the end of the world was not accidentally in progress, as he was now.

He did not enjoy being a babysitter for a monster. When General Savage asked him to run NERDS, he thought he'd be commanding a team of superspies to defend the world. He had no idea that the biggest threat the world had ever seen, a mind that could reshape reality as it wished, would be sleeping in his basement.

Ms. Holiday came through a door at the far end of the catwalk and approached him. He knew she had been busy all day, sorting through books in the school's neglected library. She was a secret agent, but she was also a librarian, and, just like Brand, she had to keep up her cover. Brand had received a few e-mails from her with the subject line "The Library That Time Forgot" and photo attachments of books like *Will Man Ever Walk on the Moon?* and *Rotary Phones: The World of Modern Communication.* He enjoyed her sense of humor, and how she approached things with a smile. Her good attitude was rubbing off on him. He was starting to relax around her and at work. She said she was smoothing out his rough edges.

"How is Paris?" he asked.

"Angry," she replied. "Every last person. Savage is arranging to have all the damage repaired, and luckily there were no serious injuries. Did you read the report?"

"Yes. Flinch wasn't ready," Brand said.

"Probably because we don't give him any responsibility," she said. "To be honest, I think he did pretty well, considering he's never been on point. I'd hate for anyone to read what happened on my first mission."

"I think fighting three mafia enforcers on an alligator farm was pretty brave," he said.

She frowned. "You read my file."

"Are you OK? You look tired."

"I had a little cold, but I'm getting over it," she said. "How is Sleeping Beauty?"

Brand nodded. "The same—for now. What are we going to do when he wakes up? The sedatives won't keep him down forever. Eventually, his body will adapt, and nothing we can do will keep him unconscious."

For a long time Ms. Holiday didn't reply. It was obvious she didn't have an answer. "I worked with him for a while," she said finally, "and he wasn't always out of control."

"I remember," Brand said.

"I'm talking about before you arrived. Yes, he was cranky and arrogant, but he could be kind of sweet, too. He was very close with his parents," Ms. Holiday said. "His mother described him as a very loving and sensitive boy."

"He changed," Brand said.

"True, but—"

"You see something else?"

"You'll think I'm silly."

"I never do," he replied.

Ms. Holiday smiled. "Well, he snores."

"Huh?"

"Heathcliff snores—a lot. It sounds like a hundred cows with sleep apnea. The staff has taken to wearing special headsets to protect their hearing."

"So?" Brand wasn't sure what she was saying.

"It means he hasn't changed so much. It means despite it all, he's still human. He still does something embarrassing. And if he snores just like everyone else, well, maybe there's a soft spot in his heart just like in everyone else's, too," Ms. Holiday said.

It was a crazy theory, but Brand wanted it to be true.

"So . . . Captain Kapow is ready for questioning," she said.

Brand nodded. "Good. I'd like to take my mind off of one maniac and put it on another. Lead the way."

He followed Holiday through the doorway and down several halls until they came to the door marked Interrogation Room. Above the door was a flashing red lightbulb, which meant the room was occupied.

"Is he restrained?" Brand asked.

"Yes, finally. I'm not sure he's ready to talk, though. He's been rambling most of the day. I think he's sick. He's feverish and disoriented. I've had one of the scientists take a look at him, but she hasn't given me a report yet."

"Pufferfish can help. She's allergic to sick people," Brand said. "And she's allergic to hundreds of different bacteria and viruses, so she might be able to narrow it down. See if you can get her here."

"The kids are already home for the day," Ms. Holiday said.

"The first day is over already?" Brand asked.

"Yes, but not without problems. It's the principal."

"One crisis at a time," Brand said with a groan.

Ms. Holiday opened the door to the interrogation room. Captain Kapow sat inside. His wrists and feet were strapped to a chair, and the chair was bolted to the floor. As soon as Brand stepped close to him, he found out why. The man growled and tried to lunge at him. Luckily, the restraints kept the Captain under control.

"Has he said anything?" Brand asked.

A small round panel opened in the wall and Benjamin zipped into the room. The orb flittered about and finally hovered in front of the agent's face. "Plenty, but not a lot that you would describe as rational. What he has said isn't as interesting as who he is. The Captain's real name is Sherman Stoop. He's been working as part of our organization for three years."

"He works for us?" Brand cried.

Ms. Holiday handed him a stack of papers. "Here's his file."

Brand flipped through Stoop's records. He could hardly believe what he was reading.

"What happened to this man?" he asked, not expecting an answer. "Record this interview, Benjamin."

"Of course, Agent Brand. Recording now."

SUPPLEMENTAL MATERIAL

The following transcript comes from an interview conducted by Agent Alexander Brand, Agent Lisa Holiday, and Communication Orb 3, a.k.a. Benjamin, with one Sherman Stoop a.k.a. Captain Kapow.

Brand: Hello, Mr. Stoop. My name is Agent Brand, and this is my associate, Agent Holiday.

Stoop: I knew that! Nothing gets past my incredible brain. My superior intellect already deduced that you would come. Naturally, you want to interrogate me.

Brand: I think most people who have committed a major crime could guess there would be someone wanting to ask them questions.

Stoop: If when you say the word "most," you mean just me, then I accept your notion! Ask what you want, Agent, but know this—many of my answers may be difficult for you to comprehend. I am, after all, a genius. But I will do my best to keep my answers simple for you and your dullard of a partner.

Holiday: Well, he's a real charmer.

Brand: Mr. Stoop, who put you up to this crime?

Stoop: Ha! How dare you! The bombing was entirely my idea!

Brand: Mr. Stoop, we've gone through your files. Your IQ is just above a house cat's.

Holiday: You were voted "Most likely to fall down a flight of steps" by your class.

Brand: When you applied for this job, they asked you for a blood test and you asked for time to study. You don't have the intellect to build the complicated devices you planted under Paris.

Stoop: My brain's full potential has recently reached great heights. Give me an IQ test, but be prepared—my scores will be so high, your tiny little minds may slip into madness trying to understand.

Brand: I think we'll pass. Whether or not that's true about your IQ, one thing hasn't increased dramatically and that's

your bank account. You don't have the funds to fly to Paris or to buy and build the bombs. So, using my tiny little mind, I have deduced that you are working for someone, Sherman.

Stoop: Don't call me that name! I'm Captain Kapow!

Holiday: He sounds like Heathcliff. He had a thing about his name, too.

Brand: You didn't do this on your own, Captain. Who helped you?

Stoop: Fine, yes, I have a benefactor. But I have no idea who he is. All I know is he's a genius—not on my level, but certainly bright. If it wasn't for him, I'd still be wasting my potential guarding that giant head.

Holiday: Did he give you the idea to bomb Paris?

Stoop: Hardly! The Antagonist merely showed me that I was special and helped me fulfill my destiny.

Brand: The Antagonist? Who is the Antagonist?

Stoop: I don't know. All I know is that he wears a mask. It's black and has a skull painted on the front.

Holiday: That can't be . . .

Brand: What kind of fool do you take us for, Mr. Stoop?

Stoop: I suppose I take you for the regular, everyday kind of fool, Agent, but what I have told you is true.

Agent Brand slams his fist on the table.

Brand: Benjamin, can you project an image of Simon for us?

Benjamin displays a photograph of Heathcliff Hodges as his alias, Simon.

Brand: Does the mask look like this?

Stoop: Yes.

Brand: That's impossible! The person who owns that mask is in this facility right now, and he's been in our custody for almost three months.

Stoop: What's that mean to me?

Brand: The owner of that mask is the giant head you were guarding! His name is Heathcliff Hodges!

END TRANSCRIPT.

6

38°87' N, 77°10' W

Flinch lived with his grandmother, Mama Rosa. She was in her late seventies but as spry as a teenage girl. After school every day, he could always find her in the same place: parked in front of the television watching her "stories." Her favorite was a Spanish soap opera called *La Luna Blanca*, which in English meant "The White Moon." It was about a beautiful housecleaner who goes to work for a very wealthy Spanish family who owns a winery. Flinch had tried to watch it once, but his Spanish was not as good as it should have been. Still, you didn't need to be fluent to know what was going on—especially with Mama Rosa around. Any time someone appeared on screen who the old woman didn't like, she hissed, pointed, and cursed at them in Spanish. Flinch didn't know what some of the words

meant, and he was pretty sure that was a good thing. Mama Rosa was in the midst of a very intense shouting match with the TV when he got home that day.

"You do know they can't hear you, Mama," Flinch said.

Mama Rosa shook her head. "Someone has to talk some sense into these people, especially poor Mrs. Lucina. Her no-good husband is trying to steal her family's fortune! Ay, Mrs. Lucina! Can't you see he is bad for you?"

Flinch couldn't have been more relieved. All the way home from school he worried that Ms. Dove had called his grandmother, but it looked as if the coast was clear. He turned to climb the stairs to his room when suddenly the television clicked off.

"So, I hear you are now a juvenile delinquent."

Flinch turned back reluctantly. He hated disappointing his grandmother. He knew the hyperactivity was bad enough, so he tried to be a good kid in most other ways. "Before you get upset, I can explain."

"Julio, today is your first day," she said. "You have never been in trouble before! Is it those kids you are always hanging around with? Are they a bad influence on you? I don't want you spending time with them if they are hoodlums."

"Mama Rosa, my friends aren't hoodlums. They're the smartest kids in the school," Flinch said. "You know Duncan as well as you know me."

"Yes, the one that eats paste," she said with a harrumph. "Well, they may not be hoodlums, but they are weird. If it's not them, then why have you turned to a life of crime?"

"It was just a detention," he said.

"It's a detention now, but what about tomorrow? Tomorrow is jail?"

Flinch frowned. Mama Rosa had a flare for the dramatic. No matter how small the mistake, she was in constant fear that Julio was on his way to the slammer.

"A bunch of kids were picking on me—"

"Julio! Julio! Julio! You know better. The bullies pick on the younger kids to get attention. If you react, then they get what they want," Mama Rosa said.

Julio shrugged. "I would have explained that to them if they hadn't shoved me in a locker first."

He felt another flash fever coming on. His anger threatened to boil over. How dare Ms. Dove call his grandmother and label him a bully? He had fought back to defend himself, and now he was the villain? Did everyone expect him to just sit and take it? Did they want him to get pushed around the rest of his life? Well, they could forget it! He was done being picked on!

"Oh, Julio, you look so tired, *cariño.* You're flushed. Are you OK?"

"I'm not feeling well," he said, as his racing heart calmed.

"Well, lie down and I'll bring you something to eat," she said, putting her hand on his forehead. "You're boiling. Go rest now, but remember: You are a good boy, and if you are not a good boy, I will see it. Your grandmother has eyes in the back of her head and in her hands and her back and her feet. I see everything—EVERYTHING! No more trouble at school. Do you understand?"

Flinch nodded. "Yes, ma'am."

He shuffled into his room, closed the door, and fell into bed with his shoes still on his feet. He felt horrible; even closing his eyes hurt. His temperature went from hot sweats to teeth-chattering chills. He'd never felt the flu come on so fast or so intense, and in his feverish haze, he wondered if he had picked up some kind of skeleton germ in the catacomb cemetery that morning. Something had killed all those people! Would he be the next victim?

He forced himself to think of other things. Chocolate-covered Easter eggs, marshmallow Peeps, Kool-Aid, maple syrup. That calmed him, and soon he fell asleep.

Unfortunately, in his dreams his happy thoughts were replaced with more frightening visions. Everyone was laughing at him. Everyone was conspiring against him. Even his friends and teammates were working on ways to keep him from achieving his full potential. In one particularly nasty nightmare, his teammates chained him to a wall in a prison cell and stood over him. He begged them to let him out, but they wouldn't. Instead, they turned their backs and walked away. Suddenly, he heard the striking of a match and a tiny orange flame danced in the dark. In its faint light he saw a boy wearing a mask with a skull painted on it.

“Heathcliff!”

“No,” the figure whispered, then took the mask off. Flinch cried out. He was looking at an exact copy of himself.

“We are great, and they know we should be in charge,” his twin said. Then he blew out his match. Only the skull on his mask still shone in the dark.

END TRANSMISSION.

OK, LET'S GET BACK TO YOUR PHYSICAL FITNESS TEST. THE FIRST ROUND WAS PRETTY IMPRESSIVE—FOR A BABY! NOW THINGS ARE GOING TO GET A LITTLE TOUGHER.

LIE ON THE FLOOR FACEDOWN, PLACE THIS BOOK ON YOUR LOWER BACK, AND GIVE ME TWENTY PUSH-UPS.

HEY, NO WHINING! THE PUSH-UP IS SORT OF THE INTERNATIONAL EXCERCISE FOR TOUGH GUYS. SOLDIERS WHO SCREW UP ARE CONSTANTLY BEING TOLD TO DROP AND GIVE THE SERGEANT TWENTY PUSH-UPS. IT'S TRUE. IT HAPPENS IN ALMOST ANY MOVIE ABOUT A SOLDIER—SO THERE!

BUT THERE ARE A FEW THINGS THAT WILL MAKE THIS EASIER.

FIRST, STRETCH YOUR PECTORAL MUSCLES, BICEPS, AND SHOULDERS. SECOND, SEPARATE YOUR HANDS SO THAT THEY ARE EQUALLY DISTANT FROM THE CENTER OF YOUR CHEST. (TOO CLOSE TOGETHER WILL WORK THE TRICEPS, THE SMALLER MUSCLES, WHICH WILL MAKE THE PUSH-UPS HARDER. TOO FAR AWAY AND YOU WILL STRAIN YOUR SHOULDERS.) LAST, THERE'S A WAY TO DO IT IF YOU ARE A BIG CRYBABY: PUT YOUR KNEES ON THE GROUND.

WHEN YOU'RE DONE, WIPE YOUR SWEATY FOREHEAD ON THE SENSOR BELOW.

LEVEL 3

ACCESS GRANTED

7

38°88' N, 77°09' W

The Antagonist had a secret lair called the Fortress of Antagonism. He had a jet called the Antagojet. He had a motorcycle called the Antagochopper. He had a boat called the Antagoboat. He had a bicycle he called a bicycle (there wasn't anything particularly evil about it, except for the jangly bell, so he didn't think it warranted its own name). He had an army of goons and minions, a handful of henchmen, and even an evil assistant named Miss Information, all of whom he called the Antagonauts. An outsider might have looked at him and said, "Wow, that madman has everything!"

But the Antagonist wasn't happy. Not happy at all! What was causing him so much grief? It seemed that every time he turned around he had to kill yet another one of his employees.

Every day, one of the hundreds of people who worked for him decided that they were smarter than he was and should be running his evil empire. They tried to kidnap him. They tried to lock him up in dungeons. They tried to toss acid into his face. It was getting annoying.

At first he had blamed it on professional jealousy. But fending off fifteen murder attempts in a single week indicated more than just envy. Something was wrong. Unfortunately, the Antagonist could not quite put his hook on what it was.

The attackers seemed to be ordinary goons and henchmen, equally eager to push a hero into a volcano or go for coffee. But then all of a sudden they were wearing costumes, planning the destruction of the planet, and building doomsday devices. Just that morning, he had discovered Betty from accounting wearing a ridiculous costume and calling herself the Terrible Tornado. She wore a machine strapped to her back that could create cyclones. To prevent the lair from spinning into destruction, the Antagonist was forced to lure Betty into the bottomless pit on level four. (It wasn't really a bottomless pit. The bottom was on level three, but no one had to know.) Betty had used her coffee breaks to build the machine, which was clearly against the rules in the employee handbook, and now the Antagonist was suspicious that the two personal days she had taken the week before were not for emergency cat delousing as she claimed.

But what was really frustrating about the entire situation was that Betty's actions seemed to inspire the others to try to destroy him, too. That morning, he had stumbled upon three henchmen, wielding swords made of electricity, hiding in his private bathroom. Then, two more assassins dropped from the ceiling and another popped up from under his desk, all armed with poisonous blow-dart guns. He broke each of their necks and then picked up his phone.

"Maintenance, this is your lord and master," he said. "I have some dead assassins in my office. Could you come up here and get rid of them? What? Yes, more dead assassins."

He hung up the phone and returned to the executive bathroom, stepping over the bodies to get to the sink. He slipped off his skull mask and splashed cold water on his face. Then he looked at himself in the mirror. At first, he wasn't sure he recognized the man staring back at him. He had a big, jutting jaw, a nose that had been on the receiving end of a few too many punches, and a brow that threatened to swallow his eyes. It wasn't the face of a man with a superior intellect. Uncomfortable, he nearly put the mask back on, but then he stopped himself. His face might not look supersmart, but there was something else—it was fierce. It was a face good at frightening people into paying their debts.

And then he began to remember who he was. He was a

goon—a professional manhandler. He was the star of his field, the most respected mauler in the industry. Not too long ago he was on the cover of *Leg-breaker* magazine as the year's Sexiest Goon Alive. How could he have forgotten? How could his snow-white hair, acquired after being struck by a massive shock of electricity, slip his mind? Did he truly forget the milky-white left eye that sent trembles of fear into his victims? His mind was so full of anger and revenge that he was losing himself.

Why had he turned his back on all the knuckle breaking and intimidation to go into management? He had never wanted to be the boss—most of the criminal masterminds he had worked for were complete knuckleheads, too caught up in their own insanity to see the big picture. None of them truly had a chance to take over the world, but they provided the goon with steady work, which was all he had really wanted.

But then something changed. The day he got that terrible flu—that's when everything went weird. That day, he felt smart. Really smart! And all he could see was weakness and ignorance in others. He was sure they were trying to keep him down—making him feel like a fool—laughing at him behind his back. And then the mask came to him in his dreams, the same mask the kid who kept trying to take over the world used to wear. The mask comforted him. If he wore the mask, gave into it, then he would have everything he ever wanted and the world would shudder for standing in his way. It was ghastly and horrible, but it was also threatening and manipulative. It was a sign of intellect used to frighten the simple.

There was a knock at the office door, so the Antagonist slipped his mask back on, left the bathroom, and crossed the office to open it. Before he turned the knob, he pressed his ear to the door and listened.

"Who is it?" he asked.

"It's Miss Information."

"Are you here to kill me?"

"Not today."

"How do I know you're telling the truth?"

"I'll be honest. I fully intend to kill you and take control of the organization, but only when you are at the height of your power. At the moment, this evil empire of yours is heavy on evil, but coming up short in the empire department. Although it does have the necessary bones to grow into something that will control the world. On that day I will strike at you with the speed and viciousness of a king cobra, but until then I'll bide my time."

The Antagonist considered this proclamation. Everyone else who worked for him smiled to his face as they tried to slide a knife in his back. Miss Information was someone whose directness he could respect, even if he couldn't tell whether her smile was wicked or sincere. He unlocked the door and found her on the other side—unarmed.

"Just so you know, one day I will push you into a pit filled with mutated spiders that will lay their eggs under your skin," the Antagonist told her.

"And someday I will subject you to a horrible medical procedure that will make you my mindless cyborg," she said. "You look tense. I mean . . . I bet you look tense under your mask. Sit down."

He sat in his desk chair and she stood behind him, rubbing his shoulders and releasing the stress that had been building for days.

"You really need to take better care of yourself, boss," she said. "Stress is not good for your heart. It raises your blood pressure, affects your sleep, and makes you prone to heart disease. I can't have you die before I get a chance to kill you myself. If you want a book on how to calm down, I can recommend one."

"Who are you?" he said, turning in his chair to face her.

The woman shook her head. "That would be telling, and besides, we have a bigger problem on our hands. It's a henchman."

The Antagonist gestured to all the bodies in his office. "It appears we have a situation with a lot of the henchmen."

"Yes, they do seem eager to kill you, but this one is a bit different. His name is Dirk Trappings," Miss Information said.

"Dirk Trappings? Which one is he?"

"We met him at the supermarket. He's the one who locked his manager in the freezer and then forcefully conquered the cereal aisle."

"Oh, yes. There were corn flakes everywhere. What has he done?"

"Well, he's built a doomsday machine and he's taken it to New York City," she said.

The Antagonist was enraged. "IS EVERYONE IN THIS ORGANIZATION BUILDING A DOOMSDAY MACHINE?"

Miss Information shrugged.

"Are you building one, too?"

"Just a little one," she replied sheepishly.

"What does Trappings's machine do? I hope he's not a repeat of that idiot Captain Kapow."

"All we really know is that he's now calling himself Mr. Miniature."

The Antagonist sighed. "It's official. I'm surrounded by crazy people."

8

38°87' N, 77°10' W

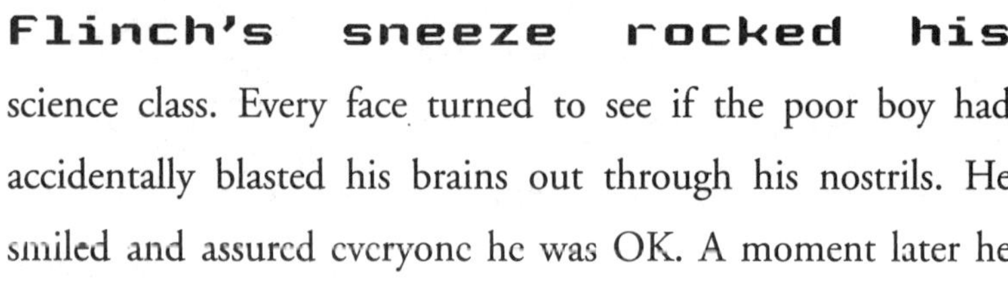

Flinch's sneeze rocked his science class. Every face turned to see if the poor boy had accidentally blasted his brains out through his nostrils. He smiled and assured everyone he was OK. A moment later he heard Agent Brand's urgent voice inside his head.

"I need the team in the Playground, now. Lunch lady, get the School Bus fueled and ready for a trip to New York City. Ms. Holiday, prep the agents for skydiving. We can't land a rocket in midtown Manhattan."

Just as he'd done a thousand times before, Flinch stood up and gathered his things. He was halfway to the door when he heard his teacher's voice.

"Excuse me," Mrs. Reinhold said. "Where do you think you're going?"

Flinch stopped in his tracks. What was he doing? He couldn't just get up and walk out of a class anymore. He was so used to leaping into action after a big sneeze that he couldn't help himself.

"Um, I have to go to the bathroom," he stammered.

"There's plenty of time between classes to use the bathroom," Mrs. Reinhold said. "Please take your seat, Mr. Escala."

Flinch knew that when an adult used your last name with Mr. or Ms. in front of it, they meant business. He slinked back to his chair and buried his head in a book. Once Mrs. Reinhold had stopped staring at him, he gave his nose a good squeeze so he could activate the two-way communication device. "I'm stuck," he whispered.

"What do you mean you're 'stuck'?" Brand said. Flinch could hear the impatience in his voice.

"The teacher won't let me go."

"Mr. Escala, your job is to save the world. If you're going to be a secret agent, you can't let a sixth-grade science teacher get in your way."

"What am I supposed to do?" Flinch asked.

"Find a way, Agent Flinch. You're a spy. You're supposed to be resourceful!"

"Maybe you guys should go without me. I mean, I did destroy Paris," he whispered.

"GET DOWN HERE!" Brand shouted.

Flinch scanned the room. What would get him out of class? Hmmm . . . The fire alarm! Back at Nathan Hale Elementary, the fire alarm was used all the time to get out of classes. He turned the dial on his harness and felt the sugary energy rush through him. Like a bolt of lightning, he zipped out of his seat and down the hall toward the alarm—only to find Ms. Dove standing right next to it. He nearly slammed into her, but he managed to turn at the last second and race back to his seat in class. No one noticed he had been gone, but the blast of wind that followed him into the room sent papers and books flying in all directions.

He needed another plan. He could always just leave. At superspeed he could be gone before anyone knew it, but they would eventually notice there was no one in his seat, and that was a sure way to get another detention. He didn't want to disappoint Mama Rosa again. He had to try to get permission to be excused.

"Mrs. Reinhold?" Flinch cried, waving his hand wildly.

The teacher turned to him with an angry look in her eye. "Yes, Mr. Escala?"

"I really need to use the bathroom. It's an emergency."

The angry look turned furious. “My answer is still no.”

“But if I don’t go now I’m going to—”

“NO!”

Brand’s voice rang in his ears, too. “Agent Flinch, the rest of the team is here. We need you now!”

Flinch growled. “I’m doing the best I can!”

Mrs. Reinhold marched down the aisle toward Flinch and stood over him. “Do we have a problem, Mr. Escala?” Flinch was so stressed he was shaking.

“Yes, we have a big problem. If you don’t let me go to the bathroom, I’m going to . . . to just go right here in my pants.”

The class erupted into laughter, but Mrs. Reinhold looked as if she had just discovered a mouse in her jar of mayonnaise.

“You wouldn’t dare,” Mrs. Reinhold said.

“Uh-oh, here it comes.”

The teacher stomped her foot. “Mr. Escala, take yourself to the office right now! Principal Dove can deal with you.”

Flinch grabbed his books and darted out of the room. Instead of heading to Ms. Dove’s office, he rounded the corner and leaped into Locker 41. A few seconds later, he was in the Playground and Ms. Holiday was helping him into his flight gear.

“I’m in trouble,” he said. “She sent me to the office, and I didn’t go. I’m going to be in detention until I’m an old man.”

Brand scowled. "I understand. That woman hounded me all day to clean up after the pack of mongrels she calls students. Have you ever had to scrape snot rockets off a library door? We will deal with her later."

He and Ms. Holiday hurried Flinch to the School Bus docking bay, where the rest of the team waited. The bright yellow ship was lying on its side like a plane, and it had been modified to ride on two tracks that led into a dark tunnel. The lunch lady stood near the open hatch.

"Let's move it, people!" he shouted. "We do not want to hit New York City during midday traffic, even in a rocket."

Seconds later, the engines roared, and with a sudden burst the School Bus hurtled into the dark tunnel, twisting around tight curves and up and down steep hills like a runaway train. There was a blinding flash of daylight and another burst of speed, and then the rocket was airborne, slicing through the powdery clouds toward outer space.

"We'll be in New York City in less than fifteen minutes," Brand said, "so we need to get prepared fast. This is a Level One threat."

"Remind me again. What's Level One?" Flinch asked.

Pufferfish rolled her eyes. "You didn't pay attention during your training! Level One is a crime using advanced technology."

"Two in the same week?" Matilda said. "What's going on?"

"I'm hoping it's just a coincidence," Ms. Holiday said. "Our target is a lunatic calling himself Mr. Miniature. Benjamin, do you have any information on him?"

Several screens dropped down from the ceiling. They showed a video of a man struggling to hold up a gigantic ray gun. Everything he pointed at got really small really fast. Flinch saw normal-size cars, trucks, buildings; one ZAP! and they were the size of children's playthings. Mr. Miniature scooped up everything he shrank and stuffed it all into a sack, like a child who won a toy-store shopping spree.

"How is he doing that?" Duncan asked, his mouth open in amazement.

"We're not sure," Benjamin told him. "We have a science team in the Playground working on similar technology, but they report that they are probably a decade away from having a working prototype. It's very advanced tech."

"And there isn't a scientist or lab in the world that is any closer than us. This guy and his machine just sort of appeared out of nowhere," Brand said.

"This guy must be supersmart to build something like that," Gluestick remarked.

"He's a stock boy at a grocery store," Ms. Holiday said, and the screen showed a picture of an ordinary-looking—perhaps even a little dull—man in a green stock-boy apron. Below his picture were the words "Employee of the Month."

"Seriously?" Wheezer cried.

"What happens if we get shrunk?" Flinch asked.

"We have no idea," Brand said. "We're hoping that his ray can also reverse the process, but we can't get close enough to see."

"We're in our descent," the lunch lady shouted from the captain's chair. "Manhattan in three minutes."

A warning light on the wall blinked. Ms. Holiday opened a panel and removed five parachute packs, one for each of the children. Flinch had never seen anything like them. The fabric seemed to take on the color of whatever it was near, making them almost invisible. It was only then that he realized his jumpsuit was doing the same thing.

"Awesome!" he shouted.

"These are the new camouflage drop suits and parachutes. They'll allow you to blend in with your background," she said. "We can't have Mr. Miniature or anyone else seeing five kids parachuting into the city."

Duncan admired his, peering closely at the fabric. "They must refract the light around us."

As Flinch pulled on his parachute, Brand opened the hatch, and the wind blasted into the rocket's compartment.

"Make this as fast as possible," he shouted. "It will be very hard to explain to the media why all the tourist attractions have shrunk."

"All right, everyone! We'll put together a plan on the ground," Pufferfish said as she put on her goggles. "Let's move!"

Brand turned to Flinch. "Actually, I want Flinch to take point on this one."

Flinch shook his head. "Um, you are aware I broke Paris yesterday?"

"He's really not ready," Pufferfish said.

Brand frowned. "It's not open for discussion."

"Time to go!" the lunch lady shouted.

Ms. Holiday pressed a chocolate-covered cupcake into Flinch's hand. "I thought you might like this," she said.

"Did you bake it?" Flinch asked. Ms. Holiday was a great librarian and an amazing spy, but her baking was downright criminal.

She shook her head. "No, this one I bought at the store. It has all the preservatives and chemicals you love."

"Yum!" Flinch said. He took a huge bite and immediately felt the sugar in his system. He beat on his chest, shouted "Grabbberler!," and leaped into the sky.

New York City from ten thousand feet was eye-popping.

The steel buildings shot skyward in a crown of silver and glass. A grid of streets and avenues covered nearly every square inch of the island. But there was something even more amazing for Flinch to gawk at—himself. His suit was a creamy blue that matched the color of the sky. When he fell through clouds, his suit turned white to mimic them.

"Pretty cool, amigos!" he shouted into the com-link.

As he was admiring the new technology, he heard Pufferfish's voice in his head. "Our target is on the move, team. He's on Thirty-third Street heading east, and I don't like where he's going."

"You're worried about a specific place?" Flinch said.

"One of the biggest and most famous buildings in New York City: the Empire State Building."

"That's not cool!" Braceface cried. "He can't shrink it until I get to see it first."

"So what's the plan?" Pufferfish asked.

Flinch had no idea, but he was smart enough not to admit it. He sorted through all the possibilities, but the boost of sugar from the cupcake made it hard to concentrate on a single plan.

"Flinch, did you hear Pufferfish?" Wheezer asked. "How do you want to handle this?"

“Let’s go beat him up,” Flinch said, tilting his body so he was facedown and plummeting fast and furious toward the ground. His teammates did the same, and together the five of them were missiles speeding toward the ground.

“Prepare to deploy parachutes!” Wheezer shouted. “On three. One! Two! Three!”

Flinch pulled his rip cord, and his parachute exploded out of his pack. Suddenly, he was jerked up as air filled his chute. He and the team drifted down like feathers.

He spotted a park, so he directed the others to it. They touched down on green grass, where crowds of people were enjoying the lovely day. The team detached their chutes, which were now just as emerald as the lawn, and tucked them into their backpacks. Normally, they would have just left them, but they didn’t need someone tripping over space-age technology.

Pufferfish had her computer out and was already tracking Mr. Miniature. “We’re about ten blocks from the Empire State Building,” she said, scanning the horizon and then pointing above the trees. “There!” Flinch glanced down the street. It was a beautiful building, like a tall, silver Popsicle.

“Let’s get moving,” Pufferfish said, but they hadn’t taken a single step when a mob of people ran straight at them, screaming and shouting for help. The mob ran through traffic into the park, and because the NERDS were still invisible, they were nearly trampled.

"I guess he's that way," Flinch said. "We need some transportation, Braceface."

Jackson's braces sprang out of his mouth, forming an enormous dune buggy. Everyone climbed aboard and they motored in the direction of the skyscraper.

"So what's the plan?" Matilda snapped. Flinch turned to her, surprised by her angry tone. Her face looked pale and she was sweating.

"Are you OK?" Flinch asked.

"Just a headache. I'll be fine. Let's do this," Matilda said.

Pufferfish was furiously at work on her computer. She pulled up a street map of the area. "OK, I've deactivated all security cameras in a five-block radius and grounded all news helicopters. Plus, I shut down cell service so whatever happens, it's not going to end up on the Internet. Now, I think the best thing is—"

"It's Flinch's mission," Duncan said.

Pufferfish's arms swelled up to the size of eggplants. She was allergic to not being in charge. "Yeah . . . OK."

Flinch cringed. It was already hard being in charge, but to not have the confidence of the team was quite another thing. The truth was, Pufferfish should have been in charge. She had the most experience, and she was good at it. He wanted to just let her take over, but he suspected giving up would land him in hot water with Agent Brand.

"OK—Gluestick and Braceface should race around the block and come at him from the left. Matilda and I will go the other way and come at him from the right. Once we've got him surrounded we'll do what we do best."

"What do I do?" Pufferfish asked.

"You're the bait," he said. "You lure him into the intersection and keep him distracted."

"Whatever!" Matilda cried.

"Huh?"

"This plan sounds like a way for you to hog all the glory for yourself," she said. "Typical Flinch."

Everyone turned to Wheezer. She had a sharp tongue, but it was rarely aimed at a teammate.

"Um, there's nothing typical about it," Flinch said. "This uses everyone's talents, and—"

"Hardly. It makes you the center of attention," Matilda grumbled. "We all saw how you undermined Pufferfish with Agent Brand. You practically stole the leadership of the team."

"What?" Flinch said. "That's not true. I didn't ask for this. I'm no leader."

"Don't I know it!" Matilda cried. "And it's about time you handed over the reins to someone who is!"

Flinch hadn't been in an argument like this since Heathcliff was on the team. Choppers, as he was called back then, spent most of his time questioning orders and grousing about his jobs. Matilda was always eager to be part of the plan. This was so unlike her that it left him and the others speechless.

Matilda wiped her brow. "I'm sorry. I'm not feeling well. This is a good plan."

Pufferfish nodded. "Fine. Let's do it."

Flinch turned the knob on his harness and felt the energy fill his limbs. Once Matilda had used her inhalers to fly into the air, he leaped out of the buggy and ran down the street to follow her.

After a few turns, they came up squarely behind their target. Mr. Miniature was firing his ray gun with wild abandon, shrinking everything in sight. A taxicab was suddenly the size of a toy car. A hot dog cart was as small as a dollhouse. Even a gigantic red double-decker tour bus was abruptly no larger than a Twinkie. Flinch shuddered to think about the people in those vehicles, suddenly finding themselves very tiny and being shoved into a sack. Miniature had to be stopped.

"I'll take him at his knees and you go for the ray gun," Flinch said.

"What kind of imbecile are you?" Matilda snarled. "Your silly little ideas smell of foolishness! I am the brains on this team. You should be listening to me!"

Again Flinch was taken aback. "Huh? What is wrong with you?"

"I'll tell you what's wrong! I have to work with a bunch of morons and nincompoops and I'm expected to keep my mouth shut and not say a word. Well, I've had it! I'm not the kind of person who takes orders from an incompetent ape."

"Wheezer, um, there's a mad scientist shrinking everything," Flinch said. "Can we talk about this later?"

"NO!" Matilda turned her inhalers on Flinch and fired. A red-hot blast of sound and light hit him right in the chest and he flew backward, slamming into a wall. His head throbbed as he staggered to his feet in a pile of brick and dust. His harness had absorbed much of the impact, but he wasn't invulnerable. Matilda's attack had hurt a lot.

Wheezer aimed her inhalers at him a second time, but Flinch wasn't about to give her another shot. He took off, going from zero to sixty miles per hour in two seconds, sending trash into the air behind him.

"This is the bait! What's going on back there?" Pufferfish's voice said in his head.

"Something's wrong with Wheezer!" Flinch shouted.

"Don't call me that name! Wheezer is no name for someone as important as me. From now on, you will call me the Asthmatic Assassin."

"Did I hear that right?" Gluestick shouted over the com-link.

"Concentrate on the bad guy," Flinch said. "I'll take care of what's-her-name."

Wheezer's inhalers fired again, nearly taking Flinch's head off. He survived only by jumping straight into the air, soaring twenty feet up, then using his incredible strength to dig his fingers into the side of a nearby building. He clung there like a spider until Matilda spotted him. She fired again, and he sprang higher, clawing into the brick with his feet and hands.

"You think you can get away?" Wheezer seethed. "You're wasting your time."

"I don't know what's wrong with you, but we're not here to fight each other," Flinch said. "We're supposed to be stopping a bad guy. You need to get control of yourself!"

"I'm in control of myself for the first time in my life!"

"Buddy, we've got a big problem," Gluestick replied. "Miniature is attacking us!"

Suddenly, a pink light enveloped the Empire State Building. Craning his neck, Flinch saw the light reaching all the way from the ground to the very top.

"Uh-oh," he said.

And then, one of the tallest buildings in New York City—in the world, even—shrank to the size of a shoe box. Mr. Miniature plucked it off the ground and shoved it into his bag. He laughed an insane, high-pitched cackle and shook his fists in the air in triumph.

"Attention, world! I am the master manipulator of size and shape. Today's demonstration is just the first of many! Soon, I will shrink all of your most precious landmarks—Mount Rushmore! The White House! The Taj Mahal! To get them back, you will have to pay my ransom. Empty your pockets and turn over all control of the world to me in twenty-four hours—or else. I'd say it's a bargain!"

Flinch hardly had time to process what had just happened, because Wheezer's attack didn't stop for a moment. She made a beeline straight for him.

He dug into the wall and braced himself for the fiery spray of her inhalers—then he got an idea. He crushed the bricks in his hands into powder and tossed the dust into her face. It blinded her and she flailed in the sky, scratching at her eyes.

While she was distracted, Flinch jumped down from the side of the wall. On the street, he opened his backpack and pulled out the invisible parachute. He shook it open and held it the way a matador holds a red cloak out to an angry bull. He just hoped he didn't get run over by this particular bull.

"Hey, Wheezer. I'm over here!" he shouted.

Still rubbing her eyes, Wheezer turned in midair and flew in the direction of his voice. Her flight was erratic, but that didn't make her any less dangerous. He shouted again, hoping to steer her with the sound of his voice. When she was nearly on top of him, he tossed the parachute directly at her. The fabric wrapped around her and she slammed into the ground. Flinch heard a groan and then nothing. After a moment he peered inside. His friend was still breathing but seemed to be out cold.

"You stay here, Wheezer," he said. He tied the ends of the parachute into a knot so it formed a bag around Wheezer, then looked for the rest of his team. He spotted them several blocks away. They were tracking Mr. Miniature, who had moved his reign of terror in the direction of Times Square. Flinch raced to catch up to his friends, guessing that Miniature was going to take a few more landmarks for his collection.

"Put your ray gun down!" Pufferfish demanded, dodging a blast from Mr. Miniature's weapon and kicking him in the calf. "You're under arrest!"

"Yeah," Braceface said. He was trying to snatch the bag of miniaturized items with his braces, which had morphed into claws. "You're in big trouble."

"Did they send children to stop me?" Miniature cried as he turned his weapon on Braceface. "How appropriate that pint-size heroes are sent to stop the Terrorist of Tiny!"

Flinch knew what was coming next, and with all the speed he had in him he bolted to the rescue, leaving a trail of fire in his wake. Unfortunately, he moved so fast, he broke the sound barrier. With a tremendous BOOM! the windows shattered in every building for two blocks. Mr. Miniature had only a split second to wonder what had caused the noise when his ray gun vanished from his hands. The wind was still blowing back his hair as he was knocked to the ground. Before he knew it, both his legs and feet were cuffed.

"What happened?" he asked, dazed.

"I happened," Flinch told him. Miniature's bag had split open in the fall, and the ground around him was covered with dozens of tiny little cars, all filled with tiny little people, honking their tiny little horns.

"We'll get you back to size as soon as we figure out how," Flinch said to the tiny crowd, but the honking didn't stop.

"What happened to the two of you?" Pufferfish asked. "Where's Matilda?"

"She attacked me. I don't think she's feeling well. She was talking crazy," Flinch said.

Suddenly, Pufferfish began to scratch, then she grabbed Flinch and together they fell to the ground. "Get down!"

There was a loud explosion behind them. They spun around to find that Wheezer had used her inhaler to blast through the parachute fabric. Little bits of flame burned around the edges of a hole that appeared to be standing in midair, and then Matilda crawled through it with revenge in her eyes.

"I'm allergic to surprise attacks," Pufferfish said.

Wheezer flew into the air, then sprayed the ground with inhaler blasts. The results were several huge, smoking craters in the street. Flinch could do nothing more than watch a circle of them appear around him, until the very ground he stood on collapsed beneath his feet.

He fell, then slammed into something hard. If he hadn't been wearing his harness, he was sure he would have broken a leg, but the impact still hurt. He clamored to his feet, feeling the agony from his injured knee and ribs.

It was dark—pitch black, just the way it had been in the Parisian catacombs, only this tunnel stretched out behind him, and there were tracks beneath his feet. His old panic returned.

"Great," he groaned, but his complaints were drowned

out by a peculiar sound filling the space—a rumbling that grew louder by the second. It was then that he understood where he was and that something big, bright, and loud was coming right at him.

Flinch spun around and ran in the opposite direction. He wanted to turn his speed up to the max, but his knee was killing him. He could barely break twenty miles an hour, limping with every step.

"This isn't my fault!" Flinch cried. "I didn't want to be in charge. I'm better as part of the team, not leading it. And now I'm going to get run over by a train."

He veered to the left at a fork in the tunnel. He hoped the train would go in the other direction, but it didn't. It followed him into the turn like a big silver bloodhound and, worse, he could feel his harness starting to sputter from a lack of fuel. He looked back over his shoulder and saw the train close behind. He turned the knob all the way to maximum and allowed the power to overtake him. Then with a sudden blast of speed he zipped ahead. But his tank was now on empty and he was running on fumes. The train would overtake him at any moment.

He didn't need speed anymore. He needed momentum. When the train was nearly on top of him, he jumped forward, and the train caught him in midair like a fly on the windshield of a car. It was jarring enough to rattle his brain, but he was aware enough to squeeze his fingers into the sides of the train to keep a good handhold. Then he rode the car into the bright, crowded station.

When the train had come to a complete stop, Flinch leaped onto the station platform.

"The train was packed today!" he said to the crowd on the platform, then darted toward the exit.

9

38°87' N, 77°10' W

Matilda's teammates subdued her before she could cause any more destruction. She was feverish and raving when Brand came in to see her. It was like watching his own daughter suffering. She was sick with something, but no one knew what. He had taken his fear of losing her out on some of the scientists, demanding answers. Finally, a scientist called a briefing in the middle school's science lab.

"Why are we meeting up here?" Brand said. In the previous school, he'd never had important conversations outside of the Playground, and he was worried Principal Dove or someone else on the staff would find them and demand an explanation.

"I don't want to frighten any of the others," the scientist said. She was Dr. Olivia Kim, a scientist with one of the brightest

minds in nanobyte technology in the world. Brand had no idea why she had been the one to call the meeting. What did the little robots that gave the kids their powers have to do with Matilda's sudden insanity?

"Why would you frighten anyone?" he asked.

The scientist gestured to a microscope resting on a table. "Take a look."

Brand peered into the lens and saw a milky white world swirling with stringy bacteria. He wasn't much of a scientist himself, and it irritated him when the big brains assumed he should naturally know what something was. "What am I looking at?"

Duncan stepped over to take a peek, followed by Ruby. Flinch was next. Jackson waved it off. Science wasn't his thing, either.

"I think I've discovered what has caused Agent Wheezer's drastic change in personality. Agent Flinch was the one who gave us the lead," Dr. Kim said. "Please, take another look."

Brand looked again. This time he saw a black dot appear and attack some of the bacteria. It was much smaller than the other creatures, but it was fierce, and soon the bacteria were dead.

"What's that black thing?"

Dr. Kim leaned over and adjusted the magnification. This time the menacing dot seemed much bigger, and Brand could make out details. It looked like a cockroach with spindly legs and pinchers on its face. It also looked mechanical.

"That's a nanobyte," Dr. Kim said.

"That's what they look like? That's what we put into the kids?" Brand asked.

The scientist nodded. "Each of our agents has millions of these in their bloodstream, enhancing and manipulating their natural talents and giving them their remarkable powers. They give Gluestick his sticky hands and feet, Pufferfish her superallergies, Braceface his morphing braces, Wheezer her supercharged inhalers, and Flinch his hyperactive strength and speed. At least that's what our nanobytes do. The nanobyte you're looking at isn't one of ours."

Brand saw Duncan arch a curious eyebrow. He was a technology geek and loved anything that needed a battery. Brand hated to admit it, but if it wasn't for Duncan, he wouldn't know how many of the team's gadgets worked. "Not one of ours?" Duncan said. "How is that possible? We're the only organization on Earth that has this technology—unless we've been infiltrated."

"No, we haven't been infiltrated. Our technology is still safe. These nanobytes aren't from Earth. They're alien."

"Like from outer space?" Braceface asked.

"No, they're from an alternate Earth—the one Heathcliff visited when he built the interdimensional bridge," Dr. Kim replied. "While he was there, he visited a mirror duplicate of our Playground and he had a new batch of that universe's nanobytes upgrade his body. They are what has caused his current condition."

"I knew the bobblehead had something to do with this," Jackson muttered.

"Is this somehow connected to Stoop's crime spree and Mr. Miniature?" Pufferfish asked.

"I'm afraid so. I found nanobytes inside of Sherman Stoop, a.k.a. Captain Kapow, and the incredible shrinking scientist, too. There were millions of them in their bloodstreams and attached to the base of their brains."

Flinch gasped. "Brain eaters!"

"No, not brain eaters. More like tiny megaphones, all blasting a specific message into their heads."

"The nanobytes are brainwashing them?" Ms. Holiday asked.

Dr. Kim nodded. "Yes, that's probably the best way to explain it."

"If these are Heathcliff's nanobytes, how did Matilda and the others get them?" Pufferfish asked, peering into the microscope again.

"I believe he's contagious," Dr. Kim said. "And worse, the nanobytes seem to be infecting people with his personality. Matilda and the others all demonstrated the same symptoms: a sudden elevated intelligence, paranoia, a sense of superiority. I believe if Matilda had the opportunity, she, too, would have begun work on some kind of doomsday device. Heathcliff is turning people into supervillains."

"How is that possible?" Ms. Holiday asked. "All the kids have nanobytes, but none of them are infecting others. None of them give people superstrength or make them crave Ring Dings."

Dr. Kim nodded. “It seems that Heathcliff’s nanobytes have been altered by his anger. His mental stability has been in question for some time, and these things are working on his brain. Perhaps the nanobytes were built differently on the alternative Earth. We have no way of checking. There are a number of things that could have mutated them.”

“So they’ve adapted to his crazy?” Jackson asked.

“I’ll have to do more tests,” Dr. Kim said. “But right now we have a much bigger problem. They’re spreading.”

“How can you be sure?” Brand asked.

“Mr. Miniature worked in a grocery store nearly fifteen miles from here. He’s never had any contact with Heathcliff and has never stepped foot in the Playground. That means he got them from someone else. It could have been someone who works in this facility, or it could have been someone who has been in contact with an employee. They could have passed each other on the street or taken the same bus, or maybe he was infected by an unknown third party. We don’t know. But we should be prepared. All three of our infected say they felt a sudden fever and fatigue, followed by a drastic change in mood. They all say they were happy, and then all of a sudden boiling with anger.”

“Um, I had a fever,” Flinch said, raising his hand.

“When?” Brand asked.

“Last night. I was tired and angry, too. I thought people

were making fun of me and I wanted revenge, but then I went to sleep and it went away. I feel like myself right now, though."

"OK, Dr. Kim, give Flinch a thorough exam and let me know if he's—"

Suddenly, all four of the children sneezed at the same time.

"Is that a call from the Playground?" Brand asked.

"It's an incident alarm," Ruby explained. "Benjamin is asking for us."

Brand ran for the door, but Ruby stopped him. "Benjamin says to sit down at the lab tables. The new entrance to the Playground has been installed and is now ready for use."

Flinch watched his boss hesitantly sit down.

"How does it—"

And then all of the seats dropped through the floor and into a deep tunnel.

Moments later, Benjamin hovered around their heads like an excited bumblebee. "Police reports are coming in," he chirped. The video screen displayed a photo of a masked man. "This one is in Atlanta. He's calling himself the Monkey Master. He's kidnapped the mayor."

"Any bets on what kind of animal he uses in his crime spree?" Jackson said.

"The lunch lady has the School Bus ready to go,"

Benjamin said. "Ms. Holiday, I suggest your mission kit include a bunch of bananas."

"Kids, let's move it," Brand said. But he snatched Flinch by the arm before he could join them. "Not you."

"But I feel great!"

Brand had no time to argue with the boy. He could tell Flinch was disappointed, but he would have to get over it. The world was in big, big trouble.

END TRANSMISSION.

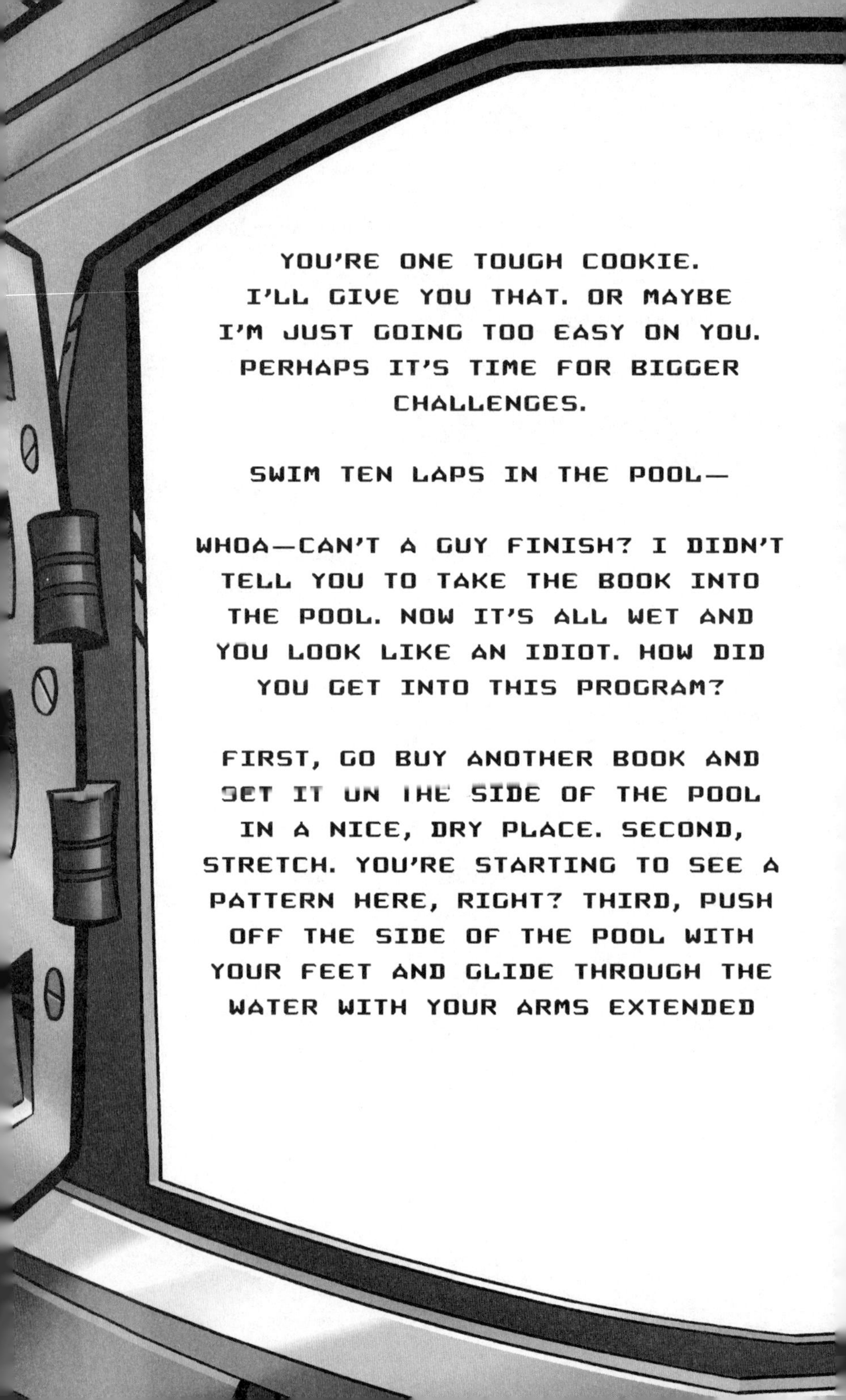

YOU'RE ONE TOUGH COOKIE. I'LL GIVE YOU THAT. OR MAYBE I'M JUST GOING TOO EASY ON YOU. PERHAPS IT'S TIME FOR BIGGER CHALLENGES.

SWIM TEN LAPS IN THE POOL—

WHOA—CAN'T A GUY FINISH? I DIDN'T TELL YOU TO TAKE THE BOOK INTO THE POOL. NOW IT'S ALL WET AND YOU LOOK LIKE AN IDIOT. HOW DID YOU GET INTO THIS PROGRAM?

FIRST, GO BUY ANOTHER BOOK AND SET IT ON THE SIDE OF THE POOL IN A NICE, DRY PLACE. SECOND, STRETCH. YOU'RE STARTING TO SEE A PATTERN HERE, RIGHT? THIRD, PUSH OFF THE SIDE OF THE POOL WITH YOUR FEET AND GLIDE THROUGH THE WATER WITH YOUR ARMS EXTENDED

AND YOUR FACE POINTING DOWN. FOURTH, KICK YOUR FEET. FIFTH, USE ONE ARM TO STROKE YOU FORWARD, THEN THE OTHER, IN A CONSTANT RHYTHM, TURNING YOUR HEAD TO BREATHE. SIXTH, DON'T DROWN.

WRITE DOWN HOW MANY LAPS YOU DID.

____

UGH, DID YOU TAKE THE PEN INTO THE POOL, TOO?

LEVEL 4
ACCESS GRANTED

BEGIN TRANSMISSION:

10

38°88' N, 77°09' W

"A virus?" the Antagonist said as he walked through his fortress's subterranean dungeon. Every one of his employees was locked in chains and raving like a lunatic. He and Miss Information were the only ones who seemed well. "You're telling me all of my henchmen are sick?"

"That's what my sources are saying," Miss Information said.

"You have sources inside the NERDS organization?" he asked, incredulous.

"They do call me Miss Information," she said. "I'm hearing that this sickness is a virus—an electronic virus."

"It's man-made?" he asked as he cupped the face of one of his henchmen. It was a portrait of murderous anger.

"They're miniature robots," she said.

"Nanobytes," the Antagonist said, recalling his former employer's obsession with them. "Do you think I'm ignorant? I know as much as anyone about that team."

"Of course you do," she said. "These nanobytes attach themselves to the victim's brain and blast it with signals. It's the reason why everyone is suddenly superintelligent. It's also why they believe the world is out to get them."

The Antagonist thought back over the past few weeks. Hadn't he suddenly gotten very smart? Wasn't he incredibly paranoid? . . . Was he infected with this bizarre illness, and if so, why wasn't he raving like everyone else who clearly had it?

"I know what you're thinking," Miss Information said.

"You do?"

"You're concerned that this infection will slow down your plans to take over the world. You wonder if you can manage the criminally insane—especially if they are more criminally insane than you. Darling, you have nothing to worry about."

"Did you just call me 'darling'?" he asked.

She wrapped her arms around his neck and pulled him close. "We hardly know each other. I don't even know what you look like, but I know all I need to know. You're ruthless, evil, and brilliant. And that hook! It's not just the masks and our need to crush our enemies that match. It's our hearts."

"But didn't you say you wanted to kill me and steal my empire?"

“I did, and someday I will, but that doesn’t mean we can’t be happy until then,” she purred. “For now, we should get married. We could have a family. Imagine it, Antagonist. The pitter-patter of evil little feet running through the fortress.”

The Antagonist found himself swept away by the idea. This woman in her skull mask was awfully cute. He loved the way she plotted the destruction of the world capitals. Could he dare to dream of love? Would it distract him from his plots and plans? But then his heart swelled in his chest and he pulled her close. They kissed—a wild, passionate kiss that sealed their love. When it was over, the two held hands; or rather, she held his hook and together they gazed into the masks’ slits where their eyes were.

"Next time, darling, we should take off the masks before we kiss," she said.

"Agreed," he said as he spit a bit of lint out of his mouth. "Now, what were you saying about taking over the world?"

"Yes, yes—look around you," she said, gesturing to his imprisoned soldiers. "What do you see?"

"A hundred lunatics all bent on taking over the world!"

She shook her head. "No, that's not what you see."

"It isn't?"

"No, you see opportunity," she said. "This virus they have inside them is spreading. Everyone who contracts it joins the ranks of evildoers."

38°88' N, 77°00' W

"And how does that help me?"

Miss Information giggled. "Oh, silly, you don't have to hide your genius from me. I know perfectly well that you are already planning to set them free."

"Set them free?"

"Yes, because if we set them free, they will cause chaos, especially for the NERDS. But better than that, the virus will spread. The infected will overrun the world, crippling governments, conquering the military, and doing all our hard work for us. Then they will turn on one another, and while they fight it out, we can sit back and watch it all unfold, ready to take our rightful place when there's no one left. It's a genius idea that only my little love puppy could imagine."

The Antagonist nodded. Of course it was genius. It was *his* idea. Though some of the details were not so clear until this amazing woman helped him flesh it all out. Right?

"Exactly," he said, pulling her close and kissing her again, this time more passionately. She returned his affection, and once more they stood and stared, as if seeing each other for the first time.

"Darling, we forgot about the masks, again," Miss Information said.

"Um, yes," he replied, spitting out another bit of lint. "Next time. For now, we have a world to conquer."

Flinch sat on an examination table in the Playground, feeling like a jerk.

"He benched me," he said to Dr. Kim. "The last two missions I've been on I screwed up. Paris is a mess and the Empire State Building is small enough to step on."

She shook her head. "Flinch, that's not why you're here, and even if it was, you can still be a big help to this mission. We need to do some tests. Maybe we can find out why you didn't suffer from the nanobytes like the others."

"While I'm on the bench," he grumbled.

Dr. Kim and several other scientists collected blood and hair samples, peered into his eyes and nose, checked his blood pressure and reflexes, and swabbed the inside of his cheeks. They

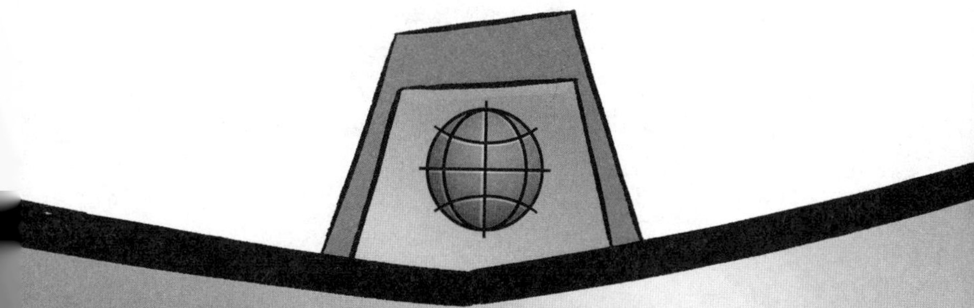

examined his harness and the connection devices that linked his bloodstream to it. They took his temperature, peered at his tongue, and had him run on a treadmill, both at superspeed and under his own natural power. Then they hurried away to study the results, leaving him alone with Dr. Kim. She was a nice lady, but she spent the next couple of hours staring into her microscope while he tried to keep himself occupied. Not an easy task after you've emptied three boxes of hot cocoa mix into your mouth. He was so jittery, he fell out of his chair seven times, but nothing could take his mind off his recent failures. As many times as Dr. Kim tried to assure him that his role in the team was important, he couldn't shake the suspicion that he was being punished. For a moment he wondered if perhaps the nanobytes were making him paranoid, but he didn't feel like a genius or that everyone was laughing at him. He knew he had screwed up. It was just normal, regular, everyday paranoia.

Dr. Kim sat down on a chair in front of him. Her face looked grim, and he panicked. "I have the disease!" he cried before she could say a word. He was going to go crazy, too! He darted across the room and into one of the empty holding cells, slammed the door shut, then took the key and swallowed it. It was the best thing for everyone, he told himself.

"Flinch, come out of the cell," Dr. Kim said.

"No! I'm too dangerous," he shouted. "I have to lock

myself up for the good of humankind. Just push a plate of gummi bears and a juice box under the door from time to time. I'll be fine!"

"Flinch, calm down. You're freaking out for no reason," the scientist said.

"Don't try to talk me out of this, Doc!" he said. "I'm better off in here, growing my toenails long and working on a big bushy beard. Don't worry about me. I'll make friends with the lint in my belly button!"

"Agent! You're not sick!"

Flinch was surprised. "Huh? But I had a fever. I wanted to take over the world."

"You had the virus, but you beat it. The alien nanobytes have been disabled," she said. "Your body created an immunity."

"Then . . . Matilda and the others will get better, too?" Flinch asked.

"No, I'm afraid not," Dr. Kim said. "Their bodies don't have the same fighting power yours does. You see, when a virus invades, white blood cells are sent to fight and kill it. Some viruses are too strong for the cells, and that's how a person gets sick. That's what happened to Matilda and Sherman."

"Then why didn't that happen to me?" Flinch asked.

"Your white blood cells are different. I've never seen anything like them. They are flooded with sugar, which gives them energy, and then your upgrades supercharge them, turning them into little firecrackers. The alien nanobytes never had a chance."

"So I'm not going to go crazy?"

"Not any crazier than you are right now," she said with a laugh. "You're not a danger to anyone, Flinch—except for those who stand between you and a box of chocolate-covered cherries. Come on out."

Flinch tried the cell door. It was locked tight. He gave his harness knob a twist and then ripped the door out of the wall.

Dr. Kim didn't seem fazed. "Agent Brand told me to send you back to class. He says the team has the Monkey Master under control and will be back soon."

"OK," Flinch said. He left and headed for the middle of the dome. In the center was a panel of blinking buttons. One was labeled RETURN TO CLASS. Before he pushed it he turned to Dr. Kim, who had followed him. "Um, sorry about that door."

"It happens," she said.

Flinch grinned and pressed the button. The gigantic fans turned on, and soon he was pushed up through the dome and into the tunnel system. He fully expected to land inside Locker 41, but instead he found himself in his chair in Mr. Gilligan's health class just as the roll was being called. Flinch popped up so quickly that no one even noticed his arrival.

"Julio Escala? Has anyone seen Julio Escala?" the teacher snapped.

"Here!" Julio said.

Mr. Gilligan sighed. "People! You need to speak up when I'm calling attendance. Tommy Friedman?"

Before Tommy could answer, there was a knock at the door. It swung open, and Ms. Dove and Mrs. Reinhold, the science teacher, entered the room. As usual, Ms. Dove was all smiles, but Mrs. Reinhold looked like a vengeful god from Mount Olympus.

If Flinch hadn't known any better, he might have thought actual flames were burning in her eyes. He didn't need to be told they were there for him. He slid out of his chair and followed the two women down the hall and into the principal's office, where they closed the door behind him.

"Mr. Escala, I find you in my office for the second time this week," Ms. Dove said with an exaggerated pouty face. "You realize there have only been three days of school so far. You are not starting off very well."

"He threatened me!" Mrs. Reinhold shouted.

"Threatened?" Flinch said. "I did not!"

"He said he would relieve himself in my classroom!"

Flinch struggled to respond. What was he supposed to say? *I had to go save the world, and that kind of thing is usually urgent?*

But he didn't have to say anything. Mrs. Reinhold launched into a fiery tirade, describing his high crimes and outlining the bleak future that lay ahead of him.

He was a troublemaker. He was disrespectful. He was a bad role model to the other children. He didn't take his education seriously. He didn't listen. He didn't follow directions. He didn't play well with others. If he didn't shape up and fly right, he was going to find himself in a heap load of trouble. He would grow up to be shiftless. He would disappoint everyone, but most important, he would disappoint himself. He would go through life sneering at authority and someday end up in prison. Yes, prison! In thirty years of teaching she had never seen anything like this. She didn't know what had gotten into kids these days. They had no respect. When she was a student she would never have been so disrespectful to a teacher. She blamed the video games. She truly thought the world was falling apart and wondered if she could find work as a waitress.

When Mrs. Reinhold finally talked herself into exhaustion, she plopped down onto a chair to catch her breath. Flinch turned to Ms. Dove, fully prepared for another lecture, but the big-eyed woman just smiled. "What are we going to do with you, Mr. Escala?"

The answer was another detention.

Mrs. Reinhold and Ms. Dove walked him down the hall to the detention room. Flinch took his seat and put his head down in disgrace. Mama Rosa was going to kill him. In three days he had gone from nerd to full-fledged juvenile delinquent.

"Psst," a voice said from behind his head. He sat up and turned. The four boys who had bullied him on the first day were all sitting in a row. He expected them to either be angry at his manhandling or completely terrified of his inhuman strength. But they were grinning at him and nodding with respect. He scanned the room and saw that everyone else was also watching him with an odd sense of awe. It was almost as if he was one of them, now that he'd been tossed into detention twice in the same week.

"Yo, bro," the kid with the red hair said. "Welcome back."

When he got home, he found a note on the kitchen table. It read, *I'm very disappointed. We will discuss this after my stories.*

Anxiety made Flinch fidget even more than usual. Mama Rosa must have thought he had lost his mind. He couldn't wait for her soap operas to be over. He needed to explain himself the best he could. He ran through the house, but before his foot hit the first stair, he was rocked by a massive explosion.

"What was that?" he cried, pushing himself to his feet.

Mama Rosa came down the steps, stomping like an angry bull. Strapped to her back were two silver canisters almost as big as garbage cans. A single tube led from the canisters to a nozzle in her hand. The nozzle was dripping something that smelled like fuel onto the rug.

"Mama Rosa!"

"That's not my name anymore! My name is Hot Tamale!"

She was infected.

If the name and the flamethrower hadn't given it away, there was also her flushed face and angry red eyes. Flinch tried to stay calm. He had to keep the old woman from doing anything drastic.

"So, that's a nice flamethrower, Hot Tamale. What do you plan on doing with it?" Flinch asked.

"I'm going to burn down Mrs. Valencia's rose garden," Mama Rosa said as she pushed past him and out the front door.

Years ago Mama Rosa and Mrs. Valencia were the best of friends. They played dominoes on the front porch and drank mojitos at an alarming rate. They loved to talk about gardening, and both considered themselves experts when it came to growing beautiful, blooming roses. But one year they both entered a contest held by the Arlington Botanical Garden, and Mrs. Valencia's roses won. Mama Rosa never spoke to her friend again. She sat on the porch, envying Mrs. Valencia as she spread her prize, a year's supply of mulch, across her bulb garden. A confrontation had been brewing for years, but no one suspected it would involve a flamethrower.

"You can't burn down her rose garden, Mama," Flinch said. The old woman tried to shoo him away, but he stayed close to her side.

"She shouldn't have laughed at me!" Mama Rosa said.

There was that phrase again. "They laughed at me." He had heard Captain Kapow say the same thing. He'd heard Mr. Miniature say it, too. When his own fever was raging, he was certain that others were snickering behind his back. How could he convince Mama Rosa otherwise?

The old woman stopped her march right in front of Mrs. Valencia's home. She raised her hose and sprayed her flames, scorching Mrs. Valencia's front yard. When she turned off the hose, the grass was black and smoldering. She cackled proudly.

Flinch pinched his nose and heard the com-link in his head activate. "I've got another infected supervillain on my hands."

"Who?" Agent Brand asked when he came online.

"My grandma!"

"Can you handle it until I can get the team there? Everyone has left for the day. I can't even get Ms. Holiday on the phone," Brand said.

"She's *mi familia*, boss. I'll handle this. I'm just letting you know Dr. Kim is right. It's spreading."

Mama Rosa blasted the weeping willow growing in Mrs. Valencia's front yard. Soon the tree was a bonfire. A moment later Mrs. Valencia, wearing an apron and carrying a rolling pin, came racing out of the house. She was angry.

"Rosa, what are you doing?" she cried.

"Something I should have done a long time ago, woman," Rosa said. "I'm going to settle the score. Don't believe what they say—revenge is a dish best served hot!"

Mama Rosa blasted fire into the sky to emphasize her point.

"Have you lost your mind?" Mrs. Valencia shouted.

"Quite the contrary! I have finally found it," Mama Rosa shouted back, blasting Mrs. Valencia's shrubs.

"You think I'm going to just let that happen, Rosa?" Mrs. Valencia asked. "You think you can stand here and burn my prize-winning roses and laugh about it? Well, I'm sick of you laughing at me. I'm sick of everyone laughing at me."

From inside her apron she pulled out a whistle. It was covered in blinking lights and knobs. Flinch had never seen anything like it outside of the Playground—which made him very nervous. Mrs. Valencia put the whistle to her mouth . . . and suddenly his eardrums felt like they were exploding. The high-pitched squeal shattered windows, set off car alarms, and knocked him and Mama Rosa to the pavement.

With ringing ears, Flinch helped Mama Rosa stand up. She was still dazed from the attack, which meant it was the perfect time to relieve her of her flamethrower.

"Every day I have to hear your stupid soap operas blasting through the window of your home, Rosa," Mrs. Valencia shouted. "All that noise is bad for the air. It's bad for the neighborhood, and it's bad for my flowers! I built this little machine to show you what it's like to not be able to hear yourself think. I guess you won't be laughing at me again, will you, Rosa? I guess you'll think twice before getting in the way of the Whistle Wizard!"

Mrs. Valencia lifted her whistle to her mouth, but Flinch was already on the move. He dashed into his neighbor's yard, leaped over the roaring fire that was once her hydrangea bush, and snatched the weapon out of her hand. Then he pulverized it beneath the heel of his sneaker.

"You fool!" the woman said. "You've foiled my plans!"

There was a massive thump that shook the ground, and everyone fell over again, even Mrs. Valencia. That thump was followed by another and then another and another, each one growing in intensity. The trees shook, and one even uprooted, collapsing onto a nearby car. A crack in the concrete grew and grew, widening into a trench and ripping the neighborhood in two. When it was finished splitting, Mama Rosa was on one side of a wide, jagged ditch and Flinch was on the other.

"Julio?" she cried. "What is causing this?"

Flinch looked down the street and nearly threw up his Twinkies. Stomping toward them was a mechanical creature nearly three stories tall. Its body had the shape of a man, but its head was a transparent orb. Inside was a very familiar face—Old Man Augustine. Every kid in the neighborhood knew the old coot, and so did every toy store in a one-mile radius. Old Man Augustine was known as "the ball bandit."

Old Man Augustine had constructed a six-foot fence around his entire property. Some said it was because he wanted privacy, but the kids knew different. Any stray ball that had the sad fate of flying over the fence and into his yard was never seen again; footballs, soccer balls, stickballs, baseballs—all vanished in the Bermuda Triangle of Fun. There were neighborhood rumors about what the old man did with the captured balls. Some said he made millions selling them on the Internet. Others said he melted them down and sold them to a third world country struggling with shortages of rubber and pigskin. Still others said he kept them all in a bizarre, underground museum dedicated to his efforts in ruining childhoods.

And now Old Man Augustine had a giant robot. Flinch couldn't help but wonder which kid had accidentally tossed that into his yard.

"I have warned everyone in this neighborhood to keep off my lawn!" the old man's voice boomed. His voice was electronically magnified, giving it an eerie, mechanical thrum. "I work hard to keep it nice, and you might think that's funny, but it's not. I've heard you all laughing about it. Well, I'll show you what's hilarious!"

There was an explosion of steam and flame and the giant robot's fist separated from its arm and flew toward Flinch. Instinctively, he leaped into the air just before it crashed into him. He landed on the other side of the trench, right next to Mama Rosa.

His grandmother shook off her insanity long enough to look stunned. "Julio, how did you—?"

"Milk does a body good, Mama Rosa," Flinch said. He didn't have time to worry about her discovering his powers and had even less time to explain them. "I'm just going to go and take care of that robot. I'll be right back."

Flinch turned and ran with a burst of speed so powerful it blew Mama Rosa's hair out of the bun on the top of her head. He burned a path toward the colossus while sorting through his possible plans. OK, superpunch? Should he try to tear its head off? Tie up its feet with a big rope?

But while pondering these possibilities, a little voice reminded him that he was a freak. He had screwed up the last two missions he was in charge of, and now he was on his way to screwing up a third. What if he just wasn't good at decisions?

"Before I put up my fence, you heathens ran through my property like a herd of cows, tearing up the flowers and turning everything to mud. All for your stupid balls! Well, do you want your balls back? Here they are!"

A cannon boom shook the air, and a hailstorm of footballs, baseballs, tennis balls, basketballs, soccer balls, a few Frisbees, and at least one Hula-Hoop flew out of the robot's chest. Flinch did his best to avoid them, zigzagging through the assault, but there were so many. A rubber dodgeball smacked him on the head, but he shook it off and kept running toward the robot. When he got close enough, he landed a massive punch right at its leg, knocking it clean off its body.

The giant robot teetered back and forth on one limb before finally tumbling over. The impact knocked down Old Man Augustine's entire fence, but in a bizarre miracle, the lawn was completely untouched.

"What in the world is going on?!" Mama Rosa demanded.

Flinch looked at her and sighed. "It's time you knew the truth."

"The truth about what?"

Suddenly, Mr. Crabapple from down the street squealed into view on a converted riding lawn mower covered in sharp, spinning blades. Not far behind him, Dean Barton from the next block over snapped pictures with a bizarre camera that seemed to steal everything it captured on film. Behind him were the Soreil twins, a couple of precocious girls in pink dresses, each swinging electrified jump ropes as if they were inviting Flinch to join them in a deadly game of double Dutch.

Flinch squeezed his nose to activate the com-link again and soon heard Agent Brand on the other end.

"Did you handle your situation, Agent?" Brand asked.

"Yes and no," Flinch said. "My grandmother is fine, but my neighborhood is losing its mind."

SUPPLEMENTAL MATERIALS

These are the intercepted text messages between the Antagonist and Miss Information. Warning: This material is highly sensitive and may include classified material. Also, it is mushy and gross.

Antagonist: How is ur day?

Msinformation: Good. U?

Antagonist: Awesome. Watching the news. There are supervillains everywhere!

Msinformation:

Antagonist: There's a crazy in Delaware calling himself Captain Cavity. Built a machine that gives people tooth decay.

Msinformation: Everyone is a captain.

Antagonist: lol. Everyone!!!!

Msinformation: Fail!

Antagonist: lol! Can't wait for our date tonight . . .

Msinformation: I can't wait to see you cooking for me.

Antagonist: I'm not really going to cook. I kidnapped the guy who won last year's goulash cook-off.

Msinformation: Love, love, love goulash!

Antagonist: I love you.

Msinformation: :<3

Antagonist: What Is :<3 ?

Msinformation: A kiss. Duh! You're so cute.

Antagonist: Not as cute as you.

Msinformation: No, you're cute.

Antagonist: Don't argue. You're the cute one.

Msinformation: Don't tell me what to do! If I say you're cute, you're cute.

Antagonist: If you don't stop and admit you are far

cuter than I am, then I can't be held responsible for the pain and misery I will heap on you.

Msinformation: And If you don't accept the fact that I think you're cuter, I will make sure that you never get another night of rest for fear of me killing you in your sleep.

Antagonist: You are going to look so cute trying to crawl out of my shark tank.

Msinformation: And you will look cute when my giant laser slices you in half.

Antagonist: We are perfect for each other.

Msinformation: That's 'cause we're cute 

12

The next morning Agent Brand found himself in the briefing room with the NERDS (minus Matilda), Ms. Holiday, the lunch lady, Benjamin, and Dr. Kim. General Savage was linked via satellite.

Dr. Kim wore a concerned expression. Brand didn't like it. Scientists were supposed to be optimistic. They put their faith in numbers and ideas, and they thought the answers to even the biggest questions were right around the corner. When they looked nervous, that didn't bode well.

"I've examined Flinch's grandmother, as well as the dozen other people from her neighborhood, and all are infected with Heathcliff's mutated nanobytes. It's likely that we're seeing the beginning of an epidemic."

"An epidemic?" Ms. Holiday repeated, horrified.

Dr. Kim nodded. "Benjamin, can you assist?"

The blue orb darted around the room. "I'd be happy to help, Dr. Kim."

The walls flipped over to reveal a collection of massive computer screens. One had a map of the greater Washington, D.C., area on it, while another had a highly magnified image of a nanobyte. Then there were charts of the circulatory system of a human body. Another screen showed a gallery of pictures, each a portrait of a normal citizen who had suddenly developed a desire to take over the world. Many of them wore masks and bizarre costumes, and all of them held some strange weapon in their hands.

"Heathcliff's nanobytes are self-replicating," the doctor said.

"And that means . . . ?" Jackson asked.

"They're cloning themselves," Duncan explained.

"Exactly," Dr. Kim said. "And they're doing it at an astounding speed. Their numbers double every ten minutes. Plus, there's another troubling discovery. As I told you before, the nanobytes are broadcasting a message into the minds of their victims. Our science team has managed to isolate it . . . Benjamin?"

Benjamin clicked and a voice filled the room. It had a determined, almost fevered intensity. "You are smarter than everyone else. Everyone you know is a fool. They don't respect your intellect. But they will pay. Oh yes, they will pay. When you take over the world, they will fall to their knees and beg for your mercy, but they will find you have none! They shouldn't have laughed at you. You will have the last laugh!"

"That voice!" Pufferfish said.

"It's Heathcliff," Brand snarled. "Even when he's asleep, he's trying to take over the world. We need to lock down the facility."

"You can't lock us in," Ms. Holiday said.

"Ms. Holiday is correct," Dr. Kim said. "We're the only group capable of dealing with the insanity out there. If the team is trapped down here, the problems will get worse."

"What are your projections, Dr. Kim?" General Savage asked. "What kind of time do we have before it goes global?"

A sectional map of the world appeared on all of the screens. It was scattered with red dots, mostly concentrated on the East Coast of the United States and Western Europe. But as Brand studied the map the dots began to spread. The map zoomed out to show the entire world, and the little red dots appeared on every continent. The dots multiplied faster and faster, and soon there wasn't an inhabited place on Earth that wasn't bright red.

"How long?" the lunch lady asked.

"Three days," Benjamin said. "Maybe longer."

"But not much longer," Dr. Kim added.

Brand looked around the room. "So what do we do?"

The group grew very quiet.

Brand slammed his hand down on a desk. "Nothing? We don't have a plan? We're just going to let the world end?" He shuddered, envisioning the inevitable. When would Ms. Holiday succumb? The lunch lady? General Savage? The team? What would happen when it was his turn and he was dreaming of taking over the world or building a freeze ray?

"If the virus is mechanical in nature, can't we just send out an electromagnetic pulse? That usually disables electronics," Duncan said.

"We tried that," Dr. Kim said. "Heathcliff's nanobytes have developed some kind of shield. Perhaps the machine that installed them in his head understood that one EMP blast could kill him, so it came with protection."

"What about Heathcliff?" Savage said. "If he's got some transmitter inside him, can't we just go in and take it out?"

"You're suggesting some sort of operation," Ms. Holiday said.

"It's in his brain, right? Would he survive it?" Pufferfish asked.

"We've thought of that, too," Dr. Kim said. "We located the transmitter, but—"

"Then cut it out!" Savage cried.

"It's not that simple, sir," Dr. Kim said.

"The transmitter is as small as a nanobyte, which is microscopic," Benjamin twittered. "If we had a surgeon who could find it, he or she would have to cut into Heathcliff's brain, which in its current state is enormous. There isn't a doctor alive who would know how to find it."

"And it could kill Heathcliff," Dr. Kim added.

There was a silence in the room.

"No," Brand said. "Heathcliff may be an insane monster and full of alien robots, but he is still an eleven-year-old boy."

"But we're talking about the end of the world here!" Savage barked.

"We still have at least three days, sir," Brand said.

"I agree with Agent Brand," Dr. Kim said. "We've got a team of one hundred of the smartest scientists to ever walk the planet dedicating all their considerable brainpower to coming up with a solution."

"So what do we do in the meantime?" Ms. Holiday asked.

"We screen everyone on the team for infections," Dr. Kim said. "We'll do it every couple of hours. Anyone who has as an alien nanobyte will be quarantined immediately to prevent him or her from infecting others."

"Everyone?" Ms. Holiday asked.

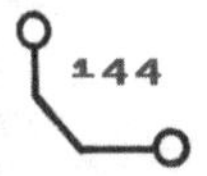

"Better safe than sorry," Agent Brand said. "Doctor, what can we do to help the science team?"

"Stay out of the way and let us do our work," Dr. Kim said. "And perhaps spend some time with the people you love while you still can. They may try to take over the world at any minute."

"If that's all, the children should get to class," Ms. Holiday said. "The new principal is watching them like a hawk."

"Can we stop with the bird references?" Jackson said.

The lunch lady nodded his head in agreement. "Listen, we're going to have to do something about her and quick. She's taken too big of an interest in the team."

Brand nodded. "It's on the list. Right now, we've got more important things to do than worry about Ms. Dove."

"Easy for you to say," Flinch remarked. "You haven't been in detention twice this week. I'm starting to get a reputation."

"Yeah, I hear some of the kids even think he's cool," Jackson said.

END TRANSMISSION.

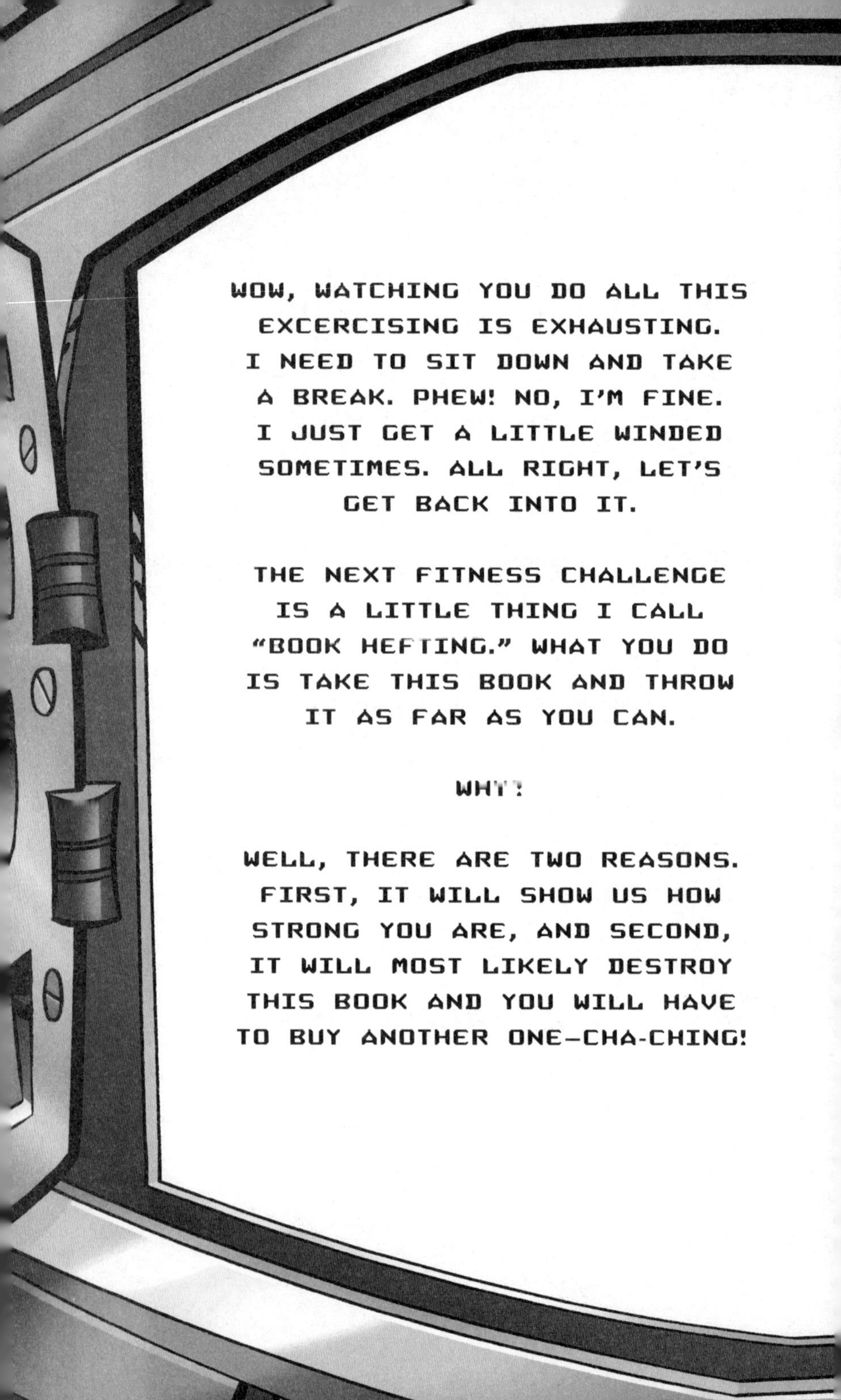
WOW, WATCHING YOU DO ALL THIS EXCERCISING IS EXHAUSTING. I NEED TO SIT DOWN AND TAKE A BREAK. PHEW! NO, I'M FINE. I JUST GET A LITTLE WINDED SOMETIMES. ALL RIGHT, LET'S GET BACK INTO IT.
THE NEXT FITNESS CHALLENGE IS A LITTLE THING I CALL "BOOK HEFTING." WHAT YOU DO IS TAKE THIS BOOK AND THROW IT AS FAR AS YOU CAN.
WHY?
WELL, THERE ARE TWO REASONS. FIRST, IT WILL SHOW US HOW STRONG YOU ARE, AND SECOND, IT WILL MOST LIKELY DESTROY THIS BOOK AND YOU WILL HAVE TO BUY ANOTHER ONE—CHA-CHING!

SO, BEND AT THE KNEES AND THROW THIS BOOK WITH ALL YOUR MIGHT. THEN USE A TAPE MEASURE TO CALCULATE HOW FAR YOU TOSSED IT.

PLEASE ENTER THE DISTANCE.

____

WOW, I HOPE THIS BOOK ISN'T FROM THE LIBRARY.

LEVEL 5
ACCESS GRANTED

BEGIN TRANSMISSION:

13

Duncan invited Flinch to stay with his family now that Mama Rosa was in quarantine, but Flinch declined. He didn't want to be too far away from his grandmother, so he stayed in the Playground on a foldaway cot. Mama Rosa was his only family, and knowing that she was sick kept him up half the night.

He wasn't alone. Agent Brand drifted from one room of the Playground to another watching Heathcliff and studying the tests the science team had done on the virus. He looked worried and frustrated, but Flinch suspected he wanted to be left alone.

In the morning, Flinch got himself ready for school. Mama

Rosa usually made a huge breakfast for the two of them, so it was strange to eat alone. With Ms. Dove's "no junk food" policy, he decided to load up on sweets before his first class. Mama Rosa would never have allowed him to eat something called Not Really Sugar Smacks, let alone four boxes of it. By the time Flinch was finished with breakfast, he was so wound up, he thought he could see ghosts. But he knew he needed all that sugar to get through the day.

When he got to his first class, he was a sweaty, panting mess. Pushing aside his fears for his grandmother, he took out his books and paper and prepared to take notes. From the corner of his eye, he caught a glimpse of a figure in the doorway. Ms. Dove's eyes were glued on him. He gave her a sheepish smile, wanting her to believe he didn't mind, but he hated being watched. He knew she would eventually see something she shouldn't, and the team's secret would be exposed. He had to find a way to distract her, but his mind was so jumbled with half possibilities that he couldn't focus. The more he thought about it, the more nervous he grew until he was ready to scream. He squeezed his nose and waited for Brand's voice.

"What is it, Agent?" the director asked. He sounded tired.

"The principal is staring at me," Flinch whispered.

"That woman!" Brand growled. "Don't let her shake you."

“Please, everyone, would you pass your homework to the front of the class,” his teacher said.

Flinch froze.

“Homework!” he whispered. “I didn’t do my math homework. Aaack! I didn’t do any of my homework. Yesterday I was too busy saving my neighborhood from giant ball-stealing robots and grandmothers with homemade flamethrowers. I went to bed without eating dinner! I didn’t even eat dessert! I never do that!”

Suddenly, his teacher, Mr. Poole, leaned over him. “Who are you talking to, Julio?”

Flinch gulped. “No one, sir. Just taking some mental notes.”

“I see. The only thing I don’t see is your homework.”

Flinch tried to smile. “I didn’t get a chance to do it.”

“You didn’t get a chance to do it?” Mr. Poole turned to the class. “Did anyone else not get a chance to do their math homework?”

The room was silent.

“I see. I wonder why they found time to do it and you didn’t. It’s a mystery. Would you care to explain?”

In a panic, Flinch tried to explain, but he was so hyper it came out as nonsense. “I broke my face on a chili pot and there were monkey pirates invading from the sun!” Then he let out a strangled cry. “Aaarrggggheeeeeee!”

“Agent Flinch, you need to relax,” Brand’s voice said in his ear. “It’s obvious Ms. Dove is after you. She’s told your teacher to give you a hard time to try to get some kind of reaction out of you. Maybe she wants you to say something disrespectful or to make a scene in class so she can have another excuse to send you to detention. Don’t give her the satisfaction.” Flinch looked at the door again. Ms. Dove was hovering there, as if waiting for her turn to smack the piñata with a stick. Brand was right, but it didn’t make Flinch feel better. In fact, he felt on the verge of a nervous breakdown.

“I’m waiting, Mr. Escala!” Mr. Poole said.

“OK, kid, listen up,” Brand said. “I went to boarding school and I know how to handle teachers who spend all their time trying to embarrass you. Just repeat everything I say and say it as sincerely as you can.”

Flinch listened to everything Brand said, and he recited it word for word, as seriously as he could.

“There’s no mystery, Mr. Poole. I didn’t manage my time well last night because I was preoccupied with family issues. I realize that by not doing the assigned work I slow down an ambitious lesson plan and make it harder on my peers to learn. I apologize to you and everyone in class for my lack of commitment and vow that this will not happen again.”

Mr. Poole blinked hard as if he had just seen Bigfoot. His

eyes were wide and his mouth seemed to be working out some kind of silent response. Flinch watched him struggle to make a sound. "Very well, Julio."

Brand's voice was in Flinch's ear again. "If you talk to them with respect, they will do backflips for you. A teacher never expects an apology. It works every time."

Flinch glanced back toward the door. Ms. Dove was still watching him.

When class was over, she followed him to the next one, and then the next, and then the next after that. In each class, Brand told him the right thing to say to the teacher to get him or her off his back. By the time lunch rolled around Flinch noticed that Ms. Dove was losing her smile. In fact, her face was curling up in a scowl fit for a hawk.

Flinch sat at his lonely cafeteria table picking at the chicken casserole surprise the lunch lady had prepared. Though Flinch had hoped the pilot had slipped in some candy corn as the "surprise," there was nothing there when he got to the bottom of the bowl.

"Hey, what's up?"

Flinch turned and saw a group of kids standing over him. They were the same four bullies who shoved him into his locker. He mentally prepared himself for a barrage of spitballs or an atomic wedgie. "Listen, guys—"

The boys grabbed some chairs from other tables, including a few that still had kids sitting in them, and sat down next to him, uninvited. A moment later they were all talking at once about a million different things, shouting over one another, and occasionally punching each other in the arm.

"So, that was pretty awesome how you threw us down the hallway," the red-haired boy said. He had introduced himself as Wyatt.

"Yeah!" his buddy Jessie said, whistling with every word. "I've got a huge purple bruise."

The short boy, who called himself Toad, lifted up the back of his shirt. "Me, too! Mine is shaped like Texas!"

"We're going down to the train station to throw rocks at pigeons after school if you wanna come," the chubby one said. His friends called him Hooper.

"You want me to come with you?" Flinch asked.

"Yeah," Toad said.

"Um, didn't you guys shove me in my locker the other day?"

"Yeah," Jessie said.

"You realize that bullies don't usually hang out with—"

"You think we're bullies?!" Wyatt exclaimed.

All the boys shouted protests.

"We're not bullies! We're juvenile delinquents," Toad croaked. His voice was much deeper than the others'.

"What's the difference?" Flinch asked.

"There's a world of difference!" Hooper cried. "A bully is a moron who has to pull down others to make himself feel big. A juvenile delinquent is an artist!"

"An artist?"

"Absolutely!" Jessie whistled. "We don't paint or sculpt, but what we create is a masterpiece of havoc, whether it's stuffing squeezable cheese into your socks or unscrewing the cap on the saltshaker in your favorite restaurant. We're the Michelangelos of Mischief."

"You guys are pulling all the school pranks?" Flinch asked. These boys must be the ones running Agent Brand ragged as a janitor. "Aren't you guys afraid of getting caught?"

The boys roared with laughter. "We get caught all the time!" Toad said. "Why do you think we're in detention? And in you, we see a kindred spirit—another artist, if you will."

"Me?"

"You must have done something to get the principal on your case," Wyatt said. "Hey! You're not the kid that keeps stealing the letters off the movie theater sign, are you?"

Flinch shook his head.

"Whoever is doing that is an inspiration to juvenile delinquents everywhere," Toad said.

Hooper laughed. "Last week there was a movie playing

called *Trouble in the Deep Water.* He changed the sign to read *The Turd in the Bowl.*"

"*Star Wars* Festival turned into *Fart Wars,*" Toad said.

"Last month the sign advertised a movie called *Eat Pray Fart!*" Hooper exclaimed.

"It's truly groundbreaking work," Wyatt said. "He's taking the juvenile delinquent world by storm!"

All of the boys laughed. Toad nearly fell out of his seat. Even Flinch laughed, right before he sneezed.

"Wow! You got some serious allergies, bro," Wyatt said.

"We should record that and make it Ms. Dove's voice mail message," Hooper suggested.

"Flinch, I need you in the Playground on the double. We've got a problem," Pufferfish told him through the com-link.

"So what do you say, dude? You hanging with us? Those rocks aren't going to throw themselves," Hooper said.

"Listen, thanks for the invite but I gotta go," Flinch said as he stood up from the table.

"I told you the guy had a secret life!" Wyatt cried.

Flinch froze. How did Wyatt know? Had he seen him sneak into Locker 41? Had he spotted him running to school at super-speed? "Um—"

"You're the one that keeps letting off stink bombs in Ms. Bailey's class!"

“Yep—busted,” Flinch lied. It was best for the boys to think he was pulling pranks instead of wondering what he was doing when he disappeared.

“Dude, that’s classic!” Toad croaked.

The other boys all agreed that it was indeed “classic.”

“All right, dude,” Hooper said. “You go do your thing. We’ve got some serious pranks to pull before the end of the day, too.”

Wyatt opened up his backpack. Flinch saw it was stuffed tight with chocolate snack cakes. They were tubes of chocolate with cream filling called Ho Hos. Flinch had eaten a million of them in his day.

“What are those for?”

“We’re dumping them in the girl’s bathroom toilets where they will magically be transformed into floating number twos. It’s going to be hilarious when the girls run out of the bathroom looking like they’re going to barf!”

“FLINCH. We need you now!” Pufferfish shouted loud enough to rattle Flinch’s brain.

“Well, have fun,” Flinch said before he left. As he hurried from the cafeteria, he looked back at the boys. What a strange world middle school was. No one was exactly who they seemed. Even the troublemakers had layers.

Moments later, Flinch leaped into Locker 41. When he

reached the floor of the Playground, his team was waiting for him—or rather, what was left of it. Nearly fifty of the scientists were now locked away in quarantine.

"They're all infected?" Flinch asked.

Brand nodded. "And there may be more, but right now we can't be certain. The results from the first round of testing were corrupted, so we're going to start over. But that's not our biggest concern right now. Suit up. The School Bus is ready."

"Where are we going?" Flinch asked.

"Pack your sunglasses, shaky," Jackson said. "We're going to Hollywood."

Ten minutes later, the School Bus was breaking the Earth's gravitational pull and making a U-turn to California. Flinch watched the red glow of the superheated ship's hull out the window while chewing on his fingernails. The last couple of missions had all been technically successful, but they were also disastrous, and it was mostly his fault. He just hoped that Agent Brand would finally see that he shouldn't be leading the team.

Ms. Holiday unstrapped herself from her seat. "Time for your mission. Benjamin, can you help me out with this one?"

"Of course," the little blue orb chirped. Spinning like a top in midair, it projected a 360-degree image along the walls of the rocket. Flinch saw a hulking giant with two heads, four arms, and four legs standing nearly ten feet tall. It was stampeding down Hollywood Boulevard, kicking cars aside and terrorizing everyone it passed. Then the video changed to a news reporter standing on the side of the very same street. She gestured toward the creature that was rapidly approaching from behind her, but much to Flinch's surprise, she didn't seem at all concerned.

"As you can see, today's film shoot is tying up traffic from here to Wilshire, and I have to say, that is one amazing-looking robot," the reporter said. "The magic of moviemaking is alive and well, folks."

The video cut to a man sitting at a desk. "Carla, how long do they say the shoot will last? I'm sure that's backing traffic up for miles."

"At this moment there seems to be confusion as to who exactly is shooting the movie, but as soon as I get word, I'll report back to you," the reporter said.

"Why are we getting involved with moviemaking?" Gluestick asked.

"That's not a movie. It's the real thing. We've told the local press we're a production company shooting a movie called *The Monstrosity*, and it's important to keep them believing it as long as we can," Agent Brand said. "People are already tense from the sudden crime wave. If they think a two-headed giant is terrorizing a major city it will lead to panic."

Pufferfish slipped on her parachute. "So, what is it—a mutant? A robot?"

"No, it's an actor," Ms. Holiday said. "I've used facial recognition technology on one of the heads and I've identified him."

"Facial recognition technology?" Flinch asked. "What's that?"

"It's a computer program. I tapped into a database filled with photos of people from all over the world. It searched every published photo, trying to match the eyes, bone structure, and nose of our giant. It took a bit longer because I was searching criminal records first. That's the problem with this epidemic. The usual suspects aren't the usual suspects; it's regular people who are causing all the problems. Well, anyway, when I expanded the search I found him right away. His name is Justin Maines."

"*The* Justin Maines?" Duncan cried.

"You know him?" Brand asked.

"Of course! He was on my favorite show of all time, *Space Trek*! He was one of the red shirts."

"What's a red shirt?" Braceface asked.

"The show was about a spaceship that investigated alien worlds. The people in charge wore yellow shirts, and the science and medical teams wore blue. But if the character had a red shirt on, he was a low-level member of the team, which meant there was a pretty good chance he was going to get killed or eaten or sucked into a time vortex and you'd never see him again."

"Gluestick, sometimes your nerdiness is frightening," Braceface said.

"But he's right, Jackson," Ms. Holiday said. "Mr. Maines was in fifty-seven episodes of that show, and he died in every single one. Since then, he's made a career out of playing dead bodies on crime shows. They call him the 'king of extras.'"

"Which makes a lot of sense when you take a good look at him—he's got a couple extra arms and legs and an extra head," Flinch said.

"Let me guess: He's got a ray gun," Pufferfish offered.

Ms. Holiday nodded. "We're not sure how it works, but it appears to duplicate the molecular structure of anything it blasts, and then it rearranges the two copies into one solid form."

"I've always wondered what it would be like to have two heads," Flinch said. "I bet I could eat twice the candy!"

"Agent Flinch, you are not allowed to get hit with the ray on purpose," Brand ordered.

Ms. Holiday helped Flinch put on his parachute, then passed him a sack of red ropes. He slurped down five like they were strands of spaghetti.

She helped Duncan next. "Wow! Justin Maines!" Duncan said, grinning. "When we stop his maniacal plot to take over the world, I'm totally going to ask for his autograph."

"We're over the drop site!" the lunch lady announced as he left the cockpit to help open the hatch.

"And remember, if you feel odd, if you get a fever or a sore throat, or feel like you're smarter than everyone else, you're probably infected," Brand shouted over the wind that whipped into the cabin from outside. "You must let us know right away."

Flinch eyed his teammates warily. Any one of them might be the next to succumb. He couldn't help but feel suspicious, but he hated to think of his friends that way. They had been through so much together as spies and as buddies. He felt guilty preparing himself to fight them.

And what about the adults? He was very concerned about the lunch lady, who, he had to admit, was a rough-around-the-edges type already. As an ex-soldier, the lunch lady had seen a lot of combat in very dangerous places. There were rumors in the Playground that he was once a demolition expert, only he thought using explosives was cheating and just beat the building silly with his bare hands. Mr. Brand was no slouch, either. Despite his cane, everyone knew the director was the United States' greatest secret agent. And then there was Ms. Holiday, who looked sweet and loving but was a trained fighter. He hoped he never had to find out what it was like to go head-to-head with any of them.

Flinch shoved three more strands of licorice into his mouth, and fearlessly jumped out of the plane into the open air. In no time he landed next to the team in the middle of Sunset Strip, one of downtown L.A.'s most popular areas. It was lined with shops and tattoo parlors, all night diners and parking garages, each with a flashy exterior that shouted "Look at me!" There weren't many people on the street, which Flinch considered a major miracle. He hoped their luck would continue.

As he was shoving another handful of red ropes in his mouth, an explosion shook the ground. A thick black plume of smoke climbed toward the sky. Emerging from the smoke was something Flinch's mind could hardly process. It was the same giant he had seen on the video in the School Bus, but now that it was live and real and right in front of him, with all those extra legs and arms and the second head . . . well, it made him feel sick.

SUNSET BLVD.
ONLY

"Flinch, you're on point on this one," Pufferfish said.

"Me? Not again!"

"Listen, this isn't my idea. Brand wants you out front more. He says you are squandering your potential being in the background. You're the strongest and fastest in the group."

Flinch shook his head. "Hasn't anyone been paying attention for the last two years? I'm the hyper one. I have a hard time concentrating. I'm the freak!"

"I don't like it any better than you do, but right now there's a very good reason you should take over. You're immune to the virus," Pufferfish said. "Any of the rest of us could get sick in the middle of the mission. So man up, Agent Flinch. You're the boss."

"Fine! I'm in charge. I'm in charge? Oh boy. What do we do? What do we do?" Julio felt like he had eaten something that had gone bad. He turned the knob on his harness just to calm his nerves and help him think. There was no more time to argue. The creature was on its way.

"We could attack the monster," Gluestick suggested.

"Good idea, buddy," Flinch said. "Let's attack the monster. So . . . maybe you could coat the street with some sticky stuff? Maybe it will slow him down a little?"

"Excellent idea," Gluestick said, and then ran off to do as he was told.

"And me?" Braceface asked.

"Uh, well . . . can you make something big with those braces? Like a big fist? Once that thing hits the glue, you could give him a big punch—you know, knock him on his back where he'll get stuck even more?"

Braceface grinned. "I'm on it."

"And me?" Pufferfish asked.

"You're allergic to lousy plans, right?"

"Yes."

"How do you feel? Any swelling of your feet or hot rashes?"

"I feel good. Must be a good plan."

While they spoke, Gluestick extended his hands and a stream of sticky paste shot from his fingertips. He coated the street with a thick layer of adhesive while Braceface's braces twisted and turned in his mouth.

"Look at me, Hollywood! I'm Justin Maines," the creature shouted, completely ignoring the NERDS. "You turned your back on me! You said I didn't have that star quality! You forced me into the life of an extra! Well, you wanted an extra, so I'm giving you an extra! Extra arms! Extra legs! And extra rage!"

The monster snatched a telephone pole and pulled it out of the ground. Its wires snapped and shimmied, sending sparks into the air like angry fireflies. He seemed unconcerned with the potential ten thousand volts of electricity that could easily kill him. Instead, he hefted the pole onto his shoulders as if he were a big league hitter, then swung for the fences, smashing a car and sending it flipping end over end into a parking garage.

"You laughed at me!" he continued. "You said I would never make it, but I've made it! I'm the biggest extra in the business. I've played a dead body over seven hundred times! I've been a diner in a restaurant on a thousand different prime-time shows. I redefined what it means to play the guy in the doctor's office! I'm not just any extra. I'm the Extra! You can't turn your backs on me. I won't let it happen!"

As he raged, he stepped right into Gluestick's trap, and his feet caught fast. He pulled and pulled, doing his best to free himself, but he couldn't budge.

"Um, I know you're in charge, and I don't want to be pushy, but right now would be the perfect time for Braceface to do his work," Pufferfish said as she scratched at her leg. Flinch knew she was also allergic to not being in charge.

"All right, Braceface!" he shouted. "Let him have it!"

An enormous fist made of orthodontic appliances shot out of Jackson's mouth. It clocked the Extra in the chin, and the monster teetered, dazed.

"Hit him again?" Flinch asked, looking to Pufferfish for reassurance.

She nodded her approval.

"Hit him again!" Flinch shouted.

Jackson's metallic mitt reared back for another punch, but this time the Extra caught it in his hand. With an angry wrench, he pulled Jackson off his feet and flung him into the air behind him. The Extra roared with anger, but he was still stuck fast in Gluestick's paste. He struggled to free himself, straining with all his might.

Just when Flinch was sure the monster was caught tight, the Extra did something no one could have expected. Instead of freeing his foot, he pulled a big chunk of the street underneath him completely out of the ground. Then he did the same with the other foot. He continued his rampage, but each step landed him in more paste, so he was forced to rip more and more chunks of pavement from the road. With each new layer beneath his feet, he grew taller and taller.

Flinch turned to Pufferfish. "OK, as the leader, I am commanding you to take charge."

"Sorry," Pufferfish said. "I'm not allowed. Time for Plan B."

"I didn't have a Plan A!" Flinch cried, eating another red rope, which didn't help calm his nerves in the least. "Gaargggggahhhab!"

"Don't freak out!" Pufferfish said as Gluestick raced to join them. "You can do this. Just keep your team and what they can do in your mind. First, Gluestick is still here. I'm still here. Braceface is probably in the next county, but you still have you, too! Supersticky, superitchy, and superstrong—what can you do with that?"

Flinch stared at his friends, then at the approaching creature. Suddenly, it came to him. "Pufferfish, you're allergic to getting killed, right?" he asked.

Ruby nodded.

"You can sense it before it happens and get out of the way, right?"

She nodded again, though this time a little hesitantly. "What do you want me to do?"

"Go fight that thing."

"Really?" Ruby cried.

"Yes. Really."

Much to Flinch's surprise, Pufferfish grinned. "I never get to fight!" Then she raced ahead to do as she was told.

"What about me?" Gluestick asked.

"Pufferfish is going to keep the Extra busy, but there's no reason we should take any chances," Flinch said. He picked his friend up off the ground and held him above his head with one hand.

"Buddy? What do you have in mind?" Gluestick said.

"Be quiet. I'm aiming for the telephone pole," Flinch said, and then he tossed his friend high into the air.

Gluestick sailed through the air and latched on to the

telephone pole the Extra was still holding like a bat. The creature was too busy trying to crush Ruby to notice Duncan, and as Flinch hoped, his friend took advantage. He sprayed glue into the monster's eyes. It reared back, and that's when Flinch leaped into the air. After a massive windup, he punched the Extra in the head. It was a knockout punch, but unfortunately this particular monster had a second head.

"OK," Flinch said with a sigh as he turned the power up on his harness. "One down, one to go."

This time, Flinch climbed the Extra's body, using his giant clothing as handholds, and when he got close enough to the creature's other chin, he delivered a powerful uppercut, then leaped down and out of the way. That proved to be a big mistake. The Extra didn't have any fight left in him, but his falling body was still dangerous. With Gluestick on the pole and Pufferfish and Flinch in the Extra's path, they were all sure to be crushed to death. Flinch closed his eyes and prepared for the worst.

But after several seconds during which he did not feel—or hear the sound of—crushing bones, he opened his eyes and saw the Extra lying flat on his chest, safely wrapped in a bed made entirely out of braces.

A crowd of onlookers clapped as if they were watching a movie shoot. Flinch smiled and waved. He had never had anyone cheer for him. "Should we sign autographs?" he asked the others.

"There he goes, taking all the credit," Pufferfish grumbled.

"Just like always," Gluestick snarled.

Flinch turned to face his friends. "What's that supposed to mean?"

"It wouldn't be the first time you've taken the glory for our hard work," Braceface said. He looked flushed and ill.

"I'm sure you'll go back to the base and laugh about it," Gluestick said. "Well, we've stood in your shadow for far too long, Flinch. It's time the real brains of this team were given the credit they deserve!"

Gluestick raised his hands and looked ready to coat him in glue. Jackson transformed his braces into a giant trident. Pufferfish punched her fist into her other hand. There was no place to go.

"You shouldn't have laughed at me!" Gluestick said.

"He shouldn't have laughed at me!" Braceface said.

"He was laughing at me first," Gluestick said. "And when he laughed at me, it was louder and more hurtful. I should get to kill him."

"No! The Prince of Paste will have his revenge!" Gluestick cried.

"No! Metal Mouth's vengeance will not wait!"

The boys raged at each other and rushed to attack. Flinch bounded skyward to escape the dual attack, and the two boys accidentally turned their powers on each other. Gluestick coated Braceface with a thick layer of sticky syrup. Jackson was locked in place, but his braces were still active. He transformed them from a trident into a giant boot and kicked Duncan down the street.

"You'll find that I'm a little harder to take down than those imbeciles," Pufferfish said. Of all the members of the team, she was probably the least powerful. Her many allergies wouldn't help her much in a fight. Still, the girl stood confidently with her hands on her hips.

"Pufferfish, you have to listen to me," Flinch said. "You aren't acting like yourself and—"

He was hoping for an argument, but he got something far more painful instead. Pufferfish took a running start, leaped into the air, and kicked him in the chest. He fell backward, stunned.

"You have all underestimated me," she said, standing over him. "You think I have the weakest upgrades, but you have no idea what I'm capable of!"

"You're sick, Pufferfish," Flinch said as he crawled to his feet. "I won't fight you."

"Then you will make it very easy for me to take you down," she said, throwing three fast punches in a row. Flinch was ready for them, and deflected each one. Undeterred, his teammate followed her assault with several kicks. None of them connected because of Flinch's speed, but he could feel their force. Pufferfish wanted to hurt him.

"You think I don't know you're laughing at me?" Pufferfish said. "When Brand gave you this mission, he chuckled. I heard him. He wanted to embarrass me and put me in my place. He's intimidated by how smart I am. All of you are!" She attacked with three karate chops followed by a roundhouse kick that, if it had connected, would certainly have taken Flinch's head off his shoulders.

"Look at you!" she continued. "You're bewildered. You have no idea what to do. You're not leadership material. You're the team freak. The joke. You're the comic relief, pal. You're only on the team because Brand has no idea what else to do with you!"

Flinch tried not to listen, but the words hurt. He was the freak. He knew that. But was he a joke? Brand had never put him in charge until recently, and he probably wouldn't have done it this time if the others weren't vulnerable to the virus.

Pufferfish kicked him in the face several times, then in the knee, knocking him down. The pain was searing, like he had hopped into a frying pan. He wasn't sure he could stand, let alone get away.

"Oh, did I hurt you?" Pufferfish taunted. "I can tell. I'm allergic to the weaknesses of others, which means my upgrades can help me pinpoint exactly where to hit you. Like for instance, your right shoulder still hurts from the fight with Wheezer."

Pufferfish ground the heel of her boot into his shoulder. It seared with pain.

"And now I can tell you want to get up and run away," she said, scratching her scalp. "I can feel what you are planning before you do it. There's nothing you can do that I can't sense before you try."

She was right. He scrambled to his feet and tried to punch her, but she deflected it with ease. All of his attacks missed the mark. Pufferfish seemed to know when they were coming as if he had written down all his moves and e-mailed them to her the day before. Her head bobbed and weaved. She ducked away from a kick at just the right time, and while his rib cage was facing her, she socked him with a powerful shot. It nearly knocked the wind out of him.

"Oh, did that sting?"

"I'm fine," Flinch gasped.

"You've forgotten that I'm allergic to liars," she said, before launching another attack. She connected with his ribs nearly six times before he backed up, hugging his arms to himself and feeling his body's agony. "You look worried, shaky. I don't need any superpowers to see that. I suspect one or two more punches might break one of those ribs."

Flinch was sure she was right, but he could do nothing to stop her. Everything he tried she could see a mile away.

But then it dawned on him. What if he were unpredictable? What if even he wasn't sure what he might do?

He turned the knob on his harness all the way to its lowest setting, stopping it from regulating the sugar in his body. At Level Zero he was all hyper and all power without any of the pesky control. She may have called him a freak, but she hadn't seen anything yet.

The next few minutes were a blur to Flinch. He knew there was a lot of jumping and running and bouncing and tossing. His voice may have sounded like a cartoon duck's. He also remembered the look of dread on Pufferfish's face when he raced around her like a hyperactive hurricane.

"What are you doing?" she cried over the wind he stirred up.

"I don't have the faintest idea!" he shouted, zipping around and around her at top speed. The mini-twister lifted the poor girl off the ground, blinded her eyes with trash and dirt, and sucked all the oxygen from her lungs. A moment later she was unconscious. He eased his speed and caught her falling body, then held his ear to her chest. She was breathing.

He pinched his nose. "Boss, they're all sick," he said.

"I know, Flinch," Agent Brand said. "Bring them home."

14

38°88' N, 77°09' W

The Antagonist was convinced that his first date with his new girlfriend was ruined. First, he burned dinner. Second, he forgot to get flowers. Third, he was attacked by ninjas who fought so hard and long that the pint of ice cream he had brought home for dessert melted in the bag.

But Miss Information didn't seem to mind. All she wanted to do was cuddle on the couch and watch television. The news was filled with fires, chaos, and mass destruction—all caused by the villain virus. The Antagonist was pretty sure he had met his soul mate. They munched on popcorn and witnessed the sorrow of others, relishing the horrors that threatened every block.

"Look, sweetie pie, there's a mall in Minneapolis encased in

a block of ice," Miss Information said. "Your plan is working perfectly."

The Antagonist grinned. "Of course it is. I'm a genius."

"My honey bun is so diabolical."

He blushed beneath his mask.

"I have some good news for you," she continued. "The NERDS are incapacitated."

"How do you know?" he asked.

"Honey, I'm not just a pretty face hidden behind a mask with a skull painted on it," she said. "I know everything."

"So they are no longer a threat," he said proudly. "I accomplished something that my boss never could. I knew he should have put me in charge."

"And now the next part of your plan can begin," she said.

“Yes,” he said quietly. What was the next part of the plan again?

“Invading their headquarters!”

“Oh, yes, invading the headquarters! We need to do that right away.”

“Imagine the amount of technology you will have access to then,” Miss Information said. “I’ll be—I mean, you will be unstoppable.”

The Antagonist grinned. How lucky this woman was to have a boyfriend as smart as him. Of course, he had no idea where the headquarters was, but he was sure that his brilliant mind would figure it out at any moment. He recalled invading their old headquarters in the depths of an elementary school, but he knew that space had been abandoned. Where could they have gone? His subconscious was probably putting together the details he had unknowingly already collected and would reveal it to him soon.

“They’re at the middle school,” Miss Information told him.

“Like I suspected,” he cried, even though he hadn’t suspected it. But that was just a tiny detail now. “Sometimes, my flower, I think you are as diabolically intelligent as I am.”

“You’re sweet,” she said, wrapping her arm around his shoulders. “Now you can crush once and for all the last obstacle between you and world domination. Apparently, there's only one active agent left and just a handful of adults in supporting roles, and most of them are scientists so they probably have the combined strength of a baby bunny. The director walks with a cane, and there's a librarian, but what is she going to do? Throw a book at us?"

"The pilot, the one that wears a smock—we have to worry about him," he said.

"It's just a matter of time before he's sick, too, darling," she purred. "Soon, they will all be overcome with evil and your empire will be unstoppable."

The Antagonist smiled beneath his mask. The sound of having an unstoppable evil empire and being at the height of his career sounded awfully good. But wait: Wasn't there something he was supposed to be worried about when he became the most powerful villain in the world? Wasn't it something she had said to him?

Just then the doorbell rang.

"That must be the Chinese food," Miss Information said. "I hope they put in extra packets of duck sauce."

"If they didn't, I will strap the delivery boy to a rocket and shoot it into space," he said.

"Darling, you make me feel like a princess," Miss Information said.

The Antagonist opened the door. There he found a young man holding a sack of food.

“Did you order the chicken lo mein?” the deliveryman asked.

The Antagonist nodded and took the sack. He opened it and took a peek.

“Honey, I’ve got bad news—no duck sauce,” he said.

Miss Information growled. “I’ll go fuel up the rocket.”

15

38°87' N, 77°10' W

The Playground was in disarray. Only fifteen scientists remained from the fifty who had been well that morning. The survivors looked exhausted. Brand guessed they were working around the clock. They were still experimenting on Heathcliff's nanobytes, and tables had been moved aside to make space for the various ray guns and doomsday devices the team had seized from the villains.

The lunch lady had returned to the Playground in a pair of his own handcuffs. "I feel the fever, boss," he admitted. "I knew if I waited, I would cause you trouble. Put me in a cell and keep working."

With his team and the entire world falling apart, Brand could do nothing but stand on the catwalk above Heathcliff's

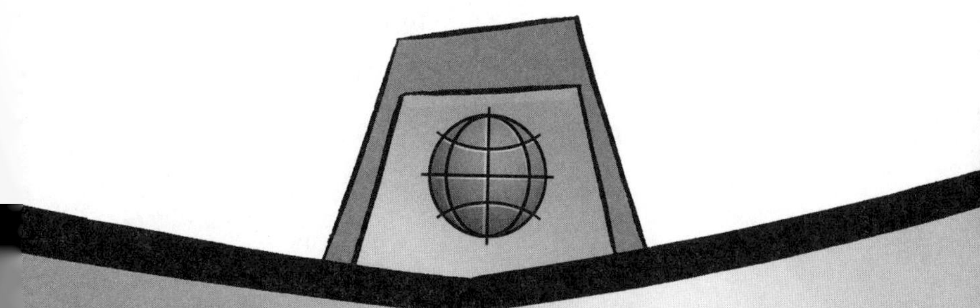

head and look down at the source of all the world's misery. He and the sleeping head were all alone. The remaining staff were busy working on a cure. All of the systems that kept the boy unconscious were running automatically, but soon they would run out of sedatives. When the boy woke up . . . well, things were going to get much, much worse. Brand wondered if General Savage was right. Should they have tried to remove the transmitter from Heathcliff's brain? Was it right to let the world go down the drain for one person? No, that was a decision he was still not prepared to make. He shoved the thought aside.

Benjamin zipped into the room. "Sir, may I be of some assistance?"

Brand sighed. "Not unless you can save the world."

"I'm afraid I'm only a superintelligent, flying computer, sir. Not a miracle worker," Benjamin said. He paused, then continued, "I've received word from the school's administrative office about Julio. Apparently, Agent Flinch is being expelled."

Twenty minutes later, Agent Brand met Flinch in the hallway outside of Principal Dove's office. He seemed more agitated than usual.

"So this is really happening?" Flinch said. "I'm not having some sort of mental breakdown? I'm a secret agent and have superpowers, and they're tossing me out of school!"

"Flinch, please relax," Brand said.

"Relax?" he cried. "How am I supposed to relax?"

Brand turned the knob on Flinch's harness, which seemed to calm the boy. "I assure you that you are not going to be expelled," he said, pinching his nose for the com-link. "Ms. Holiday, this is my fifth attempt to reach you. I need your assistance with the principal."

Ms. Holiday hadn't replied to any of his calls. He worried she was sick, but with a limited staff it was also possible that the com-link was down and there was no one to repair it. He hoped it was just a glitch. He didn't want to think about what he would have to do if she got the virus. What if she attacked him? How could he fight someone he cared so much about?

"We're going to deal with this," Brand said as he led the boy to Principal Dove's office. He knocked and was invited to enter.

Ms. Dove sat behind her desk. Her big, bulky body and huge eyes reminded Brand of a barn owl. A hungry barn owl. He and Flinch probably looked like fat mice.

"What can I help you folks with today?" the principal asked with a beaming smile.

"We've come to speak to you about Flin—I mean, Julio," Agent Brand said.

Ms. Dove sat back in her chair. "About his expulsion."

Brand nodded.

"I expected his parents to want to discuss this, Mr. Brand.

How unusual that the school's janitor has come to his defense," the principal said as she peered over her desk at him.

"Julio lives with his grandmother, and at the moment she is quite ill," he replied. "I've known Julio for a long time. I worked at Nathan Hale Elementary before I came here. I've always found him to be an incredibly respectful and cheerful young man, so I've come to vouch for him."

"Well, in my experience, children change, Mr. Brand," the principal said. "The summer between fifth and sixth grade can transform a sweet and helpful little lovebird into a cranky old pelican."

"I've seen that myself," Brand said. "I've had to scrub this school from top to bottom every day because some of these formerly sweet children are tearing this place apart. But Julio is not one of them. In this case I think we have a little less pelican and more a situation of adjustment and growing pains. Sometimes a little birdie needs time to get used to his new nest. Isn't that right, Ms. Dove?"

Ms. Dove nodded. "That's true. But I've seen a lot of birdies, Mr. Brand. I'm pretty good at picking out the sweet ones from the bullies."

"Bullies!" Flinch exclaimed.

"I hardly think Julio is a bully," Brand said.

"Mr. Brand, please don't take this the wrong way, but I

think I know my birds. I would never presume to tell you about mops and cleaners," Ms. Dove said with a smile. "I'm afraid my mind is made up. This is Mr. Escala's last day here at Thomas Knowlton Middle School."

"You must reconsider," Brand said. "He's a good boy."

Ms. Dove shook her head. "I've already put in for a transfer for him, and he's been accepted at Harris Middle School for Troubled Teens."

"Harris Middle School!" Flinch shouted. "That's a last-chance school."

"A last-chance school?" Brand asked.

"Yeah, it's the place they send kids who have been kicked out of every other school in town. It has a barbed wire fence and a guard tower. You don't graduate from there—you get out for good behavior!"

"Mr. Escala, why waste everyone's time when the inevitable is right in front of our faces? I think we all know how this story ends," Ms. Dove said.

"Ms. Dove, may I be honest with you?" Brand asked.

Ms. Dove cocked a curious eyebrow. "Please."

"I went to a boarding school when I was a child and I had a lot of teachers who liked to call themselves disciplinarians. Some of their passion came from a good place—you know, a real desire to help children. But some of it came from a bad place. Some of it was mean-spirited. Sometimes a teacher would single out a kid to make him an example for the others. I suppose they thought if they could make one kid's life miserable, the others would fall in line and behave."

"Are you suggesting I'm picking on Mr. Escala?" Ms. Dove said, her smile suddenly turning into a frown.

"Well, Ms. Dove, you may know birds, but I know people. I know a bully when I see one."

"You have quite an imagination," she grumbled. She reached into her desk and pulled out some forms and signed them quickly.

"There. That's settled," she told Flinch. "You are no longer a student at this school. I wish you the best with your future endeavors and please empty out your locker before you leave at the end of the day."

"Julio, come along," Mr. Brand said as he rose from his chair.

"But I'm a good kid!"

"Come along," Brand said. "This woman is a fool. This isn't over, but we're through here today."

Flinch followed him out the door and into the hallway.

"That wasn't exactly what I was hoping for," Flinch said. "Oh, man. I'm going to Harris! The school uniform is an orange jumpsuit with your number printed on the front!"

"Julio, I know this looks bleak, but I have considerable

power with the government. I can fix this. If Ms. Dove cannot compromise, then I will have her transferred to another school. Why, I might even have her deported just to teach her a—"

Just then, the door to Ms. Dove's office door exploded, sending wood and metal shrapnel in every direction. The blast knocked Brand and Flinch to the floor.

"What was that?" Flinch asked.

From the office emerged a figure dressed in an enormous white bird suit. It had legs as orange as a chicken's and a plume of bright red feathers on its head. It was Ms. Dove, and she was wearing one of the most ridiculous costumes Brand had ever seen. He might have laughed if not for the murderous look on the woman's face.

"Are you out here in this hallway plotting to take me down?" she cried. "Do you fools really believe that the likes of you could do it?"

"Ms. Dove, what on earth!" Brand said.

"Don't call me that! From now on you will bow to your knees and address me as Colonel Cuckoo!" She shook her tail feathers and flapped her arms aggressively, sending a shower of loose feathers to the floor.

"Those who choose to challenge me will face my wrath!" she crowed, then scratched at the floor with her feet. She let out a vicious squawk and rolled a white egg across the room.

It stopped at Flinch's feet. Flinch started to laugh at it, but then three little panels on the shell slid open and steam seeped into the air. The egg began to beep faster and faster. A bomb!

Brand grabbed Flinch and dragged him around the corner just as the egg exploded, sending chunks of the wall tumbling to the floor where they had stood.

"Flinch, we need to split up. Try to lure her out of the school," Brand said. "Those egg bombs could hurt the rest of the students."

"I'm on it, boss," Flinch said, turning and running down the hallway.

Ms. Dove stalked close behind, flapping her wings and tossing egg bombs. Explosions rocked the school.

Brand hobbled into a bathroom and shut the door. He was about to call for Benjamin when he spotted four boys huddled in the corner with screwdrivers, removing the plumbing from the sinks and toilets.

They looked at him.

He looked at them.

And then he exploded. "It's you!" he cried. "You're the kids who are making my job impossible."

"Busted," the redhead said with a laugh.

"Now, before you get all bent out of shape," the short one said. "We're just expressing our artistic freedom."

There was another explosion in the hallway and the light fixtures in the bathroom rattled.

"What was that?"

Brand ignored the boys and pinched his nose. "Benjamin, are you there?"

Benjamin's voice was on the other end. "Yes, sir."

"We've got a problem topside. The principal is infected and is roaming the hallways in a chicken suit. She's throwing egg bombs at everyone."

One of the boys, who had an annoying whistle in his voice, shouted, "We've got to see this!"

"NO! Stay where you are!" Brand commanded, then turned his attention back to Benjamin. "We need to evacuate the students, but we need to make sure they aren't running into the hallways when she's out there."

"Sensors indicate that Flinch has led her into the gymnasium," Benjamin said. "This would seem to be the opportune time."

"Do it," Brand ordered.

A second later, the fire alarms blared and Brand could hear the children exiting their classes and heading for the emergency doors.

"Who are you talking to?" one of the kids asked. "Are you crazy? A lot of janitors are—I'm not judging."

"Listen, you kids should go with the others," Brand said, but the boys shook their heads.

"No way, man," the red-haired one said. "This is the most exciting thing that has happened to us, like, ever. We're staying!"

Brand groaned. "Who are you kids?"

The chubby one grinned. "We're juvenile delinquents."

Moments later, Flinch's voice filled Brand's head. "Hey, boss, she's chasing me all over. I've got her in the library now, but she's tossing explosives everywhere. She completely destroyed the nonfiction section. I don't think anyone's going to be doing a report on beluga whales this year."

"Keep her busy, son," Brand replied.

Ms. Holiday's voice suddenly came online. "Alexander, what can I do to help?"

"Thank heavens you're safe. I thought something had happened to you!"

"Alive and well, but it's nice to know you were worried. Sorry, I know I'm not supposed to say anything like that on the com-link."

Brand grinned. "I'll let it go this time. I've got four students up here and a lunatic throwing bombs everywhere."

"I know. We're tracking your signal. You need to get to the Playground."

"What about the other students? Are they safe?"

"The building has been evacuated, sir," Benjamin said as another explosion rocked Brand's eardrums. "Would you like to activate Protocol 49?"

"What is Protocol 49?"

"As acting director, you have the ability to force a complete lockdown of the school and control all the hidden systems within the building," Benjamin explained.

Brand grinned. "There are hidden systems? Like what?"

"Laser cannons, sleeping gas, complete visual control—"

"Activate Protocol 49 and lock down the school!" Brand shouted.

Suddenly, a screaming siren filled the air. Flashing red lights popped out of the walls and steel panels slid down from the ceiling to cover the bathroom's windows.

"If you want to play with all the toys, you need to be in the Playground," Ms. Holiday said. "Bring the kids with you."

"We're on our way," Brand said, just before another explosion.

He opened the bathroom door and peeked into the hallway, gesturing for the delinquents to follow him.

As they turned a corner, they saw Ms. Dove at the end of the hall, pounding on a classroom door. Brand hurried the boys in another direction.

"Was that the principal?" one of the delinquents asked.

Brand shushed him. At Locker 41 they stopped, and Brand turned to look at the small band of people depending on him. "I guess we're going to have to redefine what the word 'classified' means around here. Get in."

"Huh?" the short one asked.

"It's the secret entrance to a spy headquarters buried far below the school. Watch." He snatched the short boy by the arm and pushed him into the locker. Before the kid could protest, Brand slammed the door and waited a few seconds. When he opened it, the boy was gone.

"Best. Day. Ever," the three remaining troublemakers said, fighting to be next.

One by one they entered the locker and vanished until Brand was alone. Just as he was about to squeeze himself inside, Ms. Dove stomped around the corner. Brand quelled his panic. Where was Flinch?

"There's my plover," she said. "You're supposed to be the bird that cleans up messes, but here you are, making one."

"Lady, you've taken this whole bird thing way too far," Brand said.

"Maybe you're right, Janitor Brand, but there's one thing you should never be confused about," Ms. Dove said as she removed another one of her egg bombs from within her costume. "This is my nest."

Brand forced himself into the locker as the little egg began to hiss. He slammed the door shut, and as he fell, he heard an explosion. He hoped the woman hadn't destroyed the entrance to the Playground. He also hoped she couldn't squeeze into the locker in that ridiculous costume. As he was whisked through the tubes, he accessed the com-link.

"Flinch! Are you OK, son?"

"I'm fine, boss," Flinch said.

"I'm en route to the Playground now, along with a group of troublemakers I found trashing the bathroom."

"Oh, you've met my friends," Flinch said. "Listen, the bombs are screwing with the electronics in my harness so it's going to take me a while to stop Colonel Cuckoo."

"I think I can help," Brand said as he floated down into the headquarters. Ms. Holiday and Dr. Kim were waiting with the boys and Benjamin. "All right, Benjamin, show me what to do."

"You're the boss," Benjamin said.

A seat rose up out of the floor and Brand slid into it. Once he was comfortable, a touch-screen panel descended from the ceiling. He could see he had access to everything in the school: lights, water, power, even the air-conditioning. He also had access to a number of things he was surprised to know were buried in the walls, including an intercom system. He pushed that button first.

“Ms. Dove, this is Mr. Brand,” he said as an image of the principal in her chicken suit appeared on-screen. She was stalking Flinch through the hallway, leaving a trail of feathers behind her.

“Who said that?” she squawked.

“It’s your plover bird, and I’m here to clean up a mess,” he said.

“Where are you?” she cried.

“Oh, somewhere safe.”

“Get out of my school!” she cried. “This is my school!”

Brand pushed a button on the panel and water showered down on the woman from the sprinklers in the ceiling. “No, Ms. Dove. This is *my* school.”

The woman raced down the hall, only to come to a screeching halt when a panel slid open and fire cannons erupted, creating a wall of flames. She fell backward and raced in the other direction. The cameras followed her every step. Wyatt, Hooper, Toad, and Jessie hovered around Brand, eyeing the action.

“What’s that button do?” Jessie asked, reaching out to touch it.

“Stop! I don’t know what it does!” Brand snapped.

“That releases a sleeping gas which renders everyone unconscious within thirty seconds,” Benjamin said.

Brand eyed Jessie with a frown but pushed the button. Jessie chuckled, and together they watched a milky white gas seeping into the hallways.

"Flinch, Ms. Dove is going to sleep for a while, and if you don't want to join her I need you down here now," Brand said.

Flinch was already floating down from the top of the dome. "Already on it, Chief."

Brand watched Ms. Dove hobble down the hall, tossing her egg bombs in all directions. It was a desperate effort to create chaos, but the effects of the gas were already evident. She was slowing down and seemed confused. Finally, she stopped in the middle of her sprint to lazily flap her wings. "You won't take this place from me," she cried. "I'd rather destroy this nest than give it to another bird."

"Good night, Ms. Dove," Brand said.

But the woman had one last bomb. She removed it from her belt. This one was as big as a bowling ball.

Brand scanned the panel for something to help. If that bomb was as powerful as it looked, it might take down the entire school—and the Playground below it—in one big blast.

"Not that I know for sure," Hooper said, "but I think this button here with the big hammer on it has potential."

Brand shrugged and pushed it. He watched on the view screen as a battering ram swung down from the ceiling. It slammed into Ms. Dove and knocked her down the hallway. The giant egg fell to the floor and lay still, as did Ms. Dove.

Brand eased back into his chair and took a deep breath.

"Good job, boss," Hooper said.

Brand rolled his eyes and then smiled. "You know, I'm starting to like middle school."

END TRANSMISSION.

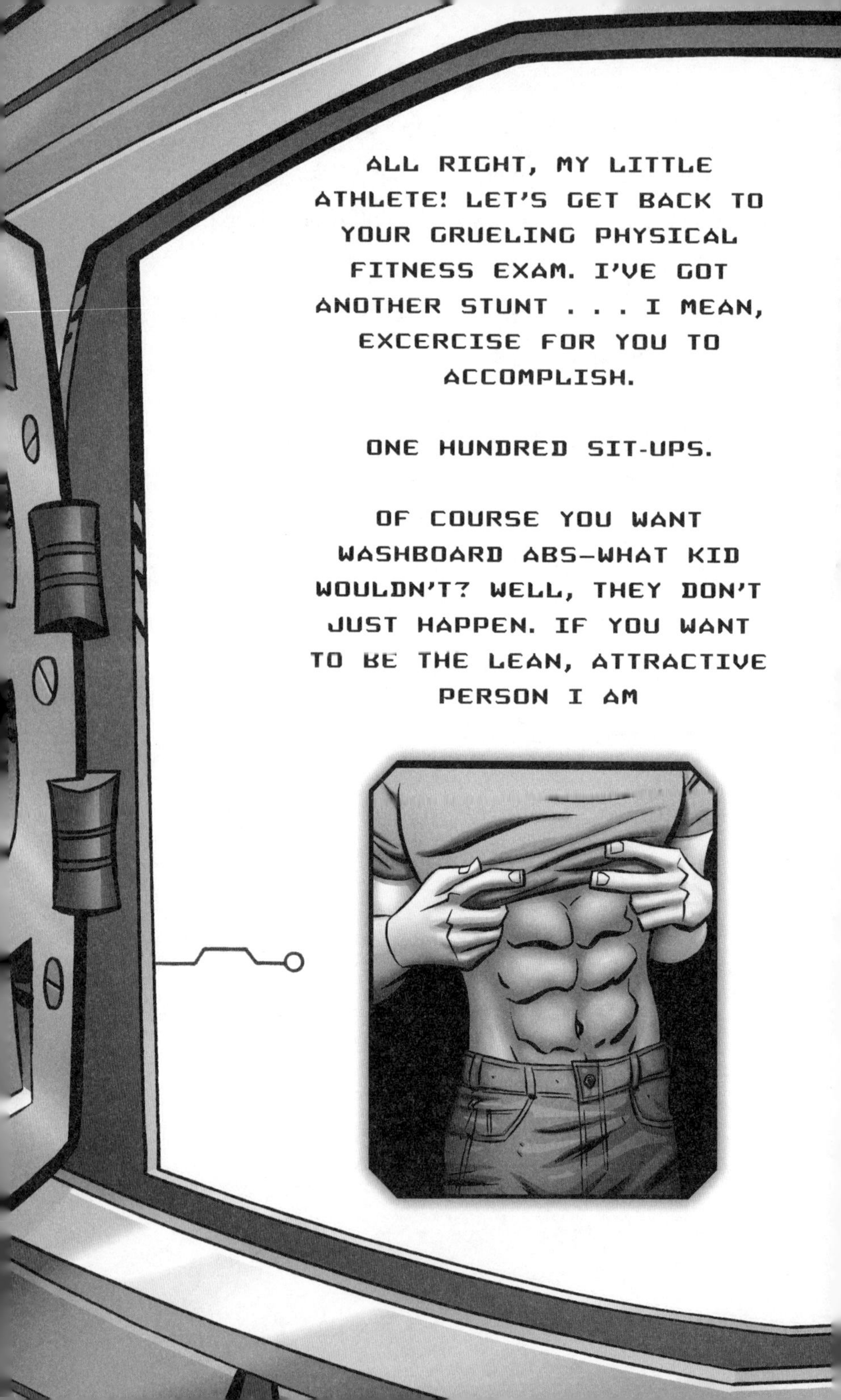
ALL RIGHT, MY LITTLE ATHLETE! LET'S GET BACK TO YOUR GRUELING PHYSICAL FITNESS EXAM. I'VE GOT ANOTHER STUNT . . . I MEAN, EXCERCISE FOR YOU TO ACCOMPLISH.
ONE HUNDRED SIT-UPS.
OF COURSE YOU WANT WASHBOARD ABS—WHAT KID WOULDN'T? WELL, THEY DON'T JUST HAPPEN. IF YOU WANT TO BE THE LEAN, ATTRACTIVE PERSON I AM

THEN YOU CAN'T WISH FOR IT—YOU HAVE TO WORK FOR IT. FIRST, LIE ON THE FLOOR AND PUT THIS BOOK ON YOUR BELLY. SECOND, SUPPORT YOUR NECK WITH A TOWEL TO PREVENT STRAIN. NEVER PULL ON YOUR NECK. THIRD, BEND YOUR KNEES. FOURTH, SIT UP AND FEEL THE BURN. BUT DON'T LET THIS BOOK SLIP OFF YOU!

YEAH! THAT'S IT! NO PAIN, NO GAIN, I'M JUST GOING TO SIT OVER HERE AND EAT MY ICE-CREAM CONE AND WATCH. WHEN YOU'RE FINISHED, RUB YOUR BELLY ON THE SENSOR SO I CAN GAUGE HOW WELL YOU DID.

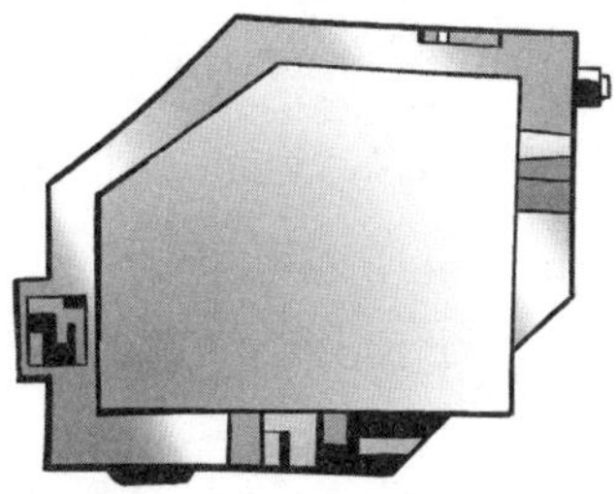

LEVEL 6
ACCESS GRANTED

BEGIN TRANSMISSION:

16

38°87' N, 77°10' W

Flinch watched as Wyatt, Hooper, Jessie, and Toad raced around the Playground, fiddling with inventions and handling weapons they couldn't possibly understand. Every once in a while there was a small explosion followed by a chorus of laughter. Brand looked like he was going to pull out his own hair.

"This place is awesome!" Wyatt said from somewhere in the science department. There was a crash and the sound of breaking glass. "Look at all this cool stuff!"

"Are you sure having them here is a good idea?" Flinch asked his boss.

"It's a terrible idea," Brand said. "But they've seen so much I can't just let them go, and it's too dangerous to have them

running around in the school all by themselves. At least down here I can keep an eye on them."

"So you come down here and save the world every day?" Jessie asked Flinch.

Flinch nodded. "They usually give us weekends off."

"Hey, what does this do?" Toad shouted. Flinch turned to see the boy hoisting Mr. Miniature's shrink ray over his head.

"Don't touch that!" Brand cried, but he was too late. Toad zapped an entire section of desks, turning them dollhouse-size.

"Cool!" the other boys said as they rushed to his side.

"My turn!" Jessie shouted.

"No! I found it! It's my shrink ray. Get your own," Toad said, wrestling the weapon away from his friend's grabby hands.

Flinch stepped in and took the ray gun from the boys. "You have to keep your hands to yourselves, guys," he said. "Some of this stuff is pretty dangerous."

"Duh!" Hooper said. "That's why it's so cool."

"Could everyone just stop for a moment so I can hear myself think?" Brand shouted. "Benjamin, I need a report."

The blue orb floated out of the mission desk. After a few clicks the dome's screen came to life with a hundred different news channels, all reporting on chaos at every corner of the Earth.

"No way!" Wyatt said. "We've got to hook up a video game to this thing!"

Flinch tried to tune the boys out and watch the screen.

"It can now be confirmed that the epidemic has spread into the hundreds of millions. France, China, and Belgium have all declared a state of emergency. Brazil, Chile, Argentina, Australia, and Ireland have established martial law. All planes worldwide have been grounded. Trains are not running. Nearly every harbor on the globe is closed."

"Dudes! There's a giant head over here," Jessie shouted. He had slipped out of the main room while everyone was watching Benjamin's report. Before Flinch could do anything, all four of the boys were racing down the hall and through the door that led to the holding cell. By the time he caught up with them, they were hooting and hollering as they gaped at Heathcliff's disturbing form.

"What is that thing?"

"It's like a hot-air balloon with a face."

"We have to take pictures!"

"Hey! This room is off-limits," Dr. Kim said. She and a handful of the remaining healthy scientists were working feverishly around the boy, clearly hoping for some kind of last-minute breakthrough. "Director Brand, Ms. Holiday, you have to get these kids out of here."

"We're doing our best," Ms. Holiday said. She and Brand each had a kid by the arm, but they were hard to move.

"They're like a bunch of excited puppies."

"Guys, you've got to go," Flinch said. "That head is what is causing all the problems. You could get sick—"

"Sick?" Hooper asked. "Is that what's going on? Everyone is sick?"

"Yes, now let's go," Brand said.

"Is it bacterial or viral?" Hooper asked, causing everyone to look at him in amazement. "What? Just 'cause I'm a troublemaker, I have to be dumb? My dad's a doctor."

"It's like a virus, but it's man-made," Dr. Kim said.

"Nanobots!" Wyatt said, which caused another ripple of surprise. "I watch a lot of sci-fi movies. So . . . those things are real?"

Dr. Kim explained that the team called their technology nanobytes, and that these particular nanobytes were corrupt and were being controlled by the transmitter buried inside of Heathcliff's brain. There was no way to shut the transmitter off without killing Heathcliff, and in his death throes he might send killing pulses out to everyone infected.

"That's wild, man," Jessie said. "So the world is screwed. Are you sure you've got nothing in this place that can stop it?"

"We're out of good ideas," Ms. Holiday said. "Unless you've got something brilliant to offer."

"You know what would be cool?" Toad said. "If it were me,

I'd take that shrink ray and make myself real tiny and then inject myself into the big head's bloodstream. Then I'd go in and turn off the transmitter."

"Yeah, that makes sense," Jessie said.

There was stunned silence in the room for a long time.

"Who are you kids?" Brand asked, then he turned to the scientists. "Could that work?"

Dr. Kim shrugged. "Mr. Miniature managed to shrink people, and they seemed perfectly well when we got them back to their normal sizes. In this case, we'd have to shrink a person down to the microscopic level, but—"

"If they went in his body, they would suffocate immediately," another scientist argued.

"Not if we shrunk an oxygen tank with them," Dr. Kim said. "If we equipped this person with the right tools, it's entirely plausible that he could reach the transmitter and shut it off without harming Heathcliff or anyone else."

"Make it happen," Brand said. "It's the best idea we have."

"Which, may I point out, was my idea. I'm, like, a genius," Toad said. Then he lifted his leg and farted.

The other boys roared with laughter.

"Classic," Flinch said, surrendering to the giggles himself. This only made the boys laugh harder.

Immediately, the scientists went to work putting together

the plan. They ran to the farthest reaches of the Playground, collecting tools and equipment. They went through all the gizmos, gadgets, and gear the team had at its disposal.

Eventually, everyone was ready, and the team assembled in Heathcliff's holding cell. Next to his gigantic head was a large contraption made up of a huge tank filled with liquid, a series of tubes that led from the tank to a hypodermic needle, and Mr. Miniature's shrink ray on a stand facing the tank. Next to this, several bizarre suits hung from a clothing rack. They were part scuba gear, part astronaut uniform, and they looked like something a Martian might wear in an alien invasion movie. Flinch marveled at the setup, even if he wasn't quite sure how it all worked.

"We had to raid a few other experiments, but we're happy to report that everything we needed was at hand," Dr. Kim told the small remaining group. "Best of all, we have these containment suits designed by Dr. Charnoff, who, unfortunately, was infected yesterday. He built about a dozen prototypes—"

"Prototypes . . . as in untested?" Ms. Holiday asked. "Do we really want to send someone on a mission with untested equipment?"

Dr. Kim nodded. "I'm afraid they're our best option. They were designed for space missions, and so they're airtight, which will keep whoever goes in safe and sound. Plus, they generate a low-level deflection technology, a sort of force field, that may help keep away trouble."

"What kind of trouble could there be in a body?" Flinch asked.

"Oh, I don't know—maybe like a million different things," Hooper said. "The acid inside the stomach could eat through the person's skin within minutes, there are substances on the tongue that could dissolve you, or white blood cells that could attack you and rip you apart. Whoever goes in is going to face a lot of danger."

"That's exactly right," Dr. Kim said, impressed. "But Dr. Charnoff's suit also has a few gadgets that will help. There are harpoon guns in both the arms and legs. These can be fired into the walls of the circulatory system to keep our hero from being swept away by the bloodstream. Then there's a laser inside the right glove that can be used to slice open passages from one organ to another. It was originally designed as a welding tool, but, shrunk down, it'll be so small that it shouldn't cause any real damage to Heathcliff."

"So how's the person going to get in?" Flinch asked as he studied the equipment.

"This is the really brilliant part. While wearing the containment suit, the agent will be placed in this tank of saline. The beam will shrink its contents, which will then fill up this hypodermic needle. Then I will inject it into Heathcliff, and the hunt for the transmitter will begin."

"And how does this person get out of Heathcliff?" Ms. Holiday asked.

Dr. Kim smiled. "That's the most important question, right? We don't want our hero floating around inside of Heathcliff for the rest of his or her life. We've created a timer system for the miniaturization process. We're going to set it for two hours, which should be plenty of time to complete the mission. When the time is up, the agent should be inside one of Heathcliff's pores or in his nostril or mouth. Then the process reverses."

"Why a timer? Why can't one of us flip the switch and just make the agent big again?" Brand asked.

"We may all be infected by then," Dr. Kim said. "It's a backup plan, in case no one's capable of operating the ray gun."

The crowd was quiet for some time before Brand spoke. "Will this work?"

"I believe it can, if things go well," Dr. Kim said. "But it's not without obstacles. First, Heathcliff's body had to go through massive mutations to make his head this enormous. Organs, skeletal structure, the entire cardiovascular system have been moved in all directions to make room for his massive brain. And then there's the problem of who to send."

"That's already settled," Brand said as he hoisted himself onto his feet with the help of his cane. "I'm going to do it."

"Alexander, you can't!" Ms. Holiday said. "Send me. I can handle this."

Brand shook his head. "I can't lose you."

"I'll go! That would rule!" Toad cried. The rest of his friends volunteered as well.

"This argument is moot," Dr. Kim said. "We have to assume that almost everyone in this room is infected with the nanobytes. We can't send anyone in that might succumb to its effects."

"Well, how do we know who has it?" one of the other scientists asked. "We tried to do blood tests, but someone deleted half the results."

"They were tampered with?" Brand scowled. "I was told it was some sort of computer malfunction."

"It's starting to look like someone intentionally destroyed the records," Dr. Kim said.

"But who?" Ms. Holiday asked. "And why?"

"Someone is infected and doesn't want us to know. He or she may already be in quarantine, or it might be one of us. We'll have to worry about that later," Dr. Kim replied. "For now, there's only one person who we know for sure is safe from the virus."

Every head in the room turned toward Flinch.

"Agent Flinch is our only candidate. He is immune to the infection," Dr. Kim said.

"I am so jealous!" Jessie cried, his breath whistling. "Do you have any idea what the potential for juvenile delinquency is inside a body?"

"I'm not going," Flinch said. "I've been the team leader now three times, and each time something crazy has happened. Paris is a disaster, they're still trying to get the Empire State Building back to its original size, and Hollywood—well, Hollywood is weird already. But anyway, I'm not good with the pressure. My brain is too scattered. The more sugar I take to fuel the harness, the harder it is for me to think. What if I get in there and screw up? What if I accidentally hurt Heathcliff? No way. There has to be someone else."

Brand put his hand on Flinch's shoulder. Flinch looked up into his boss's face and could see him struggling with what to say. The man wasn't good with words. He could take out an entire army of terrorists but often lost the battle to say something inspiring. He looked straight into Flinch's eyes and said one word: "Tough."

"Huh?"

"Tough!" Brand shouted. "So it's hard. So you've made some mistakes! You know what? Everyone does. That doesn't mean you don't have to go and do your job. Flinch, I'll admit, I kept you in the background because you're unpredictable. But during the past week I've learned to respect that unpredictability. Your plans may not always be the best in the beginning, but when the crazy stuff happens, as it always does, your mind can adapt faster and more creatively than any person I have ever met. So listen, you're in charge. Don't give me any nonsense about how you don't feel confident. It's time to save the world, Flinch. That's what you do."

"Was that a pep talk?" Flinch asked.

Brand frowned. "Get in the containment suit, buster."

Flinch was strapped into a harness and lowered into one of the containment suits, and then the remaining science team locked it closed. A number of electronic panels lit up along Flinch's arms and chest. The tips of his fingers glowed, as did his feet.

Dr. Kim handed him a helmet with a clear visor to protect his head. "The feet and hands of the suit have propulsion tech so that you can motor about—they work like Matilda's inhalers and should help you move through the bloodstream. And don't forget the harpoon guns on the side of your arms and legs for tethering yourself. Use them sparingly. There's only so many feet of cable at your disposal."

Flinch turned his head and saw a huge pack strapped on the back of the suit. "What's that?"

"That, my friend, is fruit punch," Dr. Kim said. "It runs into the helmet via a tube. There aren't any vending machines inside Heathcliff, so you have to bring your own fuel. I've calculated your daily sugar intake, which happens to be quite frightening, and have estimated how much you will need for two hours."

Ms. Holiday stood nearby. Her face was dark with worry.

"No cupcakes, Ms. Holiday?" Flinch asked.

"I don't think this is the best idea, Julio," the librarian said. "Be careful."

Flinch promised he would.

"Dude, you have to be the coolest kid we know," Jessie said as he and the rest of Flinch's new friends gathered around him. "Do you get to do stuff like this all the time?"

Flinch thought for a moment. "Yeah, I guess I do."

"Where do we sign up?" Toad croaked.

"Good luck, bro," Wyatt said, handing Flinch a can of black spray paint.

"What's this for?"

"You're going somewhere no human being has ever gone before," Hooper said. "You should leave your tag."

Flinch tapped a button on the front of his chest plate, which opened a compartment just big enough for the can. He grinned, thinking about marking the inside of Heathcliff's skull with the words FLINCH WAS HERE!

He put on his helmet, and the scientists pulled the chains to hoist him over the tank. "Agent Flinch, this is Benjamin," Flinch heard through his com-link. "Can you hear me?"

"Loud and clear," Flinch said.

"Good," the little blue orb's voice said. "A thought just occurred to me. They say if you want to stop the bad guy you have to get inside his head. This time they mean it quite literally. Good luck, Agent."

The scientists lowered Flinch into the tank. There was a dramatic dip in temperature, and he shivered until his body adjusted. He was halfway submerged when he suddenly plummeted to the bottom.

"What's going on?" he asked as he peered through the saline and the tank's glass. He saw some kind of commotion, though it was difficult to make out.

"It's nothing," Brand said. "One of the scientists is showing symptoms. The others have him under control."

Flinch took a big swig of fruit punch and felt the sugar race through him. "OK. I'm ready. Let's get *pequeño*!"

"Good luck, Julio," Dr. Kim told him, and then she turned on the beam. He wasn't sure what to expect, but he certainly wasn't prepared for it to slam into his body and nearly knock him out. This was followed by a wave of cold all around him that made his teeth chatter. Then he felt as if he were falling off a cliff. He opened his eyes, but nothing looked familiar. The tank was gone, as were the hazy forms of the scientists and his friends. He was awash in fluid. He tried to swim but could do nothing but flop about in the thick and syrupy liquid.

"You still with us, Flinch?" Brand's voice came through his com-link.

"Loud and clear, sir," Flinch said. "Did it work?"

Benjamin's voice was next. "Perfectly. You're in the hypodermic needle now. Dr. Kim is preparing the injection."

"How did it feel?" Agent Brand asked.

"Kooky."

"As good a description as any," Brand said. Flinch wasn't sure, but he thought he heard the man chuckle. "OK, Agent. Prepare for the injection."

"I'm ready," Flinch said, and then he was swept away in the liquid. The lights went out and he was suddenly floating, untethered, and unable to get his bearings.

"Flinch?" Dr. Kim's voice filled his head.

"Yes, I'm fine. I can't see anything, but I'm fine."

Benjamin's voice was next. "I'm going to remotely activate some of the more basic functions of your containment suit."

Two lamps on either side of Flinch's helmet lit up. What he

saw was incredible. He was swirling around gigantic, yellowish blobs that kept slamming into one another. He reached out to touch one and was surprised to find they were spongy and sticky.

"What are these things?" he asked.

"Just a second while we pull up visuals," Ms. Holiday said. "OK, there it is. Oh my. That's amazing."

"Flinch, what you're seeing are fat cells," Dr. Kim told him. "They're harmless, but you're going to have to use your boosters to move through them."

"Is there a lot of fat in a brain?" Flinch asked.

"Um, Flinch, we couldn't inject you into Heathcliff's brain. His skull is too tough for that. We had to find someplace softer."

He heard the troublemakers laugh.

"Where am I?"

"Um . . . well—"

"Where am I?" Flinch cried.

"You're in Heathcliff's butt!" Wyatt roared.

17

38°87' N, 77°10' W

The Antagonist walked up the sidewalk to Thomas Knowlton Middle School and eyed the steel barricades on the doors and windows. This wasn't what he'd expected. He reached into his pocket for his phone, dialed a number, and waited.

"Hi, honey bear!" Miss Information said when she answered. "I hope you're feeling evil."

"I'm feeling very evil, but there's a problem. There's no way into the school. It looks as if it's on some kind of lockdown. I'm afraid they knew we were coming."

"Does someone have the boo-boo face?"

"No."

"Is my shmuggins feeling saddy-sad?"

"It's just depressing. I wanted to take over the world today!"

"Shmookin, kissy bear, don't be sad!" Miss Information said. "I'm working on fixing the problem right now. You'll be inside sooner than you can say 'I love my superawesome girlfriend.'"

"I love my superawesome girlfriend," he said.

Miss Information laughed. "Oh, silly, be patient."

"Well, what am I supposed to do?" he groaned.

"Just relax," she said. "Listen, evil is afoot and I have to get back to it. I'll see you soon, my little love monkey."

He put the phone in his pocket and looked around at the surrounding neighborhood. It was a bright, clear day. The street was empty. The circumstances were ideal for taking over the world. He sat down on the steps outside the school and wondered how far away the closest convenience store might be. He could go for a soda—maybe a bag of chips. World-conquering gave him the munchies. But he was feeling lazy. What if his girlfriend opened the school and he wasn't there to storm in and take over?

No, he would just plant himself where he was and wait.

A car drove by.

Two birds fought over a worm.

Somewhere, someone was using a leaf blower.

He lay on his back and took out his phone again.

She hadn't called. Luckily, he had just downloaded sudoku. That would keep him busy.

18

INSIDE A GIANT HEAD

Flinch was flying through the fat cells using the containment suit's foot boosters. Occasionally, he flew right into one of the cells and bounced off it as if he were in a bouncy castle. Eventually, he came across a massive tube.

"What am I seeing, Doc?" he asked.

"That's the femoral artery, and you need to be inside it. It's going to pump you up to the lungs. We can't take you through the heart, which is the most direct route, because at your size its chambers would crush you with a single beat."

"How do I get in?" Flinch asked. "There isn't exactly a welcome mat."

"You're going to need the laser," Dr. Kim told him. "Cut a

hole just big enough to crawl through and no bigger. Platelets will come and repair the damage, but if you make it too big they won't be able to get the job done and you'll cause internal bleeding."

"Great. Now I'm a surgeon," Flinch grumbled. He pressed the button on his glove that activated the laser, then aimed carefully and fired. He cut a small incision, as he had been instructed, just big enough for his body, then fired his rocket boosters and flew right into the hole.

The second he was inside the artery, his body was swept away in a massive current as if he had fallen into the rapids of a mighty river. He was moving fast and was completely out of control.

"Flinch, your heart rate is spiking," Brand said. "What's going on?"

"I'm freaking out!"

"Just relax, Flinch!" Dr. Kim said. "You're in the bloodstream and traveling fast. You need to get ready because the lungs are coming up. When I say 'fire,' aim a harpoon at the artery wall."

Flinch struggled to get control of his body. After a while, he did the only thing he could think of and swam with the current. He glanced around. His helmet beams illuminated the way, and he saw what looked like huge red beanbag chairs floating around him.

"What are the red things?" he asked.

"Those are red blood cells," Benjamin said. "They're carrying oxygen through the body. The arteries carry them, along with white blood cells and a substance called lymph, all through the circulatory system. They shouldn't be much of a threat."

One slammed into Flinch, nearly knocking the wind out of him. "Glad to hear it!"

"How is the suit?" Ms. Holiday asked.

"It feels fine, but it's awful loud in here," Flinch said, holding his hands to his ears. Something was thumping loudly and getting even louder by the second. "I can barely think."

"That's Heathcliff's heartbeat," Benjamin chirped. "I'll remotely adjust the volume from here."

At once, the thump was quieted.

"*Gracias!*" Flinch said

"OK, Flinch, prepare your harpoon," Dr. Kim said. "Now, fire!"

Flinch pushed a button on his arm. There was a loud POP! and a long tether shot out of his hand. He could feel a rope unraveling from his chest plate as it trailed the harpoon, and then the harpoon's sharp tip punctured the spongy artery wall. Suddenly, he was jerked out of the stream, flailing.

"OK, that worked."

"Luckily, the artery you're in is taking blood to the brain

and so you've been pulled closer to your target," Benjamin said. "Look up."

Flinch did as he was told and saw a huge tunnel. At its center was a massive red muscle, opening and closing. It was the source of the pounding. "Is that Heathcliff's heart?"

"Yes, it is," Dr. Kim said.

"Good to know he has one," Flinch muttered.

"You're close to the lungs, which means you have to get out of this artery. Use the laser to cut another opening and zip through it."

Flinch did as he was told, and, once on the other side, he saw two massive pink objects that inflated like party balloons and then deflated just as rapidly. He didn't have to ask what they were.

"Do I go inside the lungs?" Flinch asked.

"Not yet," Dr. Kim said. "We need to adjust your suit's environmental controls for their increased pressure. We don't want you to pop."

He could feel something happening in his helmet and assumed Benjamin was tinkering remotely.

And then there was another commotion in his ears. It sounded like someone had tossed a chair across the room. "What's going on?"

"It's another member of the science team," Mr. Brand said.

"He's showing symptoms. We're dealing with it. Just focus on your mission. If you destroy the transmitter soon, they won't be sick much longer."

"OK. Let's go then."

But he would have to wait. From the corner of his eye he saw more beanbags, but these were white and they were coming right for him. "Um, I think the white blood cells have found me."

He took a long drink of fruit punch and went on the offensive, socking the first one with a huge punch. It exploded all over him. "Gross!"

Two more came from behind. He leaped up and delivered a roundhouse kick that exploded them as well. But that wasn't the end of the assault. A hundred more white blood cells were swirling up the artery, preparing to kill him.

"Flinch, report!" Brand cried.

"I'm a little busy," he said, drinking more juice. Full of sugar, he punched and kicked and slammed with all his might. One cell fell after another, but there were too many—more than any one person could handle, no matter how strong and fast.

"Can I use the laser?!" Flinch asked.

"Carefully!" Dr. Kim replied.

Flinch turned on the weapon, aimed it, and fired, cutting the cells in half as they approached. One after another they fell, but each one was replaced by ten more. Soon they had him backed up against the wall of the artery with nowhere else to go.

"I have to get out of here," he said, turning the laser on the wall of the lung. He cut a hole big enough for him to squeeze through, then fought his way toward the opening. The cells were everywhere. One latched on to his arms, then his legs. Others clung to his juice pack. He kicked at them, but they stuck like glue, and worse, they were trying to puncture his suit. With a huge twist on his harness, he felt a wave of sugar so intense he could do nothing but shake. He was so out of control, he couldn't speak, but it worked. The supershaking dislodged the cells. The moment he was free, he readjusted his harness then dove into the hole.

Unfortunately for Flinch, the inside of the lung was even more treacherous. He was battered and squeezed as it expanded and contracted. The feeling reminded him of a camping trip he had gone on with his parents shortly before they passed away. They had all devoured a dozen sacks of roasted marshmallows, then crawled into their brand-new sleeping bags. That's when the good times turned into a sugar-fueled nervous breakdown. His sleeping bag was so tight and constraining, Flinch felt wrapped up in the body of an anaconda. In the middle of the night, he crawled out of the tent and threw the sleeping bag in the river. Heathcliff's lungs felt like that sleeping bag.

“I’m in the lungs,” Flinch said, fighting back panic. “Get me out of the lungs!”

“Just keep moving forward. You need to find another artery. This one will be large. It’s called the aorta, and it will take you directly to the base of the brain,” Benjamin chirped.

Flinch crawled forward, unable to see more than a few feet in front of him. The noise and the wind of the lungs were so intense. It felt as if he were inside a hurricane. Benjamin turned the volume on the suit all the way down, but the sound still raged in his ears. He tried to breathe steadily so that he wouldn’t hyperventilate. The last thing he needed was to pass out inside of Heathcliff. He pressed on and finally found another of the massive tubes.

“Just a small slit,” Dr. Kim said. “The aorta is a major artery. If you cut too big it could kill Heathcliff in minutes.”

Flinch did as he was told and gingerly sliced a hole just big enough to squeeze through. This time he was ready for the fast-churning bloodstream and managed to not lose total control of himself.

“This will only take a few seconds,” Dr. Kim told him. “And then you’ll be at the base of the brain. The transmitter is buried inside the left hemisphere of Heathcliff’s brain. When you see an enormous gray mass, fire your tether into the wall of the artery.”

Flinch couldn't miss the gray mass. It was huge and right above him. He fired the tether and lodged himself in place. He eyed Heathcliff's amazing brain. Flinch could almost see the evil ideas it was conjuring.

"It's a wonder," Dr. Kim said.

"It's gross," Flinch said.

Dr. Kim laughed. "Unlike the twisted mess that is Heathcliff's body, his brain is very much unchanged—except for its size. All of the regions seem to be like any other human brain. I'm pulling up a map right now to help guide you."

But Flinch stopped listening to the scientist midway through her explanation. Hanging over his head, high in the cavernous reaches of Heathcliff's skull, were thousands of black, shiny creatures. They were clinging, heads down, to the boy's brain, like sleeping bats with eyes that glowed neon green. Every one of their eyes was turned to Flinch.

"Uh-oh," Flinch said.

Two of the creatures flew down and buzzed by his head as if they were just interested in getting a better look. Then they zipped back up to join the others. The creatures chattered back and forth and then, all at once, like a crowd that has just witnessed the hometown team lose in the final second, all of their voices roared with anger.

"Uh-oh," Flinch said again.

"What's 'Uh-oh'?" Brand asked.

"The nanobytes know I'm here," Flinch said as the creatures scurried out of the gray meat and ran toward him, clicking their legs together like beetles. Flinch took a few more greedy gulps of juice, and, with sugar racing through his bloodstream, he could only think of one thing to do: run right at them with fists clenched. He stomped through them like a rampaging rhino, snatching two by their necks and smashing them together, causing them to explode into a thousand pieces of metal and

circuitry. He punched another one's head off its shoulders, then snatched one of its spindly limbs to use as a club on a dozen more.

"C'mon, ugly, let's dance!" he shouted at one, which was soon a pile of broken robot parts. More and more came. He drank his juice and pounded his chest and shouted, "I AM MIGHTY!"

END TRANSMISSION.

WELL, SO FAR YOU'VE DONE PRETTY WELL, OR MAYBE I JUST HAVEN'T BEEN CHALLENGING YOU. SO I'M GOING TO THROW OUT THREE VERY INTENSE TASKS. IF YOU CAN ACCOMPLISH THEM, THEN I WILL TIP MY HAT TO YOU AND HAPPILY REPORT THAT YOU ARE IN TIP-TOP SECRET AGENT SHAPE. THINK YOU'RE UP FOR THIS? GOOD!

CHALLENGE #1:
ARM-WRESTLE A TRUCK DRIVER

YOU ARE A BRAVE SOUL. TRUCK DRIVERS ARE NOTORIOUSLY SURLY CHARACTERS WHO ENJOY A GOOD BOWL OF CHILI, THE OPEN ROAD, AND TEARING AN OPPONENT'S ARM OFF IN A GAME OF STRENGTH.

FIRST, FIND A TRUCK DRIVER. SECOND, FIND A DINER WITH A LOOSE POLICY ABOUT THIS MOST VENERABLE GAME. THIRD,

SAY SOMETHING MEAN ABOUT THE TRUCK DRIVER'S MOTHER.

FORGET WHETHER OR NOT YOU WON—IF YOU SURVIVED, THEN YOU'RE A WINNER IN MY BOOK.

CHALLENGE #2:
WRESTLE A BEAR

DON'T GIVE A THOUGHT TO THE FACT THAT THIS SKILL IS TOTALLY IMPRACTICAL, SINCE THERE ARE ONLY, LIKE, THREE BEARS WORKING AS ENEMY SPIES, SO THE ODDS OF BEING ON A MISSION WHERE YOU ENCOUNTER ONE SPYING ON YOUR COUNTRY IS PRETTY LIMITED.

FIRST, FIND A BEAR. SECOND, GET REALLY CLOSE TO THE BEAR AND POKE IT WITH A STICK. THIRD, THE REST WILL TAKE CARE OF ITSELF.

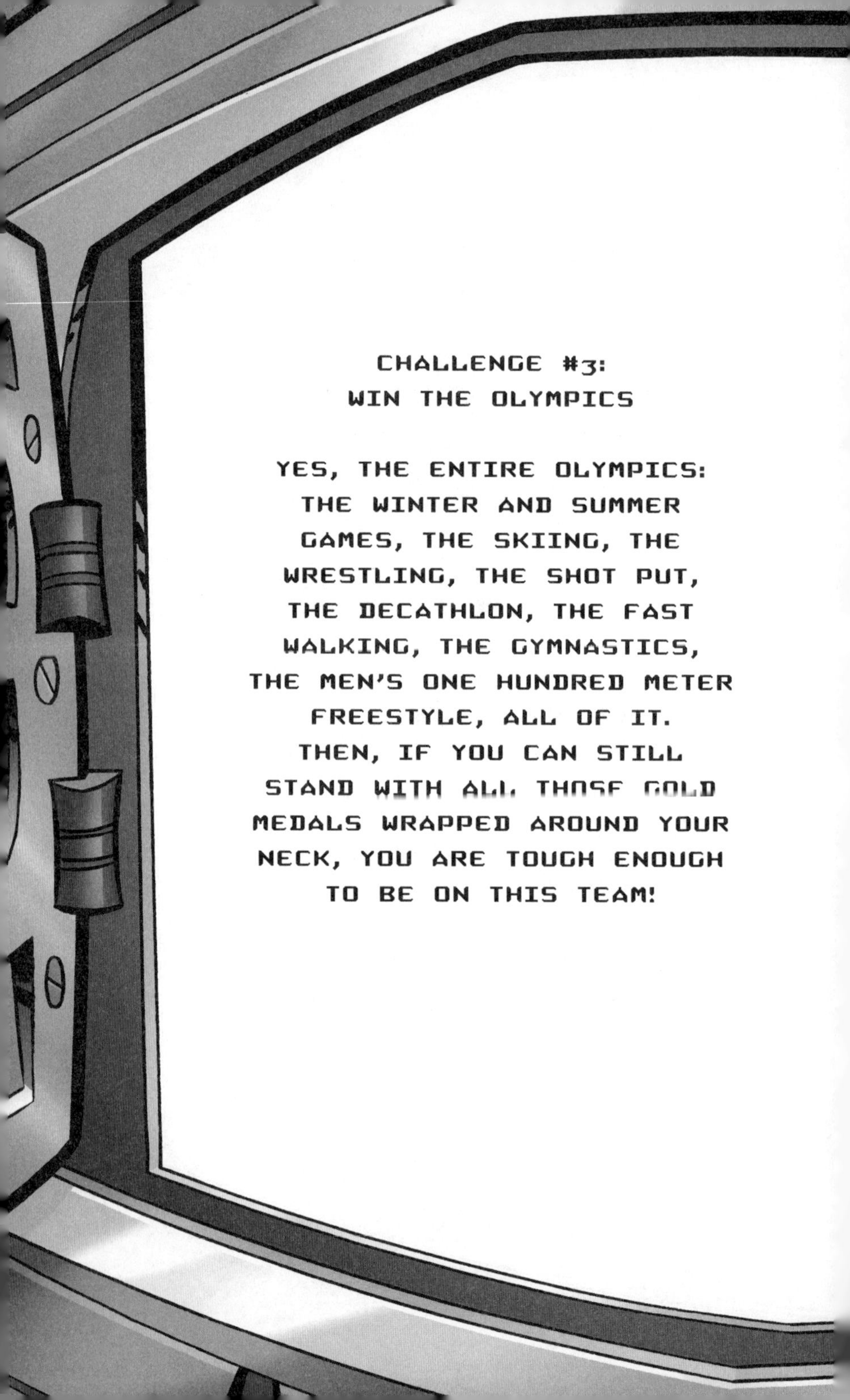
CHALLENGE #3:
WIN THE OLYMPICS
YES, THE ENTIRE OLYMPICS: THE WINTER AND SUMMER GAMES, THE SKIING, THE WRESTLING, THE SHOT PUT, THE DECATHLON, THE FAST WALKING, THE GYMNASTICS, THE MEN'S ONE HUNDRED METER FREESTYLE, ALL OF IT. THEN, IF YOU CAN STILL STAND WITH ALL THOSE GOLD MEDALS WRAPPED AROUND YOUR NECK, YOU ARE TOUGH ENOUGH TO BE ON THIS TEAM!

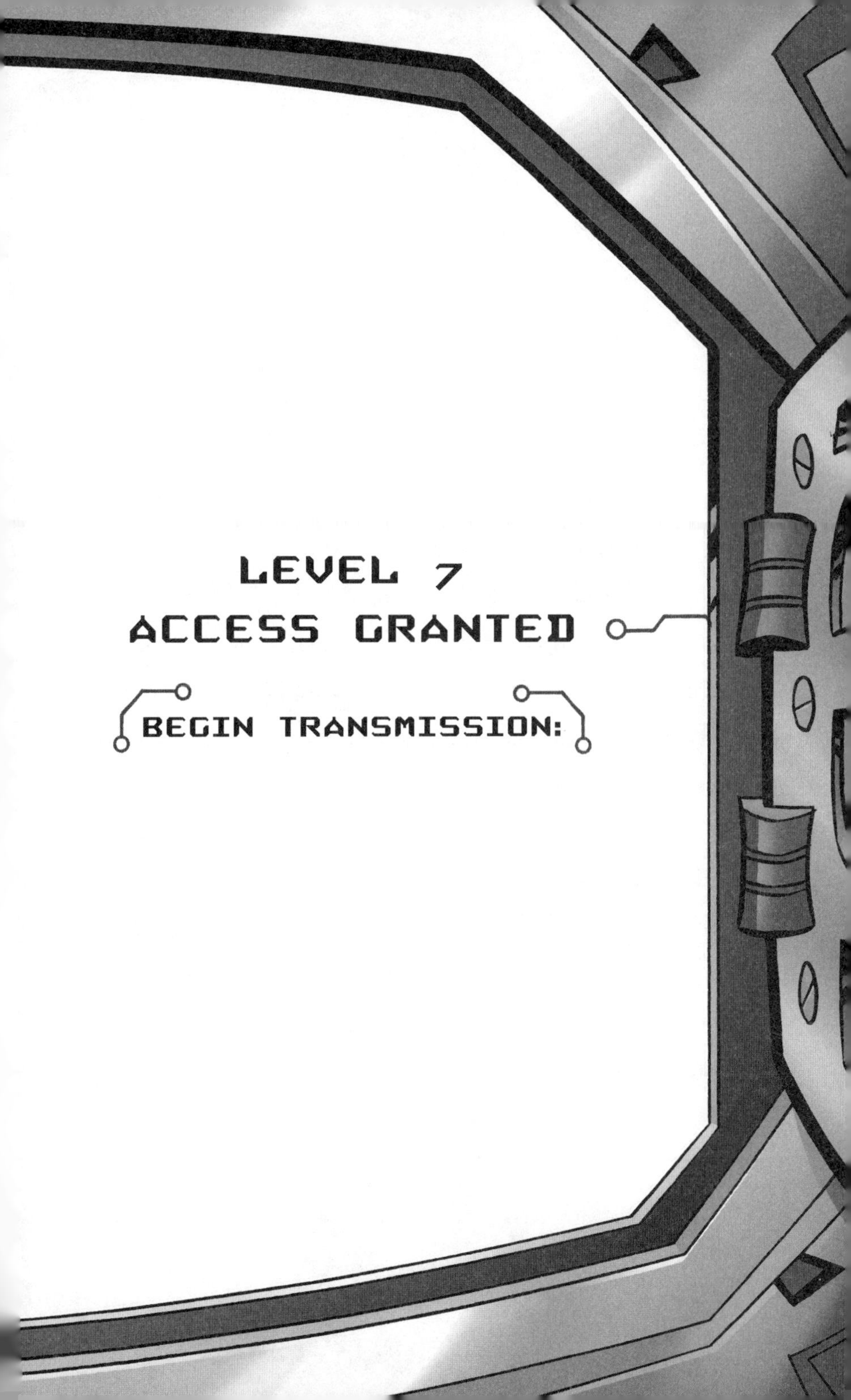
LEVEL 7
ACCESS GRANTED
BEGIN TRANSMISSION:

19

38°87' N, 77°10' W

Agent Brand and Dr. Kim stood over the monitor and watched the tiny dot that was Julio Escala move around in Heathcliff's mutated body. Flinch was doing better than Brand could have ever hoped. Now that the boy was at the base of Heathcliff's brain stem, he just had to find the transmitter, and then the world would stop being a gigantic insane asylum.

It couldn't come a minute too soon. Since Flinch had been miniaturized and injected, they had lost eight of the remaining twelve scientists All that was left of Brand's team was Dr. Kim, the three other scientists, Ms. Holiday, and the four juvenile delinquents. And it wouldn't be long before the virus got to them as well.

"Can you believe how great he's doing?" Ms. Holiday asked.

"I think I have misjudged him," Brand said.

"Don't be too hard on yourself," she said. "There are lots of things in life you just don't see until they are right in front of your eyes. Take me, for instance."

Brand smiled and got one in return.

One of the remaining scientists rushed to Brand's side. "Sir, may I have a word with you?"

"What is it, Doctor . . ."

"Yerkey, sir," he said. "It's very important and private."

"Can it wait? I have to guide an agent into a human brain," Brand said.

"It's about the blood tests from before," Dr. Yerkey said. "Some of the results were erased on purpose, and I found out who did it."

"Who?" Dr. Kim cried.

Agent Brand turned away from the screen to face the scientist, but suddenly he felt a sharp pain in the back of his head and everything went black.

38°87' N, 77°10' W 

Ms. Holiday stood over the unconscious bodies of Agent Brand and Dr. Yerkey. Her hand clutched a metal pipe from one of the experiments that had been dismantled to create the miniaturization rig. She looked at the weapon and grinned. Some things, like clobbering a person cold, were best done the old-fashioned way.

"Ms. Holiday!" Dr. Kim cried. "What are you doing?"

"C'mon, sister. You didn't see that coming?" Ms. Holiday said as she reached into her pocket, removed a mask with a skull painted on the front, and pulled it over her face. "And don't call me that name. My name is Miss Information."

"She's infected!" Dr. Kim cried.

"Duh!" Miss Information said, and then she slugged the woman on the chin. The doctor fell hard onto the floor, where she joined the others in sleepytown.

"Benjamin, it appears Agent Brand is incapacitated," she said, turning her attention to the floating orb. "Control of the school passes to me as the next in command."

Benjamin twittered. "I cannot do that. I'm shutting down all systems available to you and putting the Playground in lockdown."

The woman snarled. "Benjamin, Supreme Override Four Seven X, and my password is 'Dewey decimal.'"

Benjamin's glowing blue light turned red, and then the orb spun around several times in midair. It bobbed and weaved as if struggling with something that was happening inside its circuits. Then it righted itself, and the red light glowed brighter than ever before. "Protocol Four Seven X. Operations of school are now in the hands of Ms. Holiday."

"Very good, Benjamin," she said. "Take the school out of lockdown. My boyfriend is here."

Miss Information took her phone out of her bag and dialed it.

"I've been out here for hours, darling," the Antagonist said in a strained voice.

"Sorry, honey bun, but it took a little longer to wrap all

this up," she said. "Why don't you come and see me? I'm in the basement. Go through Locker 41."

She hung up the phone and looked over at the two remaining scientists.

"You're going to help me with a little chore," she said.

The two men shook their heads.

Miss Information frowned behind her mask, then removed a bright red ray gun from her purse. "You do realize I'm a supervillain, right? Now what would a supervillain be without a superscary weapon? Let me introduce you to mine. It's called the atom smasher. Wanna see what it does?"

The men shook their heads.

"Good! Then let's get to work. We have a lot to do."

By the time the Antagonist reached the Playground, Miss Information and the two remaining scientists had dragged Agent Brand, Dr. Kim, and Dr. Yerkey into a holding cell. Two containment suits were prepped and ready and the miniaturization ray had been adjusted and properly aimed.

"What's all this, honey?" the Antagonist asked.

"A slight change in plans, darling," Miss Information replied. "It seems the fifth member of the NERDS team has been shrunk and injected into this gigantic head."

The Antagonist looked at his former employer. Despite the boy's twisted features, he recognized Heathcliff immediately. Simon, Screwball, Brainstorm—whatever he called himself—the boy was responsible for his hook, and his white hair, and his blind eye. All of this boy's foolish plots had blown up in his face over and over again, and the Antagonist had always suffered. By the looks of him, it appeared the imbecile had finally gotten what was coming to him.

"I'm confused," he said.

"There's no time to explain, sweetie pie, only to say that inside that head is the source of the villain virus and they've sent an agent in to destroy it. If we don't want the entire world to suddenly get better, we need to stop him. Now get into your suit."

She didn't give him a chance to argue. He could be so stubborn, and worse, dim. She was his intellectual superior in every way, even if she knew he was laughing at her behind her back. Well, she had fooled him. She was running this show, even if she had led him to believe he was the one in charge. She needed his help for only a little while longer and then she would be in control of the world and he would be alligator food.

She got him into his containment suit and up the ladder to the tank before he knew what had hit him. Soon both of them were submerged in saline. Once they were settled, she tapped a button on her arm that remotely activated the ray gun. And then it was cold and dark.

21

INSIDE A GIANT HEAD

Flinch was at the bottom of Heathcliff's brain, waiting for someone to tell him what to do next. The onslaught of nanobytes had slowed, but he was still fighting them, and worse, a quick look at the timer inside his helmet told him that he had precious minutes left to finish his mission. He called out to Brand and Dr. Kim, but it was as if he had been abandoned. And then it hit him. Maybe the whole team had succumbed to the virus. Maybe he was all alone.

"Dude? Dude? Are you still there?"

"Hooper?"

"Yo! You're still alive. Bro, you won't believe what happened! The librarian clocked the janitor and he's knocked out. She did the same to the scientist lady, and then she took over the base.

She let some weird dude in here with a mask and they got into containment suits and shrank themselves. They're coming after you, man. They're going to try and stop you."

"So who is left up there?" Flinch cried.

"Just us," Hooper said. "We hid."

"'Us'?"

"Your friendly neighborhood juvenile delinquents."

The panic hit Flinch like a slap in the face. He was a tiny, microscopic secret agent trying to save the world inside the body of a monster . . . and his support team consisted of four kids whose sole goal in life was to clog up toilets.

"It's all going to work, big guy," Toad said. "We're going to help. Hooper's a doctor."

"My dad is a doctor, Toad. Not me."

"What happened to Benjamin?"

"The librarian put a whammy on it," Wyatt said. "It's on the floor, popping and hissing."

"So you're all I've got," Flinch stated.

"We are your loyal soldiers. Lead us, O great one," Jessie said.

"Lead you! I can't lead you. I'm the spaz."

"The leader of the weirdos," Toad croaked.

Flinch couldn't help smiling. Yes, he was the leader of the weirdos, and somehow that calmed his nerves. "OK, someone needs to find a picture of a brain. Dr. Kim was mapping one, so it should be there."

"It's on the screen right in front of us," Wyatt said.

"Good. Do you see a flashing dot inside it?"

"I see two!" Jessie said through his whistling nose.

"Good, one of them is me. I'm at the base of the brain."

"We've got you," Wyatt said.

"And the other beeping dot is the transmitter. I need to get to it, but I can't just cut my way through. I could kill Heathcliff. So we need to find a path that isn't going to hurt him."

"Piece of cake, bro!" Wyatt said. "Looks like right now you're hanging out on the spinal cord, and directly overhead is the cerebellum. What it does I have no idea, but it's on the map and it's in the way. So just push on through."

"No way, man!" Hooper cried. "The cerebellum is the part of the brain that affects balance and muscle coordination. You screw that up and this head will never walk again."

"It doesn't walk now," Toad pointed out.

"Please, guys, stop arguing. I need to hurry. I only have twelve minutes left before I'm back to normal size."

"Hey, don't freak," Jessie said. "You can climb up the cerebellum and reach the brain at the top."

Flinch did as he was told, activating the jet boosters to fly to the bottom of the brain.

“Awesome,” Hooper said. “Now you’re at a part called the occipital lobe. The chart says this part affects vision and, to a lesser degree, recognition of letters and numbers. So you gotta ask yourself: ‘Fate of the world, or a head that can’t sing the alphabet song?’”

Flinch cringed but used his laser to cut a small hole big enough for him to enter the brain. “I hate this,” he cried as he entered. “What if I just made this guy into an idiot?”

“Reading is pretty overrated, dude,” Toad said.

Once at the top of the brain, Flinch saw an amazing sight: a lightning display of little green electrical impulses and chemicals swirling from one place to another. He floated over it using his boosters.

“Bro, you are doing great. You’re out of the occipital lobe and approaching the temporal lobe,” Hooper told him. “The chart says it handles the memory of faces, as well as emotions and language.”

“Poke it and see if Heathcliff will suddenly start speaking Italian!” Wyatt said.

“I’m not poking it,” Flinch grumbled. “How much farther do I have to go?”

“Halfway there, buddy,” Hooper said. “You’re headed toward the frontal lobe, which deals with creative thinking and impulse control. The transmitter is buried there, right near the surface.”

Flinch kept moving through the gray mass until in the distance he could see a little red pulsing box.

"I see it," Flinch said.

"Awesome possum," Jessie said. "Uh-oh."

"What's 'Uh-oh'?" Flinch cried. "You don't get to say 'Uh-oh.' Only I get to 'Uh-oh'!"

"There are two more little dots moving in your direction and they're coming in fast. It's got to be the librarian and her creepy boyfriend."

Before Flinch could ask "How close?" the two figures were on him. The bigger of the two villains punched him in the chest, and even with the suit's deflector force field, it hurt. It also knocked him backward. When he righted himself, he could feel his pack growing lighter. The Antagonist had caused a rupture, and Flinch's fruit punch supply was seeping out. In desperation he drank as much as he could before it was completely gone.

The second figure reached down and grabbed the transmitter. He couldn't see her face, but there was something about the way she moved. He knew it was Ms. Holiday.

"Julio, you blew it," she said, proving his suspicions. Her voice wasn't sweet like always. Now it was filled with a wicked glee. "I guess that's what happens when you send the freak."

Flinch snarled and fired his boosters, making a beeline

toward Ms. Holiday's partner. Flinch put out his fists and slammed into the man, causing him to fly in the other direction, entirely disappearing within Heathcliff's brain.

"Dude, whatever you're doing in there, you'd better stop," Toad said. "The head is doing some crazy stuff."

"Like what?"

"Well, its eyes opened and then a beam came out and the entire wall turned to ashes," Jessie said. "Basically, it's the coolest thing I've ever seen."

Flinch cringed. They weren't messing around in the head of a normal person. He had forgotten about Heathcliff's power. The boy could change reality to suit him. "I'll try, but you guys need to stay as far from the head as possible."

A moment later the Antagonist pushed his way through the gray matter like a bull in a china shop. Flinch charged at him and they traded uppercuts, sending each other flying backward, only to spring back into the fight. Meanwhile, Ms. Holiday headed back the way she came, with the transmitter and without the Antagonist.

"Looks like your girlfriend is dumping you," Flinch said.

The Antagonist growled and continued his attack.

"Listen, man! You got ten minutes before you are large and in charge," Toad said.

"I'm on it!" Flinch said. He had to do something drastic. When the Antagonist drew close, Flinch punched him as hard as he could. The villain flew backward and slammed against the inside of the skull. Flinch fired several harpoon cables from his arms, stapling the villain against the hard bone.

No matter how much he struggled, the Antagonist could not free himself. He cursed and threatened, but Flinch was already racing after Ms. Holiday. The boy activated his foot boosters to catch up, knowing if he used his own speed, he would be out of power in no time. But soon the fuel was spent in his boots and he was forced to run on his own power. He ran along the surface of the skull and found her crouched at the base of an artery. She was cutting a hole in it and ready to climb in.

"Don't do this, Ms. Holiday. You're not evil."

Ms. Holiday laughed as if what he had said was the silliest thing she had ever heard. Then she dove into the artery and disappeared. Flinch went in after her and was quickly pulled through the bloodstream.

"Where am I, guys?" Flinch shouted.

"You're in something called the superior vena cava. It's a vein that's going to send you back toward the heart—that is, if you take the wrong path," Hooper said. "Or it might take you to the mouth. I can't tell. This chart has so many branches, it looks like a willow tree. Take the tunnel to the left, I think!"

Flinch did as he was told and spotted Ms. Holiday around the turn. She was swimming with the current, and so Flinch did the same. When he got close to her, he reached out and snatched her foot. She tried to kick him off, but he held on tight, clawing his way up until he had his hands on the transmitter box. She refused to release it, and the two of them fought as they plummeted through the bloodstream.

"You can't have this, Julio!" she cried. "This is my destiny. I was meant to rule the world."

"That's not true! You're infected with the virus, Ms. Holiday. You're not evil. You're my friend. You make me cupcakes. That's your destiny!"

"You're really the dumbest one of the bunch, Flinch," Ms. Holiday said. "With you in charge, it's no wonder the world fell apart. You can't stop me. You can't even control yourself!"

With a burst of her foot rockets she torpedoed toward him, but even with his limited supply of sugar he was still faster than her. He stepped out of the way and used her momentum to wrench the transmitter from her grasp. She flailed uncontrollably, slamming against the vein wall before she was swept away into the blood flow. All Flinch could do was watch.

"Which way does that tunnel go?" he asked.

“That’s a direct path to the heart,” Hooper replied. “Sorry, man.”

Flinch watched the tunnel entrance Ms. Holiday had disappeared into for a few more minutes, hoping his friend would find a way to climb back up, but she didn’t. She was gone.

“Buddy, you got two minutes!” Wyatt said. “You’re close to the mouth. Fight your way there and you can get out!” Flinch activated his laser and cut a hole in the vein wall, which he fell through clumsily. A moment later he was standing on a large, spongy mass, staring into a blinding light.

“Bro, you’re on the tongue. You are almost out,” Wyatt cheered, but the celebration came to a sudden stop. “Whoa! Dude, look out!”

All of a sudden, the Antagonist was on him. He aimed a powerful punch at Flinch’s helmet and knocked the boy loopy. Flinch struggled to fight off unconsciousness. He had never been hit so hard by anything or anyone. In his pain, he dropped the transmitter.

The Antagonist picked it up and caressed it gingerly, as if it were a precious treasure.

“The world is mine!” he laughed as he hefted Flinch into the air. The boy hung there helplessly, unable to free himself. “All mine!”

But his hands were still free. Flinch accessed the panel in his chest and reached in to get Hooper's present—the can of spray paint. He held it up and sprayed it onto the Antagonist's visor, blinding him. Flinch snatched the transmitter. While the Antagonist struggled to see, Flinch pushed a button on the front of the machine. The red light faded to black.

The transmitter was dead.

Flinch dropped it onto the tongue and stomped on it until it was nothing but rubbish.

The Antagonist pulled his helmet and mask off. Flinch recognized him at once. He was Heathcliff's goon, the one they called Dumb Vinci. The former goon looked around, confused and disoriented.

"Where am I?"

Before Flinch could answer, there was a pop and a stretching sound, and suddenly they were big. Not their normal size, but big.

"What's da big idea?" Dumb Vinci asked.

"Run!" Flinch shouted, and the two sprinted as fast as they could toward the light from Heathcliff's huge open mouth. When the next wave of growth hit them, they were leaping through Heathcliff's jaws and landing on the boy's big stretched-out face. Another wave caused them to grow to the size of small children. They jumped again so that they were back in the holding cell as the final surge hit them. Flinch and the goon were normal size again.

The goon was so disoriented that it was easy for Flinch to put him in cuffs. While he did so, and much to Flinch's surprise, an odd transformation was occurring in Heathcliff. His enormous head was shrinking and shrinking. His facial features shifted back to their normal size, and soon, he was just a little boy lying on a hospital gurney. A moment later he woke up and looked around.

"Where am I?" he asked.

"You're in the Playground—or, rather, the new Playground," Flinch said, eyeing him warily. Heathcliff was still dangerous, even without the giant head. "When you went to sleep, we were in the fifth grade. We've moved to the middle school now."

"And who are you?"

Flinch took his containment helmet off and set it down. "Now do you recognize me?"

"No," the boy said. "I've never seen you before in my life."

"I'm a friend. Do you know who you are?" Flinch asked.

The boy sat for a long moment. "No, I don't."

"Your name is Heathcliff."

• • •

Agent Brand did not come to work the next day. The team went on with the business of cleaning up the school and the Playground, and, luckily, there were no major incidents that required their help. The world was peaceful for a moment as people struggled with the universal phenomenon of not being able to remember what they had been doing recently. It was a blessing in disguise, as most would have never been able to get over what they had done while under the influence of the villain virus.

The Antagonist—a.k.a. Dumb Vinci—was behind bars. Sherman Stoop got his job back on the security team. Mr. Miniature returned to his job at the supermarket. Justin Maines resumed his life as a dead body on television shows. Even Ms. Dove came to her senses, but not before she was transferred to a middle school in the darkest, coldest reaches of Siberia. Mama Rosa returned to her sweet, lovable self—and even apologized to Mrs. Valencia for years of bitterness.

And slowly the world returned to normal.

But Brand could not return to normal. When he finally did get back to the Playground, he was changed. The soft edges Ms. Holiday had been sculpting on him were sharp once more. His ability to see his agents as more than children was gone.

In one final act as director of the NERDS, he hired Wyatt,

Hooper, Toad, and Jessie to be part of a new team called the Troublemakers, which had only one other member, a former assassin turned spy named the Hyena. Then he quit. He didn't say good-bye to the children or to Dr. Kim or to the lunch lady. He was just gone, and no one, not even General Savage, knew where he went.

END TRANSMISSION.

YOU DID IT! NOT ONLY ARE YOU A SUPERIOR PHYSICAL SPECIMEN, YOU HAVE LITTLE REGARD FOR YOUR OWN PERSONAL SAFETY AND HEALTH. THUS, YOU MAKE A FINE CANDIDATE TO BE A SECRET AGENT.

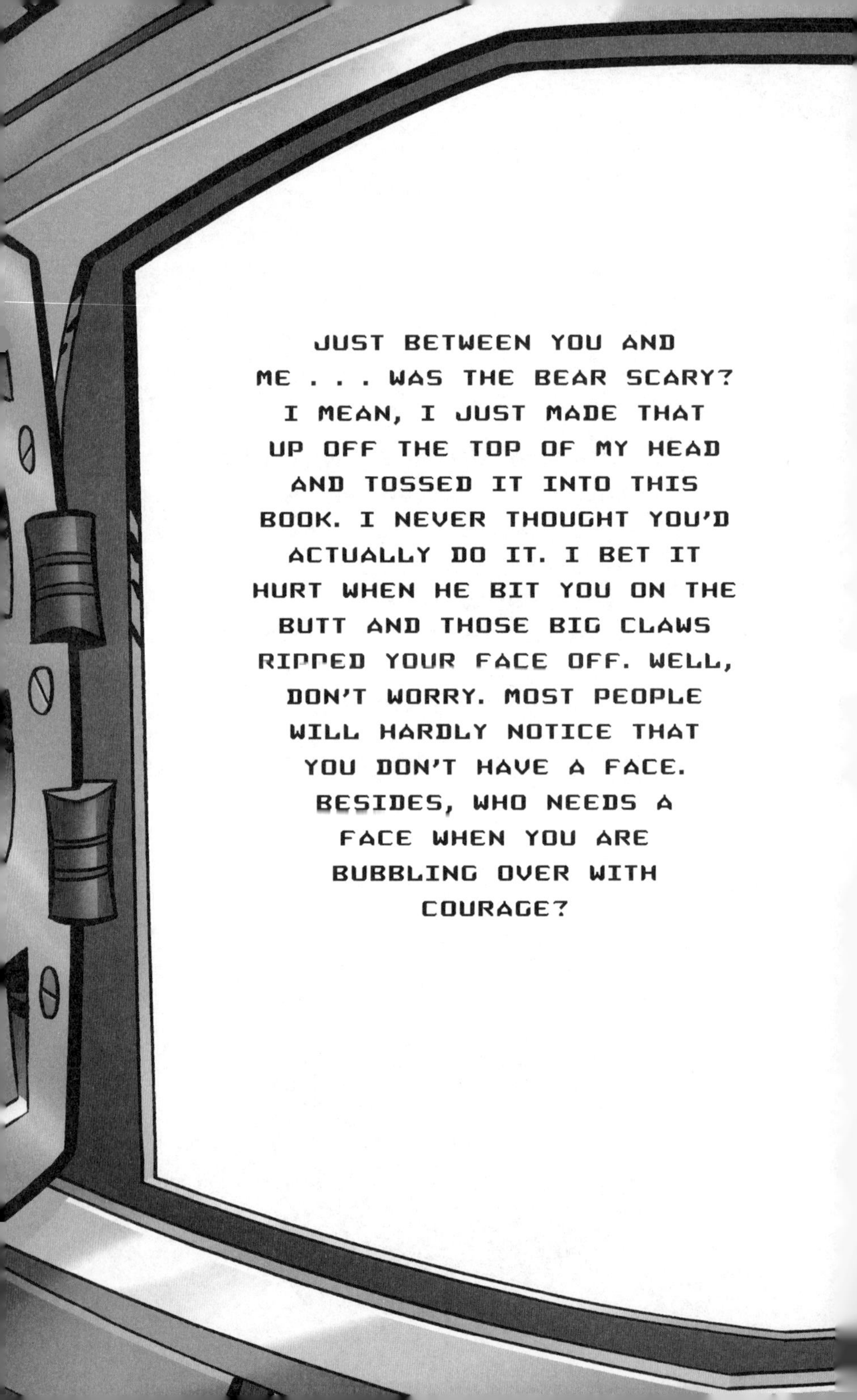
JUST BETWEEN YOU AND
ME . . . WAS THE BEAR SCARY?
I MEAN, I JUST MADE THAT
UP OFF THE TOP OF MY HEAD
AND TOSSED IT INTO THIS
BOOK. I NEVER THOUGHT YOU'D
ACTUALLY DO IT. I BET IT
HURT WHEN HE BIT YOU ON THE
BUTT AND THOSE BIG CLAWS
RIPPED YOUR FACE OFF. WELL,
DON'T WORRY. MOST PEOPLE
WILL HARDLY NOTICE THAT
YOU DON'T HAVE A FACE.
BESIDES, WHO NEEDS A
FACE WHEN YOU ARE
BUBBLING OVER WITH
COURAGE?

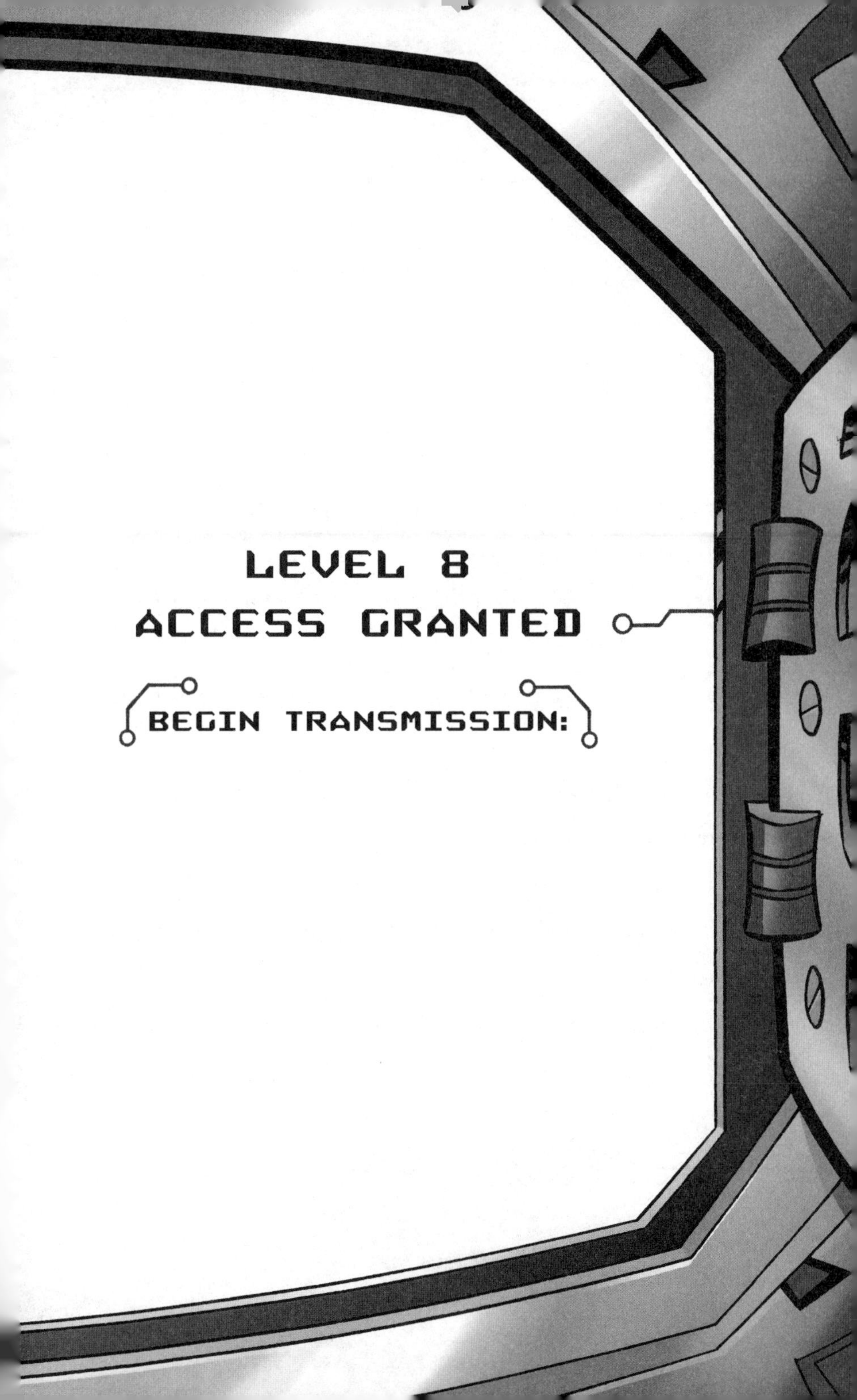
LEVEL 8
ACCESS GRANTED
BEGIN TRANSMISSION:

22

38°87' N, 77°10' W

Heathcliff lay in his bed, drift-ing off to sleep. It was nice to be around such friendly people who all seemed very concerned about him. Maybe one day soon he would get his memory back and remember them, but until then he would take it easy, just the way that nice Dr. Kim had suggested.

He was starting to dream when he felt something odd in his nose. On the table next to his bed was a box of tissues, and he snatched one. Even blowing as hard as he could, he couldn't dislodge whatever it was, and worse, it seemed to be getting bigger.

He crawled out of bed and walked over to the washbasin at the far end of the room. There was a mirror hanging on the

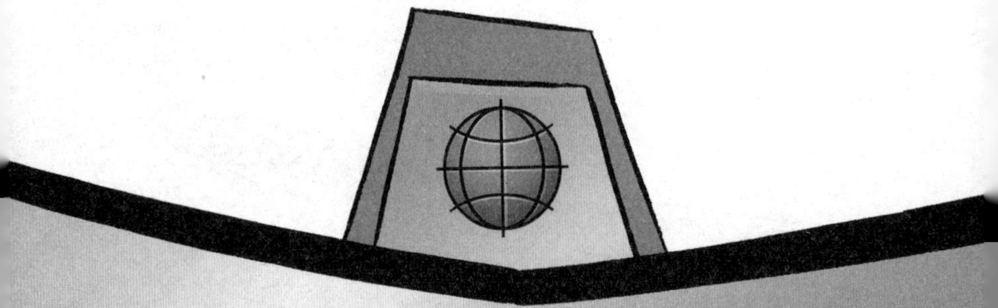

wall, so he flipped on the light and gave his nostrils a scan. Whatever was stuck up there was moving on its own, and it was starting to hurt. He could see it was pushing under the skin like a big round ball. Desperate, he blew his nose once more and this time something popped out.

With watery eyes he tried to focus on the thing, but he couldn't get a clear glimpse. He could only tell one thing: It was getting bigger—much bigger. In a matter of seconds it was as big as a dog, and then as big as a little boy. Finally, it rose to its full height and Heathcliff realized what it was—a woman. Or least he thought it was a woman. She was wearing some kind of suit—like for traveling in space—complete with a huge helmet. The figure removed the helmet to reveal a black mask covering her face. The mask had a big white skull painted on the front of it.

The woman glanced around the room as if getting her bearings. "I'm back! How long have I been gone?"

"Who are you?" Heathcliff stammered.

The woman chuckled. "Why, sweetie, I'm the lady who's going to take over the world."

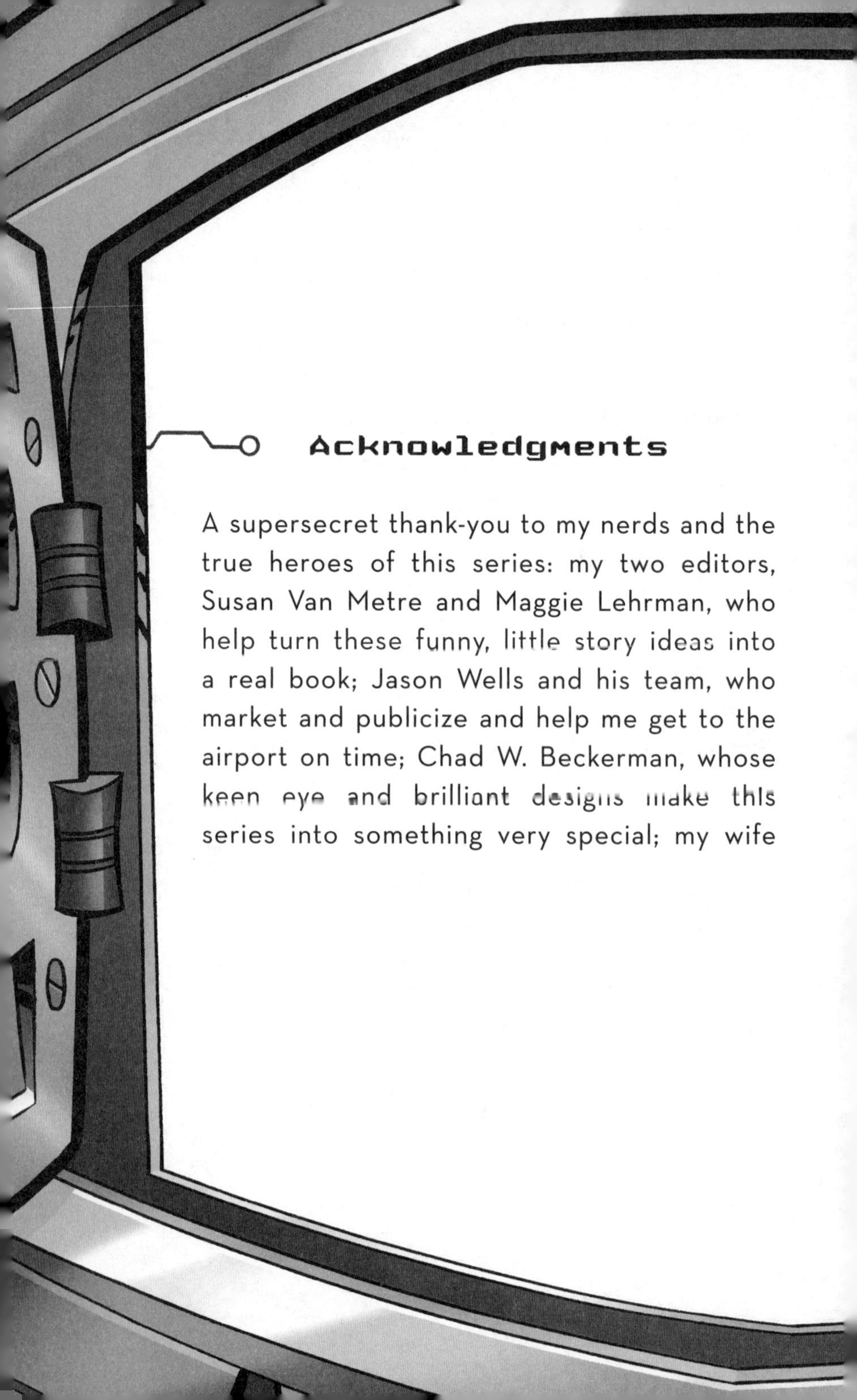

Acknowledgments

A supersecret thank-you to my nerds and the true heroes of this series: my two editors, Susan Van Metre and Maggie Lehrman, who help turn these funny, little story ideas into a real book; Jason Wells and his team, who market and publicize and help me get to the airport on time; Chad W. Beckerman, whose keen eye and brilliant designs make this series into something very special; my wife

and agent, Alison Fargis, and everyone at Stonesong—thank you, Alison, for keeping me grounded and reminding me that I, too, am a great big nerd; Nick Herman, Mariah Molina, Na-Quanda Chavis, Eileen Schorr, Bonoki-Oscar, Kari Smith, and the staff at Starbucks #11807 in Brooklyn, N.Y.; friends; family; and of course, my favorite little nerd, Finn.

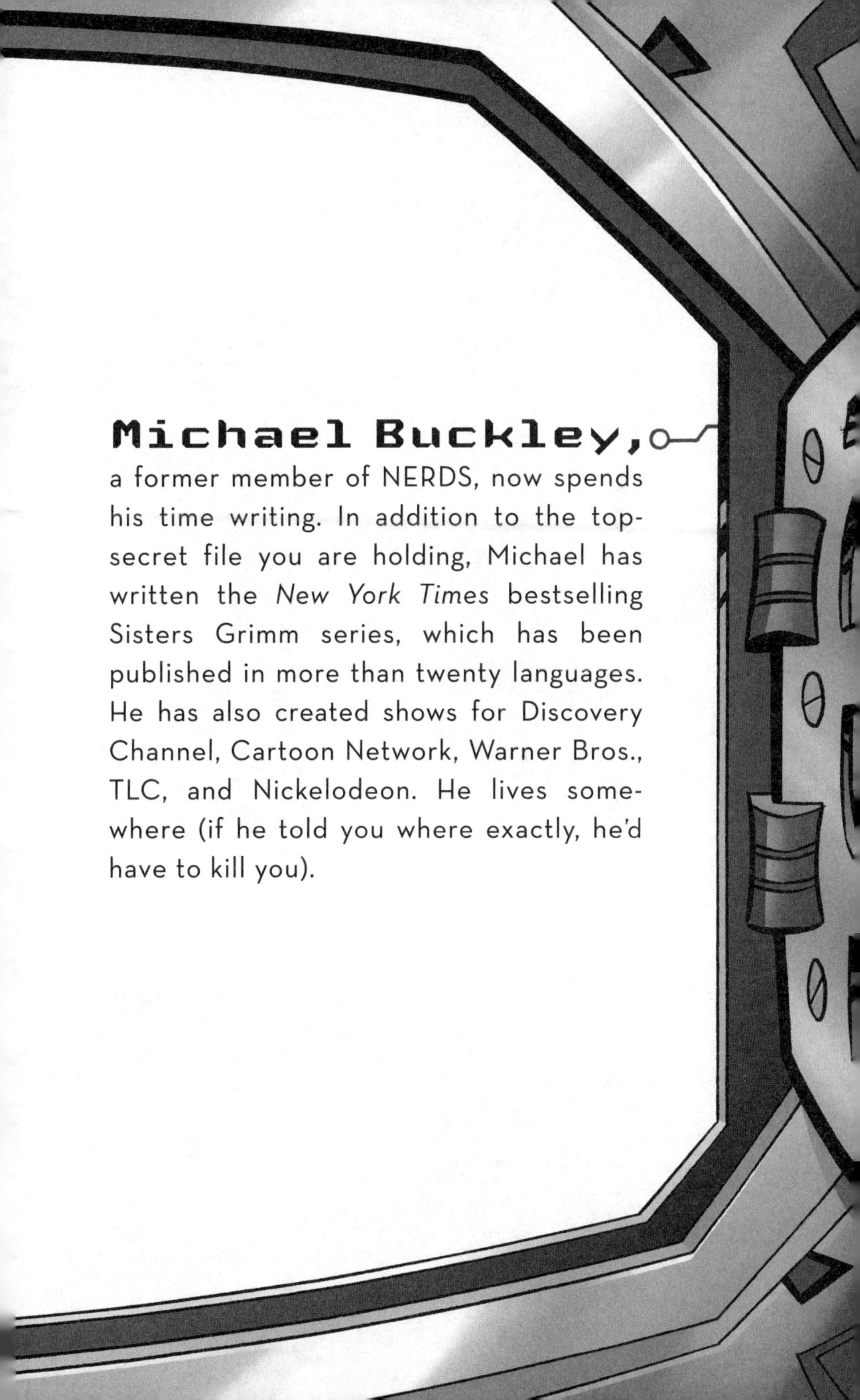

Michael Buckley, a former member of NERDS, now spends his time writing. In addition to the top-secret file you are holding, Michael has written the *New York Times* bestselling Sisters Grimm series, which has been published in more than twenty languages. He has also created shows for Discovery Channel, Cartoon Network, Warner Bros., TLC, and Nickelodeon. He lives somewhere (if he told you where exactly, he'd have to kill you).

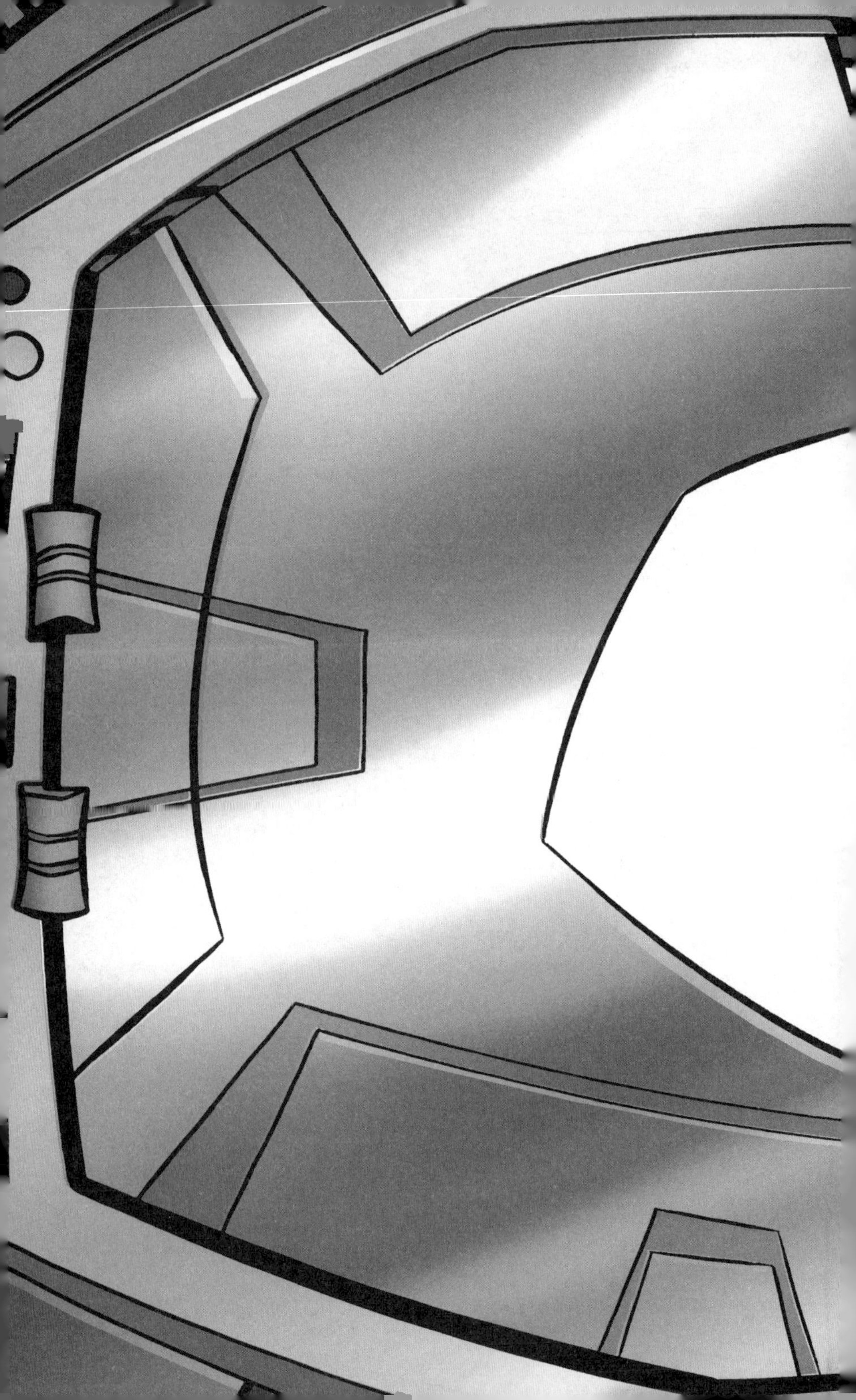

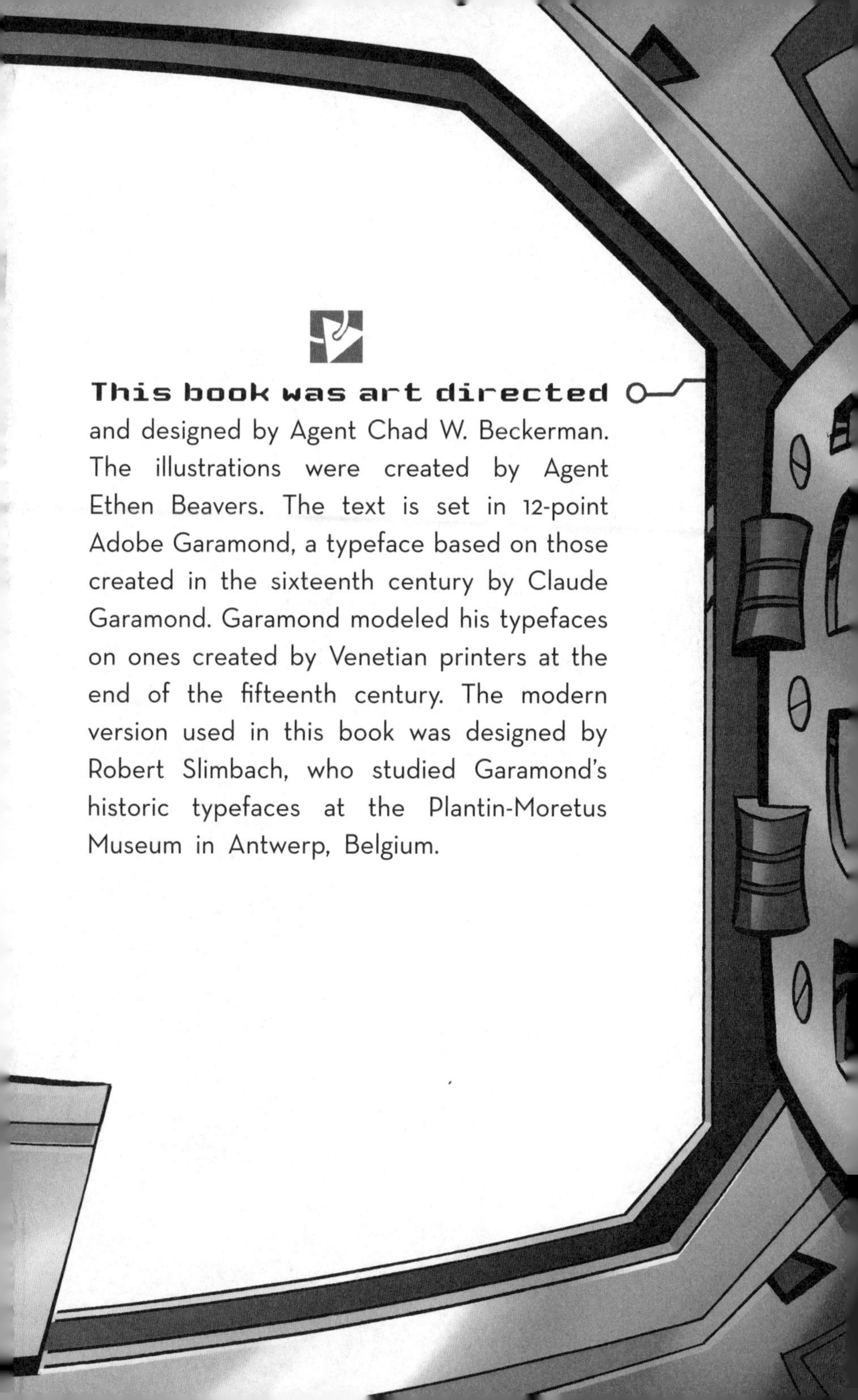

This book was art directed and designed by Agent Chad W. Beckerman. The illustrations were created by Agent Ethen Beavers. The text is set in 12-point Adobe Garamond, a typeface based on those created in the sixteenth century by Claude Garamond. Garamond modeled his typefaces on ones created by Venetian printers at the end of the fifteenth century. The modern version used in this book was designed by Robert Slimbach, who studied Garamond's historic typefaces at the Plantin-Moretus Museum in Antwerp, Belgium.